EDGE OF ANARCHY

EDGE OF COLLAPSE SERIES BOOK FOUR

KYLA STONE

Edge of Anarchy

Copyright © 2020 by Kyla Stone All rights reserved. This book or any portion thereof may not be reproduced or used in any manner whatsoever without the express written permission of the publisher except for the use of brief quotations in a book review.

This book is a work of fiction. Any references to historical events, real people, or real places are used fictitiously. Other names, characters, places, and events are products of the author's imagination, and any resemblances to actual events or places or persons, living or dead, is entirely coincidental.

Printed in the United States of America

Cover design by Christian Bentulan

Book formatting by Vellum

First Printed in 2020

ISBN: 978-1-945410-53-6

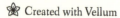 Created with Vellum

PREFACE

Much of this story takes place in Southwest Michigan. For the sake of the story, I have altered certain aspects and taken a few liberties with a real town or two. Thank you in advance for understanding an author's creative license.

The past isn't dead. It's not even past.

— WILLIAM FAULKNER

1

QUINN
DAY TWENTY

Sixteen-year-old Quinn Riley had often pictured the end of the world. She'd never imagined it quite like this. Way fewer zombies and a lot more misery.

Essentially, it sucked.

Quinn and Milo tramped through the deep snow, their boots crunching and squeaking in the stillness. A few birds chirped. The chilly air crept beneath the collar of her coat and stung her cheeks.

At least it wasn't snowing anymore.

The endless blizzards and snowstorms had finally relented. The sky was dreary and gray, with more clouds coming. It would snow again soon.

Gross. She hated winter. Loathed it with every fiber of her being.

If she ever escaped this place, she was heading straight to Florida and never coming back. They were probably spending the apocalypse on the beach hanging out in hammocks, sipping Mai Tais, and basking in the warm sun.

Quinn was pretty sure she'd forgotten what the sun was even supposed to look like.

"Next one!" Milo said. "This song is boring."

"Tom Petty's 'Free Falling' is a classic!"

He shook his head. "Too romance-y."

"Whatever. You obviously have no appreciation for great music."

"Love songs are boring and stupid."

It *was* totally lame, but she was a sucker for a haunting, forlorn love ballad as much as the next girl. "Well then, maybe you're stupid."

"That's not nice!"

She shrugged. "If the shoe fits."

Milo stuck his tongue out at her. She stuck hers out right back.

She jerked her gloves off with her teeth and clicked the next song on the playlist of the ancient iPod that Gramps had set up for her before he'd died. They'd already listened to Queen, Led Zeppelin, some Fleetwood Mac. Gramps' tastes tended toward the classics. So did Quinn's.

She slipped the iPod back into her pocket and tugged her glove back on. Over the last twenty seconds, her hand felt like it had frozen solid.

Aretha Franklin's "Respect" blasted into the earbuds currently attached to Milo's ears. She couldn't hear it, but she could imagine the fun, energetic beat. It was too difficult to stretch the short cord between them while walking. They took turns. She got one song, then he did.

The battery was low. Without the stupid sun, she hadn't been able to use the solar charger that Gramps had stored in his homemade Faraday cage down in their basement's secret stash.

Milo rolled his eyes at her, but he was grinning. He bobbed his head to the beat. "I know this one," he said too loudly over the music in his ears. "And Dad says I have great taste. He says I'm just like Mom."

Quinn's chest twinged. How could she argue with that? She wasn't completely heartless. "Fine, you win. But I'm playing 'A Little Less Conversation' next. You haven't lived until you've danced in the snow to Elvis."

Milo scrunched his nose. "How about some U2? 'I still haven't Found What I'm Looking For?'"

"Now that's a song I can get behind—"

A muffled shout echoed through the crisp air.

Quinn jerked her head up. She froze, her heart kicking against her ribs. A vision of the church flashed through her mind—bodies dropping, slugs flying, the screams and terror.

She seized Milo's hand.

He squeezed back. "What was that?"

Fear gripped her. She looked around, craning her neck, straining her ears, searching for the threat.

Everywhere she looked, there were wide expanses of white snow. Snowdrifts piled as high as her waist, as high as her head.

Big fancy houses with their circle driveways and three-car garages. Most of them were extravagant log cabins and elaborate chalets, but a few were lake cottages.

Behind the houses to her right, she glimpsed the river winking between the trunks of naked trees.

The self-sustainable community of Winter Haven was located along the widest part of Fall Creek. The community was shaped in a big oval, with smaller cul-de-sacs sticking out on either side of the main drive like the veins of a leaf.

The shout came again. Louder—and angry.

Tiny hairs lifted on the back of her neck.

"Someone's pissed off," Milo said.

"Don't say pissed. Your dad will think you got it from me."

"I *did* get it from you."

"Shhh. You're talking too loud." She twisted around to look behind them.

A man four houses down had a ladder on his deck and was balancing at the top, attempting to brush snow off the solar panels on his roof with a broom. The idiot looked like he was about to topple over backward.

He wasn't shouting, though. It wasn't him.

"It's probably nothing," she said to convince herself as much as Milo. "Probably some moron accidentally hit himself with his own snow shovel or something."

A few snowmobiles—militia on patrol—had driven past over the last hour. Quinn and Milo hadn't seen anyone else out and about other than a few people shoveling great mounds of snow from their driveways like they were tunneling to freedom.

For most of the last seven days, everyone in Fall Creek had been trapped in their houses. Noah Sheridan and a bunch of police officers and other volunteers had been busy digging everyone out, offering first aid and food to those who needed it.

The militia had helped, too. Acting like they were the big heroes when they were anything but.

Another shout.

Milo pointed. "It's coming from around the bend. Let's go check it out."

She fought down the irrational surge of panic, kept her voice light and easy. "Sure thing, Small Fry."

She told herself to calm the hell down. She told herself it was nothing. She hated how jumpy she'd become. Even a twig falling made her heart pound.

It was stupid. It made her feel dumb. Made her feel like a victim, not a survivor.

Milo tugged her forward. She trudged after him, her stupid heart still hammering, her mouth dry.

The shouting grew louder. Other voices joined in.

Something was definitely going on.

Without a word, Milo took off his earbuds and handed them to her. She stuffed them in her pocket and clicked off the iPod to conserve the battery.

Milo darted ahead.

"Stay close, Small Fry."

She hurried up to him, and they slogged through the snow together, puffing white clouds with every breath as they rounded the bend.

A three-story white house with massive windows and a big wraparound porch rose in front of them. Quinn and Milo stopped about twenty yards away.

The door to the house stood wide open. The bottom steps of the porch were buried in the snow. At the top of the stairs stood Darryl Wiggins, the priggish, sour-faced manager of Community Trust bank and all-important member of the town council.

Only, he wasn't standing.

Two men were on either side of him, gripping his arms. They'd dragged him from the house and were hauling him across the porch. Wiggins writhed, kicking and swearing, but he couldn't break free.

The men reached the top step and unceremoniously tossed Wiggins down the stairs. He landed in the snow in a collapsed heap.

A man and two women waited in the yard. They both wore backpacks and dragged sleds behind them loaded down with duffle bags, suitcases, and crates.

One of the men still on the porch wiped his hands on his

expensive wool coat. He was tall, pale, and bean-pole thin. His long, narrow face contorted in a scowl.

Quinn recognized him. It was Mr. Blair—the jerk who'd tried to steal water from the mom and two kids in Friendly's Grocery a whole lifetime ago. What a surprise.

Wiggins fumbled around in the snow, arms flailing. "You can't do this! This is against the law! You're stealing!"

"Like you stole this house from the Marcels, the rightful owners?" Mr. Blair asked, his voice dripping with condescension.

"You have no right!"

Mr. Blair shook his finger at Wiggins. "We have every right. Everyone else is taking whatever they want—including you. No one deserves this place any more than we do. We're sick of being ignored and left behind to freeze to death. This is it. Society is collapsing, the world is ending, and I'm not going to sit here and take it. I'm not going to let my family starve while you sit here in decadence you didn't earn and don't deserve. We're taking things into our own hands."

"As of this minute, you're homeless," the second man said with a smirk. He was a short, chubby Hispanic man in overalls with greasy hair and pockmarked skin. He worked at the gas station in town, but Quinn didn't know his name.

A woman strode out of the opened front door carrying a large laundry basket of clothes, personal toiletries, and other sundry items Quinn couldn't identify.

Mrs. Blair's lank brown hair was snarled and unkempt, her cheeks gaunt. She was barely recognizable as the prim, sharply-dressed lawyer that Quinn remembered.

She flung the basket's contents into the snow. Shirts, pants, and boxers fluttered around Darryl Wiggins. A sock landed on his head.

"What are they doing?" Milo whispered loudly.

"They're taking over that man's house."

"That's wrong."

"The problem is that man only has the house because the superintendent gave it to him. It's not his, either."

"I don't understand," Milo said.

"It's complicated." Quinn frowned. "And stupid. Everyone is stupid."

"That's your answer for everything."

"Yeah, well, it seems to fit everything these days, doesn't it?"

With a roar of outrage, Wiggins clambered to his feet. He wasn't wearing any boots. Or a coat, hat, or gloves. He had to be freezing.

He lunged forward, still cursing and shouting. He sank past his knees in the snow as he slogged toward the house.

Forced to lift his legs almost comically high, he staggered up the porch steps.

Mr. Blair just stood there, laughing at him. Maybe he didn't expect a fifty-something banker to throw a solid punch.

He underestimated his opponent. Wiggins was furious. Furious and desperate—a bad combination.

With a savage growl, he launched himself at Blair. He lowered his head and head-butted the man in the gut.

Blair let out a grunt and stumbled back. He tripped over the leg of a snow-covered rocking chair and tumbled to his butt.

"Hey!" Overalls swung at Wiggins and landed a punch to his face. His head jerked back. Blood spurted from his nose. Wiggins turned and slugged him back.

The woman dropped her basket and hurled herself at Wiggins, too. "Leave my husband alone!"

Blair struggled to his feet and rejoined the fray. Four adults kicked, punched, and cursed at each other. Three of them pummeled Wiggins to the porch floor. They kept kicking him, screaming and shouting in pent-up anger.

Quinn couldn't even see him anymore through the porch spindles and the legs and fists pelting his body.

"We should go, Small Fry," she said in a low voice. "Let these stupidheads work it out on their own—"

The roar of an engine splintered the air.

From the opposite direction, a snowmobile roared toward them. A second one joined the first.

The man and woman with the sleds loaded with goods jumped back. They jerked their sleds out of the way just as the snowmobiles slammed to a stop in front of the white house.

Two men yanked off their helmets and dismounted. They were dressed in gray camo fatigues and black boots with AK-47s slung over their shoulders. They looked formidable and intimidating.

Quinn's gut tightened with dread.

The militia had arrived.

2

QUINN
DAY TWENTY

Anger thrummed through Quinn. She gritted her teeth and tightened her grip on Milo's arm. She recognized both militia members: Sebastian Desoto and James Luther.

Those two jerkwads had stolen from Gran. Quinn had been forced to stand by and watch as they took half of everything she had—everything they thought she had, anyway.

Luckily, Gran and Gramps had a secret stash hidden in their basement.

Gran still had enough food and supplies to last them a few years. That did nothing to reduce Quinn's seething hatred for the militia and everything they stood for.

The sooner they were gone, the better.

Quinn wanted them out. She wanted to fight them, if that's what it took. Gran had told her to be careful, to keep her eyes open and stay watchful. And above all, not to do something stupid.

Quinn had done her best. She was impatient and impulsive by nature. She wanted to act, to *do* something.

She'd listened to Gran for once, but she was fast losing whatever threads of patience she possessed.

Desoto strode up the porch steps. He was Sutter's second-in-command. A Hispanic man in his forties, he was built like a tank and sported a military buzz cut and a hard, flat face.

Luther gripped his AK-47 and followed close behind. He was Caucasian, slim but muscular. All Quinn remembered about him was that he was a polite thief, as if manners made their armed robbery palatable. It made her hate him even more.

The two fake soldiers took stock of the situation quickly. They unclipped their semi-automatic rifles, flicked off the safeties, and aimed at the tussling civilians.

Desoto didn't hesitate. He didn't give a speech or ask for any last words or even give them a chance to defend themselves.

He jerked Overalls to his feet and flung him against the porch railing. He took a step back, raised the AK-47, and pointed the muzzle at the man's chest.

Memories flooded through Quinn's head—Octavia Riley on her knees in front of the courthouse steps, about to be executed. Mattias Sutter standing before her mother, gun aimed at her forehead.

Sour acid burned the back of Quinn's throat. Nausea swirled in her gut as dismay filled her. She knew what happened next. She'd seen it before.

She barely had time to seize Milo by the back of his coat, spin him around, and shove his face against her stomach.

So he couldn't see. So he wouldn't have to watch.

Desoto squeezed the trigger. He fired a double tap into the man's chest.

The gunshots shattered the air. The sound exploded against Quinn's eardrums.

Milo clapped his hands over his ears. A flock of birds resting on a telephone wire took to the sky in a startled flurry of wings and frantic squawking.

The force of the blast knocked Overalls' body backward over the porch railing. From Quinn's angle, she couldn't see how he'd landed. He could've landed on a cloud and it wouldn't have mattered. Two slugs punched through his ticker meant he was dead on arrival.

She stared, stunned. It all happened so fast that her brain barely had time to process it.

Desoto took hold of Blair and yanked him up. Blair flung out his arms defensively. His mouth gaped open.

He was yelling something, but Quinn couldn't translate the words. Her ears were still ringing.

Three quick blasts followed the first two. Blair fell back and sagged against the banister. He clutched feebly at his chest, staring down in shock at the three new holes in his flawless wool coat.

A few feet away, Mrs. Blair cowered on the porch, her hands over her head, weeping.

The man and woman with the sleds were already fleeing down the center of the road. They'd left their sleds—and Mrs. Blair—behind.

Outrage burned through Quinn's fear. Whatever crimes these people were guilty of, it didn't warrant death. Not like this, with these maniacs acting as judge, jury, and executioner.

This wasn't justice. She knew that much.

She longed to stop it, to freaking *do* something, but it was too late. She was no match for their guns.

For once, she held herself back. Gran was right. They needed to wait until the right moment to act. And it sure as hell wasn't now. She and Milo needed to get the hell out of here.

"Milo," she whispered. "We need to go. We need to go before they see us—"

Mrs. Blair fell over her husband's lifeless body.

Desoto aimed his rifle at her. "Do you need to die, too?"

Mrs. Blair screamed.

Milo pushed away from Quinn. She was too stunned to hold on.

He ran toward the white house, toward the murderers masquerading as militia.

"Milo! No!" She grabbed at him, but he was already out of reach.

"Leave them alone!" Milo screamed. "Stop hurting people!"

On the porch, Desoto turned in their direction. The muzzle of his weapon swung with him.

Without thinking a coherent thought, Quinn sprinted after Milo. Legs pumping, lungs burning, panic sparking bright.

Her hand found its way into her pocket, nudging aside the iPod and coiled earbuds and closing around her slingshot.

Luther grasped Mrs. Blair beneath her arms and lugged her down the porch steps. He pushed her into the snow. She landed on her hands and knees.

"Run!" he shouted. "Go!"

Mrs. Blair scrambled to her feet. She ran down the driveway erratically, arms flailing, tripping in the snow, falling, and then pulling herself up again.

Quinn didn't take her gaze off Desoto. He strode down the porch steps, carrying the rifle low, not exactly pointed at Milo but not pointed away from him, either.

"Milo!" Quinn shouted.

Brave, fearless Milo acted like he didn't even see the gun. He ran straight at the fake soldier and pummeled his stomach with his tiny fists. "Go away! Leave us alone and go away!"

With his free hand, Desoto shoved Milo away from him. Hard. "Get the hell out of here!"

Milo almost lost his balance. He stumbled, then regained his footing and launched himself at Desoto again.

Quinn skidded to a stop ten feet away. "Don't you dare lay a hand on him!"

Desoto ignored her. He dropped his rifle. He seized Milo around his thin neck with both hands and lifted him clear off the ground.

Rage streaked through her veins. She pulled the slingshot and a few rounds of ammo from her pocket with shaking hands. She planted her feet.

Milo's face turned red. He beat weakly at Desoto's muscled arms.

Desoto grimaced. "I warned you, you little—"

Quinn fitted her wrist guard, loaded the steel ball into the pouch, and drew the tapered bands taut, to her cheek, just below her right eye.

She canted the frame horizontally, lined up her sights with Desoto's ugly flat face.

She did not weigh the consequences. She did not think about anything but nailing her target. Her angle wasn't right to strike an eye with a direct shot. She lowered her sights slightly, zeroed in on a new target.

Someone was shouting. She didn't hear them, didn't comprehend their words. Sound drained away. Everything drained away.

Everything but her rage, her hate, and her absolute focus.

Quinn exhaled—and released.

The quarter-inch steel ball launched with tremendous velocity, whizzing through the air at a couple hundred feet per second.

At twenty feet away, Quinn did not miss. She never missed.

She shot Sebastian Desoto in the throat.

The steel ball struck him below and just to the right of his Adam's apple. It was not a bullet. It was not powerful enough to break the skin, but it could still do damage. And it would certainly hurt like a mother.

Desoto flinched. His eyes bulged. He opened his mouth, but no sound came out.

He released Milo. The boy dropped to the snow in a crumpled heap.

Desoto's hands went to his neck. The nasty purple bulge was already the size of a marble.

"What did you do to me?" he snarled hoarsely. His words came out raspy, like his throat was sandpaper.

Quinn already had another round loaded and the band strung to her cheek. It thrummed with tension, but her hands were steady.

"Your voice box is badly bruised," she said with a calmness she didn't feel. Her heart jackhammered against her ribs. "Nothing is broken, unfortunately."

Milo scrambled to his feet. He stood between Desoto and Quinn, nervous and indecisive. He looked scared now. Good. A little fear never hurt anyone.

"Milo," Quinn said, "get behind me right now."

He obeyed. He scampered to her side without a backward glance.

"I'll kill you!" Desoto croaked. He lunged for the AK-47, grabbed it, and started toward her.

She tightened her grip on the slingshot and kept her aim true. "Take another step, and the next one I unleash will pierce straight through your eye socket."

Desoto halted. Eight feet away now. He raised the rifle and pointed it at her chest.

Quinn's legs went weak and shaky. She could barely hold herself upright.

She did not back down. She couldn't afford to.

"If you're lucky," she said, "it'll just turn that eye to jelly and stop there. If you're not, it punches into your brain. It's just a little steel ball, but inside your soft, squishy brain? Who knows what important functions it'll scramble? I assume you enjoy speaking and thinking? Remembering your own name? Taking a piss by yourself?"

Desoto aimed at her head. "Not if I shoot you dead first, you little whore—"

"Enough!" Luther appeared out of nowhere. He stepped between Desoto and Quinn. He held up his free hand, palm out, in a placating gesture. In his right hand, he held his rifle pointed at the ground. "Slow this rodeo down, okay? That's Chief Sheridan's son right there."

Desoto's expression didn't change. "What's the police chief got to do with us?"

"Come on, now," Luther said. "Sinclair wouldn't like it. You and I both know that. And what the superintendent doesn't like, Sutter doesn't like."

Desoto sneered. "For now."

"For now," Luther acknowledged. "You really don't want to hurt these kids. We've done enough. It's enough."

Desoto blew out a frustrated breath. He lowered the AK-47. His gaze never left Quinn's face. His eyes narrowed with barely restrained rage. The welt on his throat bulged with his every swallow. "This isn't over."

Quinn didn't look away. She didn't lower the slingshot.

Milo peeked around her side. "Go to hell!"

"Language, Small Fry," she said.

"He deserves it!"

"Can't argue with you there."

With exaggerated movements, Desoto clicked on the safety and affixed the rifle to its sling. With a last parting glare, he turned his back on them and stomped across the yard to the waiting snowmobiles, stepping over the bodies like they were no more than trash.

"You just killed two people!" Wiggins cried.

Quinn had almost forgotten he was there.

Desoto sneered at him. "And?"

Wiggins visibly swallowed. He reached up and prodded the purple shiner swelling his right eye nearly shut. His face was swollen and bloodied. His clothes were torn and stained with blood splatters. He cradled one arm to his chest. Maybe it was sprained or broken.

"You should be thanking us," Desoto said hoarsely. "We just saved your life. And your house." He said "your" like it was in air quotes, with an edge of mockery.

Wiggins heard it loud and clear. "Thank you," he stammered.

"You're welcome," Luther said quietly. He was staring at Mr. Blair's body, at the blood soaking into the man's wool coat like paint.

Wiggins grasped the porch railing to steady himself. "What am I supposed to do with the bodies? How am I supposed to get this blood off the porch?"

"Leave them there to scare off the next wannabe thieves. What do we care?" Desoto took a seat on the first snowmobile. He shook his head in disgust. "Are we supposed to do everything for you? You want us to wipe your lazy butt next?"

"No."

"No, what?"

"No...sir?"

Desoto's expression didn't change, his face like a slab of granite. He massaged his throat. "That's more like it."

Luther took the second snowmobile. He slung his rifle over his shoulder and picked up his helmet. "Desoto, shut your trap already. Talking can't be good for your throat. Let's go see that nurse at the shelter, get you fixed up."

"This town isn't worth it," Desoto rasped. "I don't even know why we're doing this."

Luther didn't answer. He glanced back at Quinn. There was something in his face—remorse, regret maybe. The same as that day at Gran's house. It just made her more furious.

"What are you waiting for?" she said. "You heard Milo. Get out of here! And while you're at it, get the hell out of our town, too!"

"Make no mistake," Desoto said, his lip curling in contempt, hatred flashing in his eyes. "This town isn't yours. Fall Creek belongs to us."

3

PIKE
DAY TWENTY

Gavin Pike stopped in his tracks. After seven long days, he'd finally found what he was searching for.

The cold brittle air seared his cheeks and nose. Each inhalation burned his throat and lungs. The sky was a dreary slate gray, heavy with clouds. The bright sun reflecting off the massive snowbanks hurt his eyes.

At least it wasn't snowing. At least he was out of that stuffy, suffocating house and away from that insufferable family.

They had taken him into their home; that didn't mean he had to like them for it.

Hourly, he fantasized about breaking their fingers, one by one. *Snap, snap, snap.*

In an incredible display of self-control, he'd restrained himself. He prided himself on his discipline.

After all, the hungrier you are, the more satisfying the meal.

The single clove cigarette he allowed himself per day was the only thing that kept him sane. That and the goal he always kept fixed in his mind: find Hannah, end the soldier and the dog, take the baby.

Three days ago, the blizzard had finally ceased. Snow drifts piled higher than windows and buried stalled cars. From sunup to sundown, Pike had spent each day searching the town.

He visited every house with smoke swirling from a chimney. Ten houses. Twenty.

His camouflage was excellent. It was beyond excellent. He was polite. He flashed his reserve officer badge. The townspeople opened their doors to him. They were happy to help.

He knew his quarry was close by. Even though no more than twenty miles separated Watervliet from the outskirts of Fall Creek, they wouldn't have gone far.

In this cold, Hannah and her soldier wouldn't have survived without a fireplace. In this snow, no vehicle would make it out of here.

They were still here. He felt it. He *knew* it.

Hannah was meant for him. Her child was meant for him.

He'd finally come to a decision on the matter of his progeny. After he killed the girl, he would return to Fall Creek with the child. He would bestow it upon his mother. When the time was right, he would teach it the ways of the world. How to hunt. Who to kill.

It was ironic, fitting. He liked the poetry of it.

Door after door, he was met with helpful but confused glances, regretful head shakes.

He did not give up. He did not move on to greener pastures. He returned to the stodgy family each evening and allowed them to serve him food and provide him with shelter.

They wanted him to leave, he felt it, but they were too polite to ask.

He didn't care what they wanted. He would rely on their generosity until it ran out, and then he would take what they had left via gunpoint.

Break a few bones in that little boy's hand, and their attitudes would transform with fantastic swiftness.

He acted sicker than he was. The injury from the damned dog bite he'd sustained in the Branch library had nearly healed. The aches and bruises from the accident and the fall to the ice were fading fast, and the hypothermia had lost its grip on him.

He woke up each morning healthier than the day before. Angrier. More determined.

He kept looking. Thirty houses. Fifty.

He did not give up. He would never give up.

Yesterday evening, as night fell and the shadows stretched across the snow like claws, his perseverance had finally been rewarded. A neighbor several blocks west had caught sight of a big white dog frolicking in the snow across the street.

That night, it had been too dark to follow the tracks.

Today was a fresh day. A beautiful, brilliant day.

Now, Pike had again found what he'd been looking for. He smiled.

There in the snow was a perfect set of paw prints. Too large to be any other dog but the one he sought.

The one who would lead him straight to Hannah Sheridan.

4

HANNAH
DAY TWENTY

Hannah Sheridan felt like a different person.

She had changed so much in the last three weeks that she barely recognized herself. Her skin felt tight and ill-fitting. Like her bones were the wrong shape.

Or maybe they were the correct shape, and she just had to grow into her new self, to adjust like she was learning to adjust to everything else.

She stood in front of the mirror in the upstairs bathroom of the house she'd given birth in nine days ago. A flashlight provided enough light to see by. The house was on a septic system, so a bucket filled with water next to the tub allowed them to flush the toilet.

Her infant daughter slept downstairs. Liam was there, too—the gruff, reticent soldier who'd saved her life more than once. He had also become someone she cared for. Someone important.

She touched her soft belly. It had mostly deflated but still felt squishy. Her body was finally becoming her own again.

It was her mind that was different. The nightmares were less-ening. The terrible flashbacks of her captivity were fading before a slew of brighter, happier memories.

She was braver, less fearful. She no longer cowered.

She was shedding the old Hannah to make way for something new.

She tugged her braid over her shoulder and pulled off the hair tie. She unwove the strands and let her long hair tumble to the small of her back. It was thick, wavy, and chocolate-brown, though ratty with split ends.

Last night, she'd washed it. They still had water stored in the hot water heater. Liam had used the washing machine's supply hose to connect to the water heater valve and drain the water into several cooking pots, a couple of empty water jugs, and their water bottles.

He'd also collected the water from the back of the toilet tanks in the three bathrooms. Since it was clean and hadn't been chemically treated, it was drinkable. It had frozen in the empty house, and Liam had chiseled out the ice in chunks.

He'd warmed the water and filled the sink for her.

It felt so good to be clean. Her itchy, oily scalp was now freshly washed and tingling.

The previous occupants had left their shampoo and conditioner. Hair spray and hair gel, too. She picked up the hair spray, shook the can, and set it down.

She imagined some people were desperately missing their usual toiletries right now—make up, hair dye, and their favorite hair products.

She'd gone without for five years. She had no use for those things now.

Maybe later. Maybe when she was finally home.

Hannah picked up the hair shears she'd found in the cabinet beneath the sink. It had been five years since she'd cut her hair.

Pike hadn't allowed her something so dangerous as a pair of scissors.

Slowly, methodically, she cut the first strands. It was more than just hair she cut. It was years of nightmares, years of abuse, years of degradation, pain, and horror.

All the times he'd seized her hair and dragged her to the floor —gone. All the times he'd savagely jerked her head back—gone.

She cut off her hair, lock by lock. Strands swirled into the sink. Her hair filled the bowl until it looked like the nest of a small animal.

She kept cutting until it looked fairly even. Her new, shorter tresses swept her shoulders. Her head felt lighter. Everything felt lighter.

Soon, she would be home. Home to her family. To Milo.

She wasn't sure what she would be returning to. What Noah would be like. How they might resurrect their failing marriage.

Whatever the future held, she would be ready for it.

The new Hannah Sheridan looked in the mirror and smiled.

5

LIAM
DAY TWENTY-ONE

The house that Liam and Hannah had taken refuge in was located on the outskirts of town.

It was at the end of a cul-de-sac, surrounded by trees to the west, with the river directly behind it. They hadn't seen or heard any people or vehicles since they'd arrived.

That was a good thing, but Liam Coleman wasn't going to let his guard down. He never let his guard down.

While Hannah recovered physically from the ordeal of childbirth, Liam had spent the days strengthening their defenses.

He barricaded the plywood he'd nailed to the sliding glass doors with a sofa. He used the wedges from his go-bag to block the doors and whittled shims to jam the windows shut. Even if the glass was broken, they wouldn't open.

He cleaned his weapons and sharpened his knife. He always kept his Gerber tactical knife and holstered Glock on his body, a round ready in the chamber.

He studied the map and plotted the remainder of their journey to Fall Creek, which they should make in less than a day if he could scavenge them a working snowmobile or truck with a snowplow. He'd searched the nearby houses—many of them already scavenged—but he didn't want to stray too far from Hannah.

He found deadfall among the trees behind the house and chopped more firewood. He cooked breakfast, lunch, and dinner for Hannah, Ghost, and himself, assembling creative meals based on the cans of soups and beans and boxes of pasta in the pantry.

Ghost happily gulped up anything. He was basically a garbage can on legs.

Liam's back twinged as he bent over the counter to finish up the dishes. He missed the convenience of dishwashers. Washing everything by hand was a pain—literally.

Liam had spent his life preparing for any threat, any disaster, any eventuality. He'd trained for decades, becoming a soldier, a warrior, strengthening and hardening his body until it was a smooth, well-oiled killing machine.

But the crushed disc injury he'd sustained as an operator with Delta Forces continued to haunt him. In the last three weeks, he'd pushed his body further and harder than he had in years. His spine had protested, but he ignored it. The pain wouldn't be ignored forever.

He winced and rubbed his aching lower back with wet, sudsy fingers.

"Is your back bothering you?" Hannah asked.

She stood in the doorway between the living room and the kitchen, her head cocked, her lip caught between her small white teeth.

She wore gray sweatpants and a soft pink sweater that she'd found in one of the closets upstairs. They fit her nicely. The pink brightened her cheeks.

She was looking healthier. It was more than that, though.

Her green eyes were shining. Her chocolate-brown hair was brushed, clean, and swished around her shoulders.

She'd cut it. It looked...good. She looked good. Beautiful, even.

As if she could read his thoughts, she blushed and gave him a shy smile.

He cleared his throat awkwardly. "It's fine. I'm fine."

Liam found it difficult to look at her for too long. It was a bit like looking into the sun. Warm and inviting, but painful.

Her presence did something to him, unnerved him in a way he wasn't prepared for. She threatened to awaken a longing inside him that he didn't deserve and could never have.

He dropped his gaze and concentrated on the dishes. He scrubbed the last plate with a bit of melted snow and soap and let it soak in a second pot of warmed water. "We should go soon."

After she'd nearly died in childbirth, he'd been hesitant to push travel, even though he was antsy and hated being cooped up day after day. She was already exhausted from her ordeal, not to mention everything that had come before.

But she was recovering well. Last night, she'd helped him prepare cornbread slathered in honey, Kraft macaroni and cheese with water instead of milk and butter, and canned peaches for dessert.

Her company had been enjoyable. More than enjoyable. And the food wasn't terrible, either.

If he was completely honest with himself, maybe he'd been putting it off. Three weeks ago, he'd been eager to deliver her home and be rid of the burden of responsibility.

Now, the thought of delivering her to her husband and heading north alone to his own isolated homestead left him feeling strangely bereft.

Hannah bit her lower lip. She nodded. "It's time."

"I've been looking for a snowmobile, something that can get

through this deep snow. I'll go out again today. If we leave first thing tomorrow, we could be in Fall Creek by lunchtime."

A complicated mix of emotions flashed across her face—anticipation and joy mingled with a hint of anxiety. She was probably anxious about the reunion, worried about the well-being of her family after such a long separation.

Guilt pricked him. She needed to get home to them. She deserved to see her son again.

She cleared her throat. "You should have a good meal before you go out. Do you feel like fettuccine alfredo for breakfast? I think there's a jar of alfredo sauce left in the pantry."

"Not sure that's part of a complete breakfast."

"I'm certain that it is. If donuts make the cut, I don't see how pasta wouldn't."

Hannah hesitated. She rubbed her damaged hand, then took the long way around the kitchen island, avoiding the basement door located at the far end of the kitchen.

The door to the basement was in a small hallway alcove that shared the door to the garage and the back door, leading to a small patio with outdoor furniture covered in snow.

Liam's brow furrowed, but he said nothing.

All week, she'd studiously avoided approaching the basement. Maybe she would shun basements for the rest of her life. He understood her reluctance. He didn't blame her.

He had his own demons that he'd rather evade than face. Some memories were too awful to relive—ever.

They hadn't spoken Pike's name since Hannah had told him what the monster had done to her and her second child. Just the thought of Pike filled him with outrage, loathing, and disgust.

Liam was sorry he hadn't gotten the chance to finish Pike himself, with his own bare hands.

The smallest sliver of unease wormed its way into his gut. He hated the fact that he hadn't seen Pike's body. That he hadn't drilled the kill shot into his skull himself.

Liam didn't like leaving anything to chance. The hole in the ice haunted his thoughts, invaded his nightmares. Swallowed his certainty.

After they'd driven Pike's snowmobile off the bridge, Liam had wanted to scale the embankment and hunt for that maniac until he'd found his body and made 100 percent sure.

Hannah's preeclampsia had made the decision for him. Though it defied his training and soldier's instinct, he couldn't risk her life.

His instinct to protect—to save—had been stronger.

The dishes finished, Liam wiped his hands on a hand towel next to the sink and moved to the rear door. He tugged aside the blackout curtains that he'd duct-taped to the window to do a security check and watch for Ghost.

He wouldn't leave Hannah alone without the Great Pyrenees there to guard her. In addition, he'd found a whistle in the garage which she wore around her neck beneath her sweater.

If she was in trouble, she would blow on the whistle, and Liam would come running. He made sure never to stray out of range, though he might have to in order to find a snowmobile.

He peered through the narrow sliver of window, instinctively checking the woods and scanning the back yard for threats. He didn't see Ghost.

The dog had gone out exploring a few hours each of the last several days. He always came back covered in snow, dirt, and burs, tired but happy.

A dog like a Great Pyrenees was meant to be outside. Ghost hated being cooped up as much as Liam did, but the time to recover was good for him. His fur was already growing back over the bald spot that Dr. Laudé had shaved when she'd alleviated his brain swelling.

As much as Liam didn't want to admit it, these last nine days had been a godsend for both Hannah and Ghost. And maybe for Liam, too. A vital break from the constant chaos and threat of death always nipping at their heels. A chance to regroup, to heal.

The baby awoke with a startled cry. Charlotte Rose was sleeping in the fire-warmed living room, tucked inside a makeshift bassinet—a dresser drawer stuffed with the softest sheets they could find.

Liam had cut up another pair of sheets to make diapers. They only sort of worked. Real diapers were high on the list of needs, along with wipes, bottles, pacifiers, butt powder, and everything else that came with a baby.

Hannah hurried into the living room and returned a moment later with a small bundle in her arms. He watched her, serene and radiant and full of a deep, abandoned joy.

Joy wasn't an emotion he had much experience with. Love, either.

Unless you counted unrequited love, which came with an equal share of pain and heartache.

Suddenly uncomfortable, he fished around for something to say. "She sleeps so well."

She looked down at the infant with a soft smile. "So did Milo."

She held the bundle out to Liam. "Can you hold her? My mom used to make alfredo with rosemary and garlic. I bet they have some rosemary in a drawer somewhere."

Liam took the baby easily, cradling the small human being in the crook of his arm. It hadn't always been that way. The first time Hannah had asked him to hold her, he'd blanched.

"I don't do babies," he'd mumbled.

"I call B.S." Hannah had rolled her eyes. "How many people

other than OBs can say they've helped birth a human? Not many."

He didn't say he'd done it twice. He didn't tell her how the thought of his nephew skewered his heart. How Jessa's death played out in the theater of his mind every night, a terrible film that never ceased.

He wanted to, but he didn't. He couldn't. The words stuck in his mouth like nails.

"I'd say your expertise already outdoes most males on the planet," Hannah said. "Here, take her. You'll do fine."

He swallowed, about to protest again, but somehow the bundle was in his arms and Hannah was already moving away, a sly grin on her face.

"See?" Hannah said. "She likes you."

He'd held the baby stiffly at first. She was so small, so fragile. So tiny—just a breath, a bird in the hand, almost nothing at all and everything at once.

Now, he held her with more ease, but just as much care.

She scrunched her delicate little face and stared up at him with wide slate-blue eyes, so different than her mother's jade-green, but just as beautiful. She wore the tiny gray and green knit hat that he'd given her the day she was born.

He remembered the squishy cord wrapped around her neck, the fear twisting his gut as he'd frantically unwound it, begging her to breathe.

He remembered the first child he'd delivered. How his nephew's entire head had fit into his hand, a warm little body snuggled against his chest, pressed against his neck.

There was nothing that could prepare you for bringing another life into the world. No amount of training or discipline that could gird a man against the rush of emotion—and sense of responsibility—that he felt every time he laid eyes upon little Charlotte Rose.

She was Hannah's through and through, but she was more than that to him. Liam would be damned if he allowed anyone to lay a hand on her.

Something long frozen had begun to melt inside him. He didn't fight it. He didn't want to fight it anymore.

He cradled Hannah's child in his arms and felt that fierce protectiveness again. And not just protectiveness. Tenderness. Maybe even something deeper, stronger.

He glanced at Hannah, at her shining face, warm and open and full of affection. It did something to him that he didn't want to admit, was still afraid to acknowledge but knew was there, all the same.

Maybe it was because of this place, this house that felt somehow disconnected from the rest of the world of consequences and repercussions. In this moment, it felt like the three of them were the only people left alive in the whole damn world.

"Hannah," he started, feeling incredibly foolish but bumbling ahead all the same. "I need to tell you—"

Outside the back door, Ghost barked.

6

PIKE
DAY TWENTY-ONE

Pike crept closer. Hiding behind the trunk of a large pine tree, he raised the binoculars that he'd scavenged from one of the nearby homes and watched the house.

In his coat pocket, he carried a handgun. Most vacant houses had already been ransacked, but he'd discovered the Smith and Wesson M&P Shield handgun tucked beneath a mattress.

It held seven .40 S&W rounds in the extended magazine. No backups or spares. It wasn't much, but it would be enough.

A plan hatched in Pike's mind. He liked it more and more the longer he thought about it. If he could lure Soldier Boy out, Hannah would be alone in the house.

Pike had learned from his previous errors. Going after Hannah before Soldier Boy was eliminated would be a mistake.

Besides, he wanted to take his time with her. He needed to know that no one was coming to her rescue.

Not this time. Not ever again.

Just the thought set his blood buzzing. He tugged out his lighter and listened to the soothing *click, click, click.*

This was one of his favorite games. Let the prey get close. Lay a trap and wait for the jaws to snap shut.

It wasn't without risk. Pike normally didn't care for this level of risk. He liked to have more time to prepare, to make sure that everything went according to plan.

There were many ways for things to go wrong, but the reward was utterly tantalizing.

Click, click, click. He closed his eyes, relishing the delicious sound.

He fantasized that it was the crack and snap of Hannah's bones instead: phalanges, the radius, the ulna, the carpals and metacarpals, maybe even a rib or two.

Pike opened his eyes and went to work.

7

LIAM
DAY TWENTY-ONE

The kitchen filled with the delicious scent of alfredo sauce. Cold air blew through the window over the sink they'd opened temporarily to diffuse the fumes.

Hannah kept watch over the small pans of sauce and noodles cooking on the small propane camping stove that Liam had found stored in the garage.

Ghost had flopped himself in the center of the kitchen. They nearly tripped over him constantly, but he didn't seem to mind. Liam had dried off his paws and fur with a wet towel. He'd found dog food in one of the nearby houses, so Ghost had already eaten his fill and was ready for a pleasant nap.

"We're almost out of propane," Hannah said.

"Another reason to leave as soon as possible," Liam said gruffly.

Maybe it was for the best that Ghost had interrupted what he'd started to say. It would've come out all wrong anyway.

He moved to the front of the house and checked the windows, Ghost padding along behind him. Nothing out of place. Still no movement in the streets. The gray sky was filling with dark clouds—another storm was headed their way.

He adjusted Charlotte in his arm and returned to the kitchen, pausing by the back door to study the yard again. He felt something. A prickle against the back of his neck. A sense he couldn't name or quantify but trusted implicitly—the feeling of being watched.

He looked harder. Something snagged the corner of his eye. A glint in the trees twenty-five yards to the left of the house. The flash of binocular lenses reflecting off the snow.

With a low warning growl, Ghost leapt to his feet and bounded to the door.

Every muscle in Liam's body went tense. "Hannah."

Hannah immediately went to him and held her arms out for the baby. Liam handed Charlotte to her and seized the Bushmaster AR-15 leaning against the wall next to the back door.

He was already wearing his boots and two pairs of wool socks, plastic Ziploc bags wrapped between the layers to keep his feet dry. His coat was draped over a kitchen chair, but he didn't waste time putting it on. He wore a long-sleeved undershirt and two sweatshirts.

"Get down. Stay away from the windows."

She nodded and turned off the propane stove with one hand. Liam quickly closed the window and replaced the shim.

He went to the back door, peered through the glass, then threw the door open. He moved into the narrow space that he'd shoveled for Ghost's potty breaks during the blizzard, Ghost at his heels.

He clambered up the steep drift on the right side, lifting his muzzle over the edge cautiously, then peered over the rim himself, rapidly scanning his surroundings for the threat.

Ghost ran back and forth in a tight circle, barking fiercely at the tree line.

His senses alert, pulse thudding, he climbed up and stood looking over the lawn, stock against his shoulder, muzzle up, straining his ears and searching for the telltale glint.

The freezing air bit at his exposed skin, tunneling straight through his sweater and long-sleeved shirt. The clouds were thick and low. Snow spiraled down from the gunmetal gray sky, faster and faster.

He studied the houses that lined the empty street, searching the windows and roofs for movement, for the glint of a rifle barrel. He scanned the trees behind the house.

He circled the house, his boots sinking deep, and studied the snow for tracks, for any sign of the intruder.

There it was. A mass of fur and bloody entrails staining the pure white snow. The carcass was hidden just inside the tree line, downwind about thirty yards from the back of the house.

It used to be a wild hare but was now a message from an enemy—an enemy who should be dead but wasn't.

Pike was alive.

Liam rocked back on his heels. Darkness opened up inside him. A black rage sprouted in his chest, his whole body thrumming with revulsion.

The psycho was goading him, provoking him.

If this was an attempt to get him to abandon his training and rush headlong into a trap, Pike would be sorely mistaken.

Liam would hunt him down and kill him. Today. Right now.

"Ghost!" Liam commanded. "Stay with Hannah."

The dog let out another great booming bark, his muscles straining in his eagerness to seek out the threat, but he obeyed.

Liam went to the rear door, moving backward, keeping his rifle trained on the woods. Ghost followed him.

Hannah was waiting for them. She held her daughter close to her chest. Her face was bone-white, her lips pale. "He's not dead."

"No."

"You're going to kill him."

Liam hesitated. He felt conflicted to his very core. He did not want to leave her. Every instinct warred against it. She was his vulnerability. It put him between a rock and a hard place—for he needed to both protect Hannah and kill Pike.

"Go," Hannah said. "He needs to die."

Liam put on his coat and scarf and pulled his hat low over his ears. He pulled on his gloves and took three loaded magazines—two for the AR-15, one for the Glock—and stuffed them in his pockets. He missed his chest rig and military-grade cold weather gear.

"When I come back, I'll whistle 'Happy Birthday.' Shoot anyone else. Don't hesitate."

She nodded, her features tight. "You'll come back."

"I will."

Ghost paced from the living room to the kitchen and back, alert and wary, a low rumbling growl deep in his chest. He felt a little better with the dog with her. Only a little.

"Use your whistle if you need me," Liam said. "Where's your .45?"

She shifted, holding Charlotte with one hand, and pulled the gun out of her sweatpants' pocket. "It's loaded. Round in the chamber, like you taught me."

"That never leaves your hand."

Her expression hardened. "I know."

8

PIKE
DAY TWENTY-ONE

Pike doubled back on his own tracks.

Soldier Boy erroneously believed he was the hunter. Alas, he was not.

Along the outskirts of town, the houses along the river ended abruptly as the ground dipped into a steep ravine near the river's edge. Woods lined the ravine on both sides.

The snow had started up again. Even under the canopy of the trees, the powder rose midway between his knees and thighs. He waded through it. His boots made muffled squeaking sounds with every step.

Snow built up on his head and shoulders, drifting into every crack and crevice, sneaking between the folds of his scarf, dripping down his neck and back, and slipping between his gloves and coat sleeves.

The rapidly falling snow made it impossible to see more than thirty feet in front of him. It would get worse. Pike wasn't worried.

He'd created the necessary tracks before doubling back, planting the fresh kill, and waiting for the trap to be sprung.

The soldier would follow the plan perfectly. He believed that

Pike was ahead of him; he'd never see him sneaking up from behind.

Pike had no sense of fairness, no honor. As soon as he saw the man, he intended to shoot him in the back.

The storm offered cover. The soldier wouldn't hear his approach over the wind. Wouldn't be able to smell him or sense him. Hell, Pike couldn't trust his own senses.

He plodded through the snow, stepping in Soldier Boy's methodical footprints that trailed his own, pushing blindly forward. It was becoming more difficult to see. The wind was picking up, sending clouds of ice crystals swirling across the packed snow.

He tightened his grip on the pistol and quickened his pace.

A sound ahead of him. Fifteen, twenty feet. Directly ahead? Or a little west?

Pike whirled around, gun up, searching the trees. Everything looked the same. The same ugly barren oak and maple trees. The same pine and spruce laden with snow.

A flicker of unease curdled through him. It wasn't a feeling he was accustomed to. He didn't like it.

Another noise, this time behind him. A soft squeak, like careful footsteps sinking into the snow.

He twisted around, craning his neck wildly.

He sensed movement to his left. Then ahead.

He didn't hear a sound. He didn't see a thing.

The forest was a tangle of black straggly trees that pressed in on him from all sides. The menace was palpable, the frigid air heavy and smothering.

To the southwest, a branch overloaded with powder snapped beneath the weight. A mound of snow thudded to the ground.

He gritted his teeth in irritation. Just his overactive mind playing tricks on him. This brutal cold getting into his head.

He kept going, pushing hard through deeper drifts. The tracks were partially buried and becoming harder to locate with each passing minute.

His legs felt leaden and stiff. He tripped over something buried in the snow and nearly fell but regained his footing.

He was fast growing tired of this.

The girl was waiting for him in the warm house. He wanted Soldier Boy dead—he didn't care how anymore. It was time to end this and be done with it.

A branch creaked. Powder thudded to the ground. A chipmunk skittered through underbrush.

Sound drifted. It was impossible to tell where it came from.

Behind him. Ahead. To the left or right.

That disconcerting feeling niggled at his gut. Maybe the soldier was smarter than he'd anticipated. More wily and cunning.

Maybe Pike was no longer the only one playing the game.

He felt the ground sloping beneath his feet and recalled the location of the ravine. It should be directly to his left. Ten feet? Fifteen? In the near white-out conditions, he couldn't see the drop-off past the thin line of trees.

He visualized the topography in his mind. It was a sharp incline and steep. Easy to fall over a cliff of snow and tumble fifteen yards down to the river below, the water black as blood.

With the inclement weather, an unsuspecting person wouldn't even see it coming.

Pike stepped into the next footprint and halted abruptly. His unease growing, he blinked the ice from his eyelashes and squinted down at the prints.

Something was off. Nothing he could put a finger on, just a gut feeling.

He brought his pistol up and twisted left then right, neck craning, squinting hard, searching for any hint of danger.

Nothing. He could see nothing. But he felt the soldier like a sinister presence, lurking just beyond his line of sight.

His apprehension transformed into something else—an alien feeling, but one he still recognized, an instinct every mammal possessed, even him.

Fear.

Like prey, Pike ran.

9

LIAM

DAY TWENTY-ONE

The snow drove into Liam's face, stinging his cheeks, forehead, and nose.

It was miserable. His lower back ached in protest. He'd been crouched in the same position for too long.

His teeth chattered. His hands were stiffening. He flexed his fingers on the trigger guard of the Bushmaster AR-15 to keep the blood flowing.

Liam squatted behind the cover of a cluster of trees about fifteen feet to the left of the trail of breadcrumb tracks that Pike had left for him to follow. He'd followed them around a bend and was lying in wait, ready to ambush his target.

Pike had attempted to circle around and sneak up on Liam from behind. It wouldn't work. He would use Pike's own plan against him.

Liam had checked for double-backed tracks. He'd swept in a semi-circle from the obvious trail outward until he'd found it, and then he'd set up his ambush after checking the ground conditions around his firing position.

From Liam's vantage point just behind a V-split in the trunk of an oak, he would see Pike before Pike saw him. And then he would kill him.

Liam shivered. He was surrounded by white static. When he turned to look the way he'd come, there was nothing but white, like the houses had been blown away completely. Or had never existed.

The snowstorm had blown in seemingly out of nowhere. Snowstorms blew in across vast Lake Michigan all the time. It wasn't unusual. But without weather alerts, they no longer had forewarning.

Even with his parka, layered clothing, and the Ziploc baggies between his socks, he wouldn't last in conditions like this for very long. No one could.

Cold was a far greater threat to survival than it appeared. It decreased the ability to think and subdued the will to do anything, even to survive.

The cold was an insidious enemy. And Liam already had Pike to contend with.

He needed to end this, and quickly.

As if on cue, a dark shape appeared around the bend.

Just a shadow through the snow at first, then a deeper, darker outline trudging forward, slow and purposeful, head down against the wind. Thirty-five feet away.

Adrenaline kicked through him, rage a clenched fist in his chest. Liam brought the Bushmaster AR-15 to bear on his target and thumbed off the safety. He tapped the bottom of the loaded magazine to ensure it was properly seated and squinted through the scope.

Conditions had deteriorated so rapidly that Liam could barely see past fifteen to twenty feet. The wind and snow effectively deafened him and limited visibility. His senses, which he urgently depended upon, were blunted.

He needed his target closer to make sure he nailed the shot.

Liam tensed. He focused his breathing and slowed his heartrate. Anger slashed through him. He felt it thrumming through every frozen cell in his body.

This deranged psychopath was dying today. Full stop.

In his military career, Liam had killed hundreds of men. He'd killed dozens more just in the last few weeks. They were the enemy; he was the soldier who took them out.

This, however, was personal.

After what Pike had done to Hannah, the irreparable harm he had caused her... Liam wanted the scumbag to die a slow, painful death. For Liam's face to be the last thing he ever saw.

Twenty-five feet away. The wind cut through his clothes and whipped the snow into a frenzy. Liam blinked, clearing his vision, and aimed, finger applying pressure to the trigger.

The figure stopped. Pike moved abruptly to the right.

Liam fired. *Boom!*

Pike's body jerked. He stumbled but kept moving.

Due to the poor conditions, Liam's shot had gone wide, winging him in the shoulder instead of the chest.

He quickly shifted to adjust his aim, but Pike had already slipped between two towering pines and vanished into the swirling snow.

He resisted the urge to squeeze the trigger. To fire now would waste ammo and give away his position.

Patience was bred into an operator's DNA. He would wait for Pike to make a mistake and reveal himself first, then take a confirmed shot.

"She's mine!" Pike shouted.

Liam gritted his teeth and didn't answer. Pike was provoking him to betray his location.

"I'm going to take my time with her! Nice and slow!" His

voice was muted, stolen by the wind and flung away, echoing off the snow and trees. It sounded like it was coming from nowhere and everywhere at once.

Liam remained crouched, tracking with the rifle muzzle, blinking snow out of his eyes, finger poised on the trigger.

The crack of a gunshot. Bark splintered from a maple tree ten or fifteen feet to his right. Muffled by the snow, it was difficult to determine the origin of the shot.

Another shot boomed. Twenty-plus feet ahead and on his left, bark sprayed from a pine tree. Pike shouted another curse and fired again.

Pike was shooting blindly, hoping to flush him out. It had the opposite effect.

This time, Liam was able to get a bead on where he was likely hiding.

Liam moved. Electric pain shot through his spine in protest, his discs threatening to lock up after so long in the same position.

He blocked it out. He had a mission, and nothing would get in his way.

Keeping low, stock pressed against his cheek, Liam dodged back between the trees and made a wide circle as he flanked Pike's suspected location. Even with his aching back, he stepped as quietly as he could in the deep snow.

He ducked low, spine twinging, and peered out from around a thick trunk, leading with the AR-15. He squinted, searching through the driving snow and wind for shadowy movement or the glint of metal.

He swept the weapon from left to right, steadily searching in a grid pattern—scan left to right. Bump down five degrees. Scan right to left. Bump down five degrees. Repeat.

There.

Liam glimpsed a blurred figure. Twenty feet to the northwest, barely visible, a small, dark shape poked out behind the tall trunk of a birch tree. An odd contour that didn't belong. Liam squinted through the scope.

Pike's shoulder protruded. A thin strip of the back of his skull. He was facing away, searching for Liam to the north, back the way they'd come.

Liam carefully stepped backward to get a better angle, always mindful of the ground conditions around his shooting position. The discs in his spine shifted, fresh pain jolting through him. He stumbled.

Abruptly, the snow beneath his feet gave way. He tried to leap forward, but his boot snagged on a fallen log hidden beneath a drift of white powder.

The shelf of snow collapsed beneath him.

Liam fell.

10

LIAM
DAY TWENTY-ONE

Liam scrambled for purchase on the collapsing snow, but there was none. His boots skidded, his arms flailing.

He tumbled down the steep slope, tree trunks and fallen logs battering his body, his pants and coat snagging and ripping, twigs scratching his face.

He came to a sudden, jarring stop. His back struck the base of a large pine tree. Pain knifed from his lower back to his neck. His spine felt like it'd been filled with molten lava.

Dizziness flared through him. Black spots behind his eyelids. He blinked rapidly, disoriented and in incredible pain.

He gasped. Snow spilled into his opened mouth. He lay prone in the snow, jammed sideways against the trunk at the base of a steep ravine.

Trepidation speared him. He had to get up, had to get to his feet and reassess the situation. Pike had the high ground now. Liam was a sitting duck.

Urgently, he tried to sit up, instinctively reaching for his weapon. Nothing happened. His body refused to obey.

He moved his arms, flexed his fingers, and shifted his shoulders. His upper body seemed to be in working order.

His legs wouldn't move. He couldn't feel his feet.

He couldn't feel anything from the waist down.

He was numb. No, worse. He was paralyzed.

Fear and dread pressed down, suffocating him. A part of him had been waiting for this for years—the moment his injured back finally failed him.

The moment his own body betrayed him.

He would die here. Unable to climb the ravine, he would succumb to hypothermia within an hour. And Pike was still out there.

The cold was already burrowing into his bones, sinking deep inside him. Thickening his thoughts, the pain blurred everything to a distinct white haze.

You're not dead yet, Jessa whispered in his mind. *Don't give up now.*

She was right. He couldn't move his legs, but he could still move his arms. He could still shoot. As long as he had breath in his lungs, he could fight.

He thought nothing of his own survival. Only one thought drove him—ending Pike before he could get back to Hannah.

He shifted, ignoring the pain, and got his right elbow under him. He pushed in the snow, managed to raise his torso enough to snag his tangled AR-15, and pulled it out from beneath his ribs.

He pushed himself into a seated position against the trunk, legs splayed uselessly in front of him, and positioned the rifle stock firmly against his shoulder. He peered through the scope, his finger stiff on the trigger, and spanned the ridge top.

Normally, he could shoot a half-dollar head shot cluster at twenty-five yards. Not now. Not in conditions like this.

"Come on!" he shouted. "Come fight like a man!"

A blurry figure moved furtively through the trees along the ridge line. Twenty-five, maybe thirty feet above him.

Liam waited. The wind and the driving snow made it a difficult shot. His hands were like blocks of ice. The creeping cold bore down on him.

A gunshot splintered the air. Fifteen feet away, bark sprayed from an oak tree. A second and third round tore into pine trees ten feet to his right. Shredded bark and pine needles showered down on him.

"The hunter always wins!" Pike shouted from the top of the ravine.

Liam waited until he glimpsed movement. There. He exhaled, shifted slightly, and the AR-15 barked twice. The hot shells fell smoking into the snow.

Pike's curse was nearly swallowed by the storm as he went down. Liam sought him through the scope. By the time he found him, he was up again and had shuffled back behind the trees.

He was limping. Liam had nailed him in the leg. How badly, he couldn't tell.

"Come out!" Liam shouted. The cold seared his lungs, the wind snatching his voice and hurling it away. "Show yourself, you coward!"

"You lose!" Pike screamed from behind the safety of the trees. "You've already lost!"

Liam waited, not breathing, ready to fire. The second he showed himself, Pike was dead.

No movement from the top of the ridge line. No sound other than the creaking trees and the moaning wind.

Snow drove into his face and eyes. He blinked the flakes away, his heart in his throat, an ill feeling slick-sliding through his guts. *Come on, come on.*

Pike did not come out. He did not show himself.

And why would he? Liam wasn't his target. Liam wasn't his end game.

All Pike had needed was to get Liam out of the way. He'd accomplished that goal. Pike was already gone.

Anger like he'd never felt slashed through Liam. Rage mingled with gut-wrenching fear. Not for himself; never for himself.

A monster was heading Hannah's way.

This time, there was nothing Liam could do to stop it.

11

JULIAN
DAY TWENTY-ONE

Julian and Rosamond stood in her expansive kitchen, all glossy white cabinets, smooth marble, and shiny high-end appliances. They faced each other across the island.

"What the hell just happened?" Rosamond asked Julian. "Why do I have two dead bodies on my hands?"

Julian still wore his coat, hat, and gloves. Snow dribbled from his boots onto the polished wood floor. He inhaled the delicious scent of cooking pizza wafting from the oven.

Heat bathed his face. The electric lights cast a soft, warm glow. Rosamond constantly kept the generators on to back up the solar power.

It was evening. The windows were dark. Outside, the cold, wind, and snow lurked.

Nothing could get inside this house, where everything felt untouched by the chaos, like a fly caught in amber. The furniture pristine, the shelves dusted, everything immaculate; just like his mother.

Here, lights still flicked on and off and water poured from the tap on command. Only three weeks had passed, and a hot shower already seemed like a miraculous, precious commodity.

Fresh anger flushed through him as he explained the attack on Darryl Wiggins and the townspeople's attempt to take over a Winter Haven house. "They think they deserve Winter Haven. They want it for themselves."

Rosamond steepled her fingers on the counter. Her polished scarlet nails flashed in the light. "I see."

"They don't deserve it. They could've bought one of these houses years ago. They didn't. That's their choice. Now they have to live with it. Everyone else here has earned it. We're the ones putting ourselves on the front lines to keep the town safe. The least we can do is give them a roof over their heads."

"Not everyone understands that."

Julian took off his gloves and stuffed them in his pocket. "We should just let them starve. Why are we working so hard to feed them when they repay us like this?"

"This is our town," Rosamond said quietly. "Our people. It's our job—my job—to provide for them. As long as I am able, I will do that." Her expression hardened. "But neither will I stand by and allow them to harm each other and act like spoiled children."

"What are you going to do?"

The oven timer beeped. Rosamond pulled oven mitts from a drawer. She opened the oven, pulled out the pizza tray, and set it on top of the stove to cool.

The cheese bubbled deliciously. Catching a whiff of the tantalizing smell, his stomach rumbled.

She pulled off the mitts and returned them to the drawer. "You know what I miss most of all? Salad. What I wouldn't give for a bowl of mixed baby greens slathered in balsamic vinegar right now."

He'd always hated salad. "What happens next?"

His mother moved to the large stainless-steel refrigerator and opened the freezer. It was stuffed full of food—fruits, vegetables, meats, and ice cream. Julian knew she had two other freezers in the garage, both bursting at the seams. Not to mention the crates in the basement.

She took out a bag of frozen strawberries and a loaf of garlic bread and set them on the marble island. "Tell Sutter's men to stop feeding anyone who participated in the attack. And their families."

"That would work. Except there's one problem. Those particular families aren't going to the community distribution center at the middle school."

"What do you mean?"

"They're getting all the free food they want from Atticus Bishop."

His mother's mouth twitched. The skin around her eyes tightened. "This is only a problem because of *you*."

He couldn't help it; he flinched.

"You were supposed to stop Bishop weeks ago."

Resentment boiled through him. "I did! I tried! How was I supposed to know—"

"That's the problem, isn't it? You never know. You never plan. You never think things through. You just act—rashly and recklessly, without regard to consequences. All actions have consequences, Julian. They're like dominos, one tumbling after another. If you don't know exactly where that last domino will land, then you're acting blind. The strongest leaders—those that last, those that leave a true legacy—they never act rashly. They're never blind. They know exactly what they're doing, and why, every single step of the way. Do you understand?"

"Yes!" he said defensively, anger slashing through him. "Of course."

For a long moment, she didn't say anything. She opened the garlic bread packaging, tugged out the frozen bread, and put it in the oven. She pulled a large bowl from the cupboard beside the sink and poured the fruit into it.

Julian waited with barely restrained impatience. He shifted from foot to foot, his hands balling into fists at his sides. He wanted to defend himself, explain his actions, place the blame on someone—anyone—other than himself.

He fought to curb his anger, biting his tongue so hard that he tasted copper. He knew better than to interrupt his mother when she was like this—using her silence as a weapon to cow him.

It worked. His face burned with humiliation. He felt small and impotent, like a bug squirming beneath her thumb.

Finally, she settled her gaze on him. She pursed her lips and lowered her brows, her eyes as sharp as ice. A look of intense displeasure, of disgust.

He hated that all-too-familiar look. Despised it. For a blistering second, he imagined slapping it off her smug face. How satisfying it would feel. How empowering.

His mother gave a long-suffering sigh. "Gavin would have taken care of this problem. He knew how to use a scalpel rather than a hammer. He always knew what to do."

Jealousy bit deep into his soul. His face went hot. "I know what to do!"

She stared at him, her eyes hard, appraising him and finding him wanting. "Do you really?"

"I'm not stupid," Julian said petulantly. "I know what you're trying to do. He who controls the food controls the people."

"It's so much more than that. We can't afford dissent. If we are divided, we won't stand against the outside attacks that will come." She shook her head wearily. "That's what no one understands. They don't want to understand. They want safety, but they don't want to pay the cost. By the time they understand the truth, it will be too late. They're small-minded and stubborn as children. They don't know what's best for them. But *we* do. *I* do. I have to make the hard decisions for them. That's why I'm in charge. That's how I must lead."

"If the only place they can get supplies is through us, then they have to obey us," Julian said, scrambling to satisfy his mother. "That's how we force them to do what we want. Anyone attacks Winter Haven again, we take the food away. Let those stubborn fathers and mothers watch their kids starve. See how the people like that."

She sliced the steaming pizza with a pizza cutter and slid two pieces onto a china plate. She added a piece of garlic bread dripping with butter and the bowl of fruit. She sat down on the stool at the island, unfolded a cloth napkin, and smoothed it over her lap.

She stared down at her food without taking a bite. "I do not understand why some people insist on acting against their own self-interests. I wish there was another way."

Julian's stomach rumbled with hunger. He'd been working all day. Gone were the days when he could pull through the McDonald's or Taco Bell drive-thru.

His mother did not put out a plate for him or offer him a slice. He knew better than to ask for one.

"There isn't another way," he said.

"You're correct, son." She straightened her already perfect posture. "We have no choice."

"Bishop is out on that rescue mission of yours. A couple of volunteers are running the Crossway food pantry right now. I know them. They aren't like Bishop. They won't be trouble."

"And when Bishop returns?"

"I'll handle him. And Noah, too."

"Noah will handle Bishop."

Resentment speared him. "Noah? Why Noah? I can do it—"

"I will decide what you can or cannot do!" She shot him another displeased look. "Noah is on our side."

A surge of jealousy burned through him. Bitterness mingled with loathing. Julian was supposed to be chief of police. Julian was supposed to be running this town.

Not Noah Sheridan, his former best friend. "Is he? Are you sure about that?"

"Let me deal with the new police chief. Noah requires more—finesse. But he's loyal. I trust him to do what needs to be done."

The words she didn't say echoed through the room. Julian stiffened. "You can trust me, too."

"We'll see." She cocked her brows in that condescending, mocking way of hers. "Can I trust you to take care of the food pantry, or do I need to get Mattias involved? Do you think you can handle it this time? Are you up to the task?"

He swallowed bitter bile. "Absolutely."

His mother stabbed a small frozen strawberry with her fork and raised it to her lips. "There's nothing like freshly-picked strawberries, but these still have a sweet tartness to them."

Rosamond chewed slowly, thoughtfully. The sneer faded from her face. For a moment, she looked pensive, almost haunted. "In times of great crisis, we are forced to do what we must to protect the whole group. I thought what had happened would be enough. That everyone had suffered enough."

She set the fork down, her expression softening, and gave him a warm, motherly look. "You weren't the only one who made a mistake, son. So did I. We must fix it now, by any means necessary."

He drew himself to his full height. "I'm ready."

She nodded. "Then shut it down."

Julian was already heading for the door, a dark smile creasing his face.

12

NOAH
DAY TWENTY-ONE

"One more chapter?" Milo begged.

Noah Sheridan closed the book. "We've already read four chapters. I need a break, buddy."

"A break from what?"

"My throat is getting sore, for one. Plus, to be honest with you, I'm a bit tired of thinking about the end of the world."

Milo tugged the book out of his hands, stroked the cover lovingly, and tucked it under his pillow.

Quinn had let him borrow it from her personal collection. It was titled "Life as We Knew It" and was about the moon shifting from its orbit and basically destroying life on Earth.

Like anyone needed yet another world-ending scenario to worry about.

Noah and Milo were snuggled in Milo's bed at their new house in Winter Haven, a half-dozen blankets piled on top of them.

The solar panels hadn't gotten much solar energy in days, so they were using portable propane heaters for warmth and flashlights and lanterns at night. Many of the homes had backup generators that the militia kept stocked with fuel. This particular house did not.

Outside, yet another snowstorm raged. Wind and snow battered the house. The walls creaked and moaned. Visibility was less than six feet. Venturing anywhere—even to the next house—was a death wish.

The whole town had hunkered down, bracing themselves against the onslaught, determined to wait it out.

For once, Noah was stuck at home, too. He didn't mind the time to catch up with Milo, but he knew the workload would triple as soon as the storm relented.

Just like the other storms over the last weeks, people would need to be dug out of their homes. Stores of food, toiletries, and firewood replenished.

Some—the elderly, the sick—would have run out of anything to eat or drink or keep them warm during the storm. They wouldn't make it.

Noah would have to send out a team to go house to house and remove corpses.

It was a grim thought, but a part of their lives now. They'd lost another eleven residents to hypothermia in the last eight days.

It was only mid-January. They had a long way to go before winter finally ended.

Noah rolled over to face Milo. He double folded a pillow beneath his arm. "Hey, buddy. Before you slip away into dream world, I just wanted to check in with you to see how you're doing."

"I'm fine, Dad."

"Quinn has you taking your meds twice a day like clockwork, right?"

"Yep. Every single day."

Sutter and the militia brought Noah more hydrocortisone pills with every scavenging trip, though they hadn't been able to go out like usual due to the blizzards rampaging through southern Michigan.

Noah wasn't worried. He had several years' worth stashed in a duffle bag in the master bedroom closet. The constant anxiety that had stalked him in the first weeks after the EMP had dissipated.

But not his worry for his son. That never went away.

"You know I have to make sure."

"Quinn says you're overprotective."

Noah lifted his eyebrows. "Does she now?"

"She says I should be able to climb the tallest tree that I want to. She says I can jump out of airplanes if I want to." He chewed his bottom lip. "Just as soon as there are airplanes again."

"I'm pretty sure you have to be eighteen for that."

"Fine, whatever. Can we put it on my pail list?"

Noah smiled. "You mean your bucket list?"

"The list you make of stuff you wanna do before you die."

"Yes, that." Noah's chest tightened. He hesitated. "Why are you making a bucket list?"

"Quinn says everybody dies."

"Well, technically, but—"

"Everybody dies, but not everybody really lives. I said we should make a list of all the stuff we wanted to do while we're still alive. Because you don't know how long it'll last."

Noah swallowed a sudden thickness in his throat. He was only eight years old, but Milo had already seen horrible things and lived through a lifetime of terrors.

First, the dead bodies on the chairlift the day of the EMP. Then the Crossway Massacre. And now the shootout at Darryl Wiggins' place yesterday.

Thomas Blair and his friend, Ted Nickleson, were dead. The Blairs, Nicklesons, and a few others had gotten it into their heads that they could forcibly take a Winter Haven house for themselves.

The militia had quickly disabused them of that notion. Desoto's tactics were brutal but effective. Anyone who'd been thinking of trying something similar would seriously reconsider. Noah didn't agree with them, but what was done was done.

Rosamond had taken it a step further. None of the family members associated with the guilty parties would receive any supplies from the town's distribution center. Nothing. Not a can of beans or a roll of toilet paper.

Mrs. Blair was a widow. Her daughter Whitney was mourning her father.

Noah couldn't help it. He pitied them.

Once this snowstorm let up, Noah would pay Rosamond a visit. He'd talk to her, get her to lighten up, walk the orders back a bit.

Things would be okay. He'd make sure of it. He was the police chief now, after all.

"You know I make rules and check on you because I care about you," Noah said. "I'm just trying to keep you safe."

Milo rolled his eyes. "I know, Dad."

Noah reached out and brushed Milo's curly hair back from his face. It was getting long and hung in his eyes. Noah would have to track down some cutting shears and give him a home haircut.

Yet another aspect of society's collapse that he'd never thought about.

Though Noah was half Hispanic, he took after his Irish-American father, with dark brown hair but a fair complexion. Milo had inherited the olive skin-tone of Noah's Venezuelan mother, with his unruly black curls and big dark eyes.

His round, little-boy face was thinning, his features resembling Hannah's more and more every day. Noah's heart swelled with love for this sweet, serious kid.

"I mean it. We have to be careful. The world's unsafe. Anything could happen. Milo, you watched two people die yesterday."

"Quinn smushed my face into her stomach. It hurt. I didn't see anything, just heard the loud bangs. I wanted to help. She wouldn't let me."

Noah exhaled. Quinn to the rescue. Again. She'd told him as much, but it was reassuring to hear it from Milo's mouth.

"I'm glad she did that, son. The world—it's different than I wish it was. I can't protect you from everything, much as I want to."

"That's what Quinn says."

Sometimes, he listened to Milo's versions of Quinn-isms and Molly-isms all day long. There were worse things. "What does Quinn say?"

"That you can't stay safe from everything. That trying to do that ends up being worse in the end. That living your life means taking some risks. That you just have to be smart about it, not stupid like most people. It's like a trampoline. No, a balancing act. Like in the circus."

Irritation flared through him. Noah pushed himself into a seated position on the mattress. He raked his hand through his hair. "That's Quinn's opinion. She's sixteen years old."

"That's lots of years older than me."

"Not that much older. Not nearly old enough," Noah snapped. "When you both are as old as I am, then maybe you can start making the decisions. Until then, I'm the one in charge. And I'm the one who decides about safety. You got it?"

Milo's face fell.

Guilt pricked him. Noah had spoken too harshly. He hadn't intended to.

He cared about Quinn, but she was still a kid, idealistic and naïve. She had a kid's notions about how the world should be. Should be, not the way it was.

In the real world, you had to make concessions and compromises. Sometimes, you even had to do things that made you dislike yourself.

He squeezed Milo's shoulder. "Hey. That wasn't cool. I'm stressed out, but that was no excuse. I'm sorry. Forgive me?"

Milo nodded, relieved. He scooted up onto his elbows and buried his head against Noah's chest. Noah wrapped his arms around his son. So small, so thin. Noah's entire heart caught in this little boy's body. His love for his son beat hard and fierce, aching in every cell.

"I love you, son. There isn't anything I wouldn't do for you."

"I know, Daddy," Milo said, his voice muffled. "I love you, too."

13

HANNAH
DAY TWENTY-ONE

Hannah waited.

Ghost whined at the front door.

Hannah wanted to give in to him, to fling the door open and send him out into the night to help Liam. But she didn't.

Liam's words rang in her ears. *Do not open the door for anyone but me. Keep Ghost here to protect you and Charlotte.*

He'd left over an hour ago. If it were just her, she'd release Ghost anyway, despite Liam's order.

But she had Charlotte to think about. Charlotte to keep safe.

"I'm sorry, boy," she said. "We have to wait for Liam to come back. We have to wait."

Ghost growled his displeasure. He glanced back at her, ears cocked, his brown eyes giving her a pleading look.

"I hate it, too."

She sat in the middle of the living room facing the front door. She sat straight-backed in a kitchen chair that she'd pulled in from the dining room.

Her Ruger American .45 lay in her lap. The safety was off.

Charlotte slept in her drawer beside the fireplace. She'd been sleeping for an hour. She'd wake up soon, hungry again. Newborns ate a lot more than she remembered.

In the fireplace, a log popped and whistled and settled onto its bed of coals. Small flames leapt for the flue and vanished in midair.

Outside, the snowstorm beat at the house. Trees creaked. A branch thrashed against the roof.

Hannah's heart was a wild thing in her chest. She jumped at every noise, every creak and thud. Every second that Liam was gone stretched her nerves tighter and tighter.

She fought the fear, the dread. For eight days, she'd believed Pike was dead. Now, like some sort of demon, he'd returned from the grave. A man with no soul. A man who represented evil in its purest form.

She believed in God. Maybe belief in a god necessitated a belief in its opposite—a supernatural force bent on evil. Maybe that force was sustaining him, bequeathing him with otherworldly powers no mere mortal could possess.

She shook those thoughts out of her head. That was ridiculous. That was her fear talking.

Pike was a man. Just a man. He could be killed. He *would* be killed.

Liam would do it this time. She had to believe that. The alternative was untenable.

Her fingers tightened on the grip of the Ruger .45.

A small cry came from the dresser drawer. Charlotte was awake.

Hannah rose and carried the gun with her. She set it on the floor at her feet, squatted, and gathered the babe into her arms. She rocked her gently, lovingly, murmuring into her soft, downy scalp.

The knit cap Liam had made had fallen off while she was

sleeping. Her lower half was damp.

Hannah changed her on the sofa—removing the soiled makeshift diaper and placing it in the small trash can they'd reserved for that purpose, washing her bottom with rags she dipped into a kitchen mixing bowl half-full of warm water, and re-swaddling her in fresh strips held in place with safety pins.

There wasn't a rocking chair, but rather a stuffed reading chair sat invitingly in one corner of the living room. She sat and nursed Charlotte back to sleep. Charlotte's little eyes drifted closed, a sweet, satisfied expression on her tiny face.

She trusted in her caregiver completely. She had no idea what was out there. The evil in the world. The things that hunted them.

Love for the infant in her arms tightened her chest. She had been so afraid she wouldn't be able to love her, that she would feel the same loathing and revulsion for the child as she did for the monster responsible for creating her, who shared her genes.

What if she'd looked like Pike? What if she had his darkness, his evil? What if every time Hannah looked at her, she saw her captor reflected in her child's eyes?

But she didn't. She looked like Hannah. She looked like a baby: innocent and blameless. Pike had no part in this. Her daughter was hers and hers alone.

For all that Hannah had endured and would endure, this burden was not one of them. She loved her daughter, wholly and completely, and without reservation.

Hannah held Charlotte. She hummed tunelessly but didn't sing. The words, the notes—they wouldn't come to her. Her eyes ached, but she was too anxious to sleep.

The snowstorm outside created heavy, wavering shadows. The day was bleeding into late afternoon. She listened to the branches scraping the side of the house and the moaning wind and fought the fear creeping in.

She felt the snow all around her, pressing down on the roof, slowly creeping up the walls, crouching beneath the windows.

She counted the books in the bookcase—one hundred and thirty-three—the blinds over the windows—fifty-six—and the stripes on the comforter—forty-two.

Tiny and warm, Charlotte pressed against her chest. Anchoring her, keeping her present.

She held the baby with her good hand; with her bad hand, she dug into the front pocket of her sweatshirt and tugged out her pocketknife with the four-inch blade.

It was difficult to grip with her misshapen fingers. They had been broken, healed crookedly, only to be broken again. Bones, like anything else, were strong—until they weren't.

They were crippled and ugly. Useless. Well, almost useless.

She'd been practicing as much as she could over the last week. Learning to adjust her mangled grip so she could hold things. Working the aching joints and coaxing movement from stiff, arthritic fingers.

The gnarled bones grated against each other. Every small movement caused pain. She didn't stop until her crippled fingers had closed over the handle.

She closed her eyes for a moment, relieved.

It wasn't something she'd ever wanted to do—to hold a knife, to wield a gun.

It was necessary. She would do what she had to do.

Ghost stiffened. His hackles raised. His tail stood straight out.

He gave a savage, booming bark. The explosive sound rang in her ears. Ghost jumped up and scratched at the front door.

Every hair on her neck stood on end. Her arms tightened around Charlotte. The baby squirmed but didn't wake up.

Hannah stilled, straining her ears.

Ghost kept barking. His nails scrabbled on the wood floor as he sprinted from the front door in the living room into the kitchen.

She heard a crashing sound as he threw his body against the door leading to the garage in the hallway nook between the kitchen and living room.

His barking was relentless, ferocious, and terrifying. She'd heard that bark only once before.

Terror sprang into her chest. She folded the knife, stuck it back into her sweatshirt pocket, and rose swiftly to her feet with the baby in her arms. She crossed the living room, bent, and placed the sleeping infant in the dresser drawer.

Ghost's barking deepened. Threatening, fierce.

Something was out there. Something that was trying to get inside.

Not *something*. She knew what it was. Who it was.

She had to hide the baby. She picked the .45 off the floor, flicked the safety back on, and slipped it into the pocket of her sweatpants. She couldn't carry the gun and the drawer. She needed to be quick.

Heart in her throat, she squatted, hefted the drawer with Charlotte sleeping peacefully inside, shifting so her bad hand helped balance the weight though she couldn't grip the edge with her fingers.

She moved swiftly from the living room to the stairs, where she turned sideways so she could press her back against the banister and see a bit better as she climbed the stairs carefully, her arms already straining from the ungainly weight.

At the top of the stairs, she headed for the little girl's purple bedroom on the right, just before the guest bathroom. The master was all the way at the end of the hall. The gray light from the upstairs windows was dim and shadowed, but enough to see by.

It was cold up here. Much colder than the living room with

the fire. Hopefully, she'd bundled Charlotte in enough blankets to keep her warm.

She squatted again and set the drawer down in front of the guest room dresser. She moved to her knees, picked up the drawer again, and attempted to slide it into the empty slot.

Her hands were shaking, and she fumbled, nearly dropping the drawer. Her stomach lurched. She couldn't have Charlotte waking up now. She needed her quiet and hidden.

She tried again and this time the sides caught and she slid the drawer closed with trembling fingers. She left a few inches of open space for the baby to breathe.

If anyone were to glance into the darkened room, they would see nothing unusual. Nothing out of place. They wouldn't notice the precious infant tucked inside the dresser.

At least, that's what she prayed for with a desperation that thrummed through her entire being.

Liam wasn't here. She knew that in her heart of hearts.

If it was Liam out there, Ghost wouldn't be acting like this, like he wanted to tear the entire house down to get at whoever lurked outside these walls.

She could not think about what might have happened to Liam. Not now.

It was up to Hannah to protect herself and her child. Hannah and Ghost.

She seized the pistol from her pocket and looked down at her baby one last time.

"I love you, sweet girl," she whispered. "Sleep, and don't wake up until it is safe. Whatever you do, don't wake up."

14

PIKE
DAY TWENTY-ONE

Pike circled the house.

The wind whooshed through the brittle, leafless branches. Ice crystals blew into his face like thousands of tiny pinpricks. His feet and hands were numb.

He floundered through deep snow. He staggered and lurched, clutching his wounded side. Sluggish blood leaked between his fingers. The outside of his right thigh burned like someone had pressed a hot poker against it.

Two bullet wounds. He'd been shot twice, but he was still going.

Adrenaline kept the pain from overwhelming him. Sheer will power kept him on his feet.

He didn't care. He didn't care about any of it. The blood would stop. The wounds would heal, just like every injury he'd suffered before this.

Pain was nothing but a distraction—one he'd learned to conquer long ago.

He'd barely been able to follow the tracks back to the house through the storm. Luckily, Liam's tracks were deep. He was a big man. A dead man, now.

It hadn't gone down the way Pike had envisioned. The way he'd fantasized for days, for weeks.

No matter.

He was a hunter. Hunters were adaptable. Flexible. They adjusted on the fly, recalibrating every plan of action as needed.

Liam was no longer a threat. That was the important part. That was what counted.

The soldier no longer stood between Pike and the girl.

She was in the house. Alone—but for that damned dog.

He could hear the beast barking over the soughing of the wind and the creaking trees. It would be a problem.

He had never wished for a gun more acutely. With his ammo gone, the Smith and Wesson was a useless chunk of metal. He'd chucked it into a snowbank.

Pike would find a way. He always found a way.

He continued his examination of the house. He trudged through driving snow, carefully and quietly checking every door and window on the lower level.

The sliding glass door was nailed with plywood. The windows wouldn't budge. The soldier had blocked them with wooden shims.

Even if he broke the window, he wouldn't be able to pry the frame open. And the jagged glass would make it nearly impossible to climb inside without adding more grievous injuries.

Structurally, the garage door was the weakest part of the house. Once he got through the garage door, he could escape the brutal wind and take his time lock-picking the door to the inside.

Earlier in the week, he'd scavenged a scrap of a two-by-four and a wire clothes hanger from one of the nearby houses and reshaped it to suit his needs. He'd straightened the hanger and formed a hook shape with one end.

He wedged the block of wood into the space between the top of the garage door and the frame, creating a two-inch gap. He stuck the hook end of the hanger up through the slim gap between the top of the garage door and the frame and threaded it through.

It took a minute of fishing around blindly, feeling for the tug of the hook snagging on the garage door's emergency safety release. He felt the hook catch and pulled down steadily. The door released, free from the carriage, so that all he needed to do was grab the garage door from the bottom and slide it open.

Even if he hadn't been able to reach the contraption, the hook could also grab the handle at the end of the cord dangling from the lever and disengage the release that way, too.

Less than a minute and he was in. In better weather conditions, he had gotten inside a garage in under ten seconds.

Most garages included such a security flaw. This one was no different.

It always surprised him how few people considered their garage security. How easily thieves could gain entry to the garage to pillage its contents or worse—have all the time in the world to pick the lock of the exterior door, unseen by neighbors or looky-loos, and get into the house.

He kicked the snow that had drifted against the garage door, wincing at the pain spearing his side and thigh. The wind battered him, nearly knocking him off his feet. The dog's incessant barking pounded in his ears.

He forced open the flimsy aluminum door just enough to slide beneath it. Snow snuck beneath the neck of his coat and trickled down his back as he rolled beneath the door into the garage.

He inhaled sharply. The air was cold and stale. The storm raged outside, not in here. He blinked, adjusting his eyes to the meager gray light spilling from the opened garage door and the single window on the left-hand side.

He clambered to his feet more slowly than he wanted. The gunshot wounds and the exhausting trek through deep snow had depleted his energy more than he wished to admit.

His lungs burned for a clove cigarette to settle his nerves, but he didn't want to take the time. He was close. So close.

He paused, taking in his surroundings. In front of him, a tan sedan and a hulking gold SUV crowded either side of the garage. Along the back wall stood a row of three tall metal shelves bristling with junk—totes and crates, shovels, rakes, toolboxes, a snowblower, and a chainsaw.

To his right was the side entry door. A chest freezer lined the wall just past the door. A hand-push mower sat next to it.

The dog's frantic barking grew louder. A thudding sound. And then another. The door shuddered in its frame.

Cursing silently, Pike moved to the shelves at the back. He tried the chainsaw. That would shut the stupid animal right up.

Out of gas or rendered useless by the EMP? Either way, it didn't start.

He scanned the shelves, searching for something better. He settled on the gardening shovel. The handle was sturdy, the steel blade tapered to a wicked point, and the shorter length allowed him to swing it like a club.

Shovel in hand, he strode to the side door, set it down, and examined the lock.

The exterior door lock was a simple pin tumbler lock. It didn't even have a deadbolt. He silently cheered his good fortune. It was about time something went his way.

It was not difficult to pick the lock, though the frenzied dog on the other side was disconcerting, to say the least.

It smelled Pike, sensed him just like Pike sensed Hannah's nearness.

Its claws scratched metal. It hurled itself against the door, shaking it in its frame.

Pike unlocked the door and hefted the shovel. He paused. His heartbeat accelerated, his mouth dry with anticipation. Eagerness thrummed through him. A dark thrill.

Get this right, and he was seconds from Hannah. Seconds from having all the time in the world with her.

When the moment felt right, he twisted the handle and kicked the door inward as hard as he could. As he'd expected, the door slammed into the dog.

The beast let out a pained whimper. It hesitated, shaking its head, momentarily stunned.

Pike seized the shovel handle with both hands and swung it at the dog's head.

At the last second, the creature darted to the side. The spade of the shovel missed its skull and struck its burly shoulder instead. The impact thrummed up the shaft and knocked the handle from Pike's hands.

The dog fell sideways into the frame of the doorway. It was on its feet faster than Pike thought possible. It gave a ferocious growl, black jowls peeling back to reveal sharp white teeth.

The enormous dog filled the doorway, all gleaming fangs and snarling fury. A memory slashed through him—the library, the beast looming over him, savagely snapping at his throat.

Pike stumbled backward. He whirled and fled.

He dashed around the rear bumper of the tan sedan as fast as his legs could carry him. He barely felt the knifing pain in his side, the searing burn in his thigh.

With a snarl, the dog followed.

Pike rounded the back of the sedan and ran up the center

between the two cars. His right leg gave out, and he stumbled hard against the side of the sedan. Fresh adrenaline spiked through him.

He limped forward, grasped the passenger side mirror and dragged himself along. He had to keep a vehicle between himself and the dog just long enough to get away. Just a few seconds were all he needed.

The beast chased him, barking and snarling. The animal slid as it rounded the back of the car, its paws scrambling for purchase, and slammed into the rear fender of the SUV.

It regained its footing with record swiftness and came at him again.

Pike hobbled to the front of the car. He lunged for the metal shelving, seized the nearest one with both hands, and jerked it backward. The shelf wavered, then toppled with a mighty crash.

Pike juked to the side and ducked beneath it, coming out on the left side in front of the sedan as the shelf collapsed behind him —right on top of the dog.

It yelped in surprise and pain.

Pike didn't bother to look back. He dodged around the front of the car and lurched for the open side door.

Metal scraped against concrete. Objects pinged and thudded against the garage floor. The dog barked in fury.

Pike didn't risk a glance back, but he could imagine the animal clawing and clambering out from beneath the toppled shelf as it fought to free itself.

Pike reached the door. The dog scrabbling only feet behind him, about to pounce.

Pike dove inside. He turned, fumbling for the handle, and threw the door shut.

The dog slammed into it. The door shuddered. The resounding *thud* reverberated in Pike's ears.

Pike took a step back into the darkened hallway, pressing his hand against his bloody side and breathing hard.

The dog barked in furious indignation. It threw itself at the door again and again.

Stupid animal. Dogs were supposed to be smart and loyal. This one was utterly worthless. Pike should've put it down long ago.

With his free hand, he pulled out his Zippo lighter as he moved into the kitchen in search of a knife. *Click, click, click.*

How soothing that sound was. How pleasant.

Despite the pain, despite the weariness pulling at him, Pike smiled.

He would come back to finish off the worthless mutt later.

Now, though, it was time for Hannah.

15

HANNAH
DAY TWENTY-ONE

Hannah met Pike in the hallway.

Distantly, she heard Ghost barking from another part of the house. He was still alive, but he was trapped somehow. He couldn't get to her.

Instinctively, she understood. She was alone in this.

Fear shook her entire body. Gut-clenching terror like a train roaring at her, the harsh light blinding her, filling her vision.

There was nowhere to go. Nowhere to run.

Her tongue was coppery, her mouth filled with nails. Part of herself threatened to fall away into darkness. She fought it with everything in her.

She had overcome too much to let fear rule her now.

Her legs had felt like concrete as she'd forced herself to move from the purple bedroom where Charlotte was hidden through the long hallway to the stairs, then down to the shorter hallway that led to the living room and kitchen.

Every step that brought her closer to Pike felt like treachery. Every fiber of her being screamed at her to *run*, to *hide*.

She held the .45 with both quavering hands. The butt was nestled in the crook of her bad hand the way Liam had taught her.

The safety was off. The seven-round magazine was full, with an additional round in the chamber.

CiCi had given her this gun. CiCi, the feisty old woman who'd helped them, befriended them, only to be murdered by this monster. The monster who'd stalked her to this place, who'd invaded her sanctuary and threatened everything she loved.

She took the last step, entered the short hallway, and moved cautiously toward the living room. Pistol held high. Her socks slipped on the wood floor. Her breaths were too loud, her pulse a roar in her ears.

She heard it first.

Click, click, click.

Horror froze her in place.

Click, click, click.

The scent of cloves stung her nostrils.

In the center of the living room, Pike appeared.

Ten feet separated them. He stood silhouetted in the dim light. An apparition, a demon from hell.

Still, she recognized him instantly. The shape of him. The smell of him. The sound of him.

He saw her and smiled. That slash of a red mouth. Those dead eyes. "Hannah, Hannah, Hannah."

Hannah couldn't move.

Pike slipped the lighter into his coat pocket. In his other hand, he held a kitchen knife. The long, sharp blade glinted in the firelight. "It's been far too long, don't you think?"

She'd forgotten words. Forgotten how to speak. Forgotten everything but the fear.

His gaze shifted to the weapon in her hands. "What do you think you're going to do with that? We both remember what happened last time. It's useless with that crippled hand of yours. Why don't you put it down? It's useless to fight. You know that. You've always known that."

Her bad hand ached. Her arms felt incredibly heavy. Her finger slick and shaky on the trigger.

She managed to raise the Ruger until it was even with Pike's head, trying frantically to remember everything Liam had taught her. Plant her feet. Steady her hands. Aim down the sights.

"Let's finally end this, shall we?" He took a step toward her, that awful smile still painted on his face. "Put it down, little mouse."

"I'm not a mouse," Hannah said.

She squeezed the trigger.

The pistol bucked in her hands. The gunshot exploded in the narrow quarters of the house. The concussive sound stunned her, rang in her ears. She blinked, trying to refocus.

Pike stumbled backward.

She didn't know if she'd hit him. She squeezed the trigger twice in quick succession. The gun jerked, the blasts slamming into her ears.

She took a step forward. Fired. Then another step. Fired again.

She had no idea if she was shooting where she was aiming. Her heart beat frenzied wings against her ribs. Adrenaline shot through her. It was hard to see straight, to think, to focus.

She wasn't used to this. Hadn't trained for it.

Her practice sessions meant little in the heat of the moment, with panic breathing down the back of her neck and everything on the line.

Pike moved back. He clutched at his left shoulder with his knife hand. His face contorted in a grimace of rage and pain.

She fired again as he turned and darted deeper into the living room.

She wouldn't let him get away. Not again. On shaking legs, she followed him.

Frantically, she scanned the room. The two couches and the coffee table pushed against the far wall. Her mattress with the purple princess sheets in the center of the room. The fire in the fireplace crackled and popped.

As she emerged from the hallway, Pike appeared, bursting from behind the living room wall. He sprang at her. He came in low, below her line of fire, lunging for her legs.

Panic seized her. She squeezed the trigger once, twice, three times. *Boom! Boom! Boom!*

Pike grunted a curse and dove for the floor.

She aimed low and fired. The Ruger clicked. The chamber was empty.

Pike was on his hands and knees. Six, seven feet away. Breathing heavily. Blood stained his left shoulder, leaking down his arm. A two-inch gash in his coat.

The round had skimmed him. Enough to hurt, but not enough to do serious damage.

Reflexively, she pulled the trigger again. *Click.*

She didn't have another preloaded magazine. She knew where Liam kept more rounds, but it would take far too long to reload with her useless hand. The gun in her hand was just as useless to her now.

Dimly, she heard Ghost's frenetic barking. She heard her heart roaring in her ears, felt it bucking in her chest.

This couldn't be happening. She and her worst nightmare were in the same room, breathing the same air. And she had nothing with which to defend herself.

Pike climbed slowly to his feet. He brushed himself off and checked his shoulder.

She couldn't move, couldn't breathe; her legs were rooted to the floor.

Pike looked at her. He still held the knife in his hand. Grimacing, in pain, but with a dark light flashing in his eyes. "This is the part where you run."

16

HANNAH
DAY TWENTY-ONE

Hannah ran.

Pike stood directly in front of her, blocking her exit. The doors and windows were all blocked. They would take time to open. Time she didn't have.

There was no time to think, no time to formulate a plan.

She spun and stumbled for the stairs behind her. Her thoughts a blur. Panic turning her brain to mush.

She stumbled down the short hallway and hauled herself up the steps, gripping the railing with damp palms, her socks slipping on the slick hardwood.

Pike clambered after her, cursing.

She reached the top of the stairs and sprinted down the narrow hallway. Past the guest bathroom on the right, the two little girls' rooms on the left. The first one pink, the second purple.

The purple room where Charlotte slept—peaceful, innocent, and utterly oblivious to the darkness hunting her. She bypassed it.

She had to keep Pike away from it, away from her daughter.

The only coherent thought in her head was a desperate prayer. *Stay asleep. Please, dear God, make her sleep.*

That, and *escape*. Find a way out. Get away. Stop him.

She reached the end of the hallway. Only one direction to go. She swerved right into the master bedroom. Her socks skidded on the floor, and she crashed into the bedroom door.

She heard him grunting behind her. He'd just reached the top of the stairs.

She pushed the door shut and fumbled for a lock. It wouldn't stop him for long. The doors weren't even real wood; the handle locks were flimsy.

Her frenzied gaze skipped over the darkened room, the shapes looming out of the shadows. A massive bed, a mirror on one wall, two dressers covered with picture frames.

She scrambled behind the tall dresser next to the door and pushed with all of her might. It rocked on its squat legs.

The door handle rattled. Pike punched the door. "Open the hell up, Hannah!"

Her breath came in rasping gasps. A stitch in her side. Her belly, her whole body ached in protest. She'd given birth a week ago. She was out of shape, still recovering.

With a desperate cry, she lowered her shoulder and rammed into the dresser again. This time, it tipped over. She knocked it on its side across the door just as Pike slammed into it from the opposite side.

Even that would only give her a few precious seconds.

She turned and examined the room again. Two nightstands on either side of the bed. Two small lamps stood on the nightstands.

Her thoughts came jumbled and frantic. She couldn't *think*.

Could she hit him on the head with the base of the lamp? Maybe. The lamps were small, their bases slender.

She ran alongside the bed, reached the nearest nightstand, and seized the lamp with her good hand. She tried to pull it. After a few feet, the lamp stopped short.

The cord was caught between the nightstand and the wall. It was stuck. She fumbled for the nightstand, tried to move it with her bad hand. It moved a few inches.

She swallowed a moan of despair and knocked the nightstand over with a mighty heave. She yanked the cord from the wall.

Only then did it register how light the lamp was. Not even real metal. Some fake composite thing from Hobby Lobby. It wouldn't even stun him.

The bedroom door shook and rattled. A steady *thud, thud, thud* as Pike inched the door wider and wider. He'd be inside in seconds.

She couldn't try to wrestle the knife from him or hit him on the head with something that wouldn't be enough to knock him out anyway.

Not with her withered hand. Not in her weakened state. Not with blind terror thrumming through every cell of her body.

She dropped the lamp and fled into the master bathroom.

She took in the room with a glance. She already knew where everything was. She'd washed her hair up here just yesterday.

A shower stall to her right, the toilet in its own tiny room just beyond it, the double vanities crowded with hair products and huge wall mirror directly ahead, the oversized tub and closet to the left.

Hannah crouched beneath the sink and opened the cabinet door. The hair shears she'd used to cut her hair. That's what she needed.

Her hands were stiff and shaking so hard, she fumbled just to get the door open. The shears were in a black plastic case buried in the back of the cabinet.

Terror made her clumsy. Every movement was slow, jerky, and uncoordinated. Her quivering, ruined hand couldn't get the damn case open.

The bedroom door bashed open.

Time slowed.

She heard every sound. Ghost barking distantly downstairs. The wind moaning, the trees creaking against the house.

Pike lumbering through the bedroom toward her. His footfalls squeaked with every step.

She heard him breathing. Smelled coppery blood and cloves.

Pike jerked open the bathroom door. She glimpsed his reflection in the mirror. The shape of him a dark mass, his eyes black holes.

Too late for the scissors. Too late for anything.

Hannah rose to her feet. Her heart galloped inside her chest.

She seized the can of hairspray from the counter, spun as she raised it, and depressed the nozzle. She sprayed it directly into his eyes.

He screamed in agony.

She barreled past him. She shot out of the bathroom, racing through the master bedroom, toward the hallway.

Fear drove her. She wasn't thinking, wasn't planning. She was a fleeing animal, nothing but panic and instinct.

She tore down the hallway and nearly fell down the stairs. She slid the last few steps on her butt and was up again, stumbling through the living room toward the kitchen.

Ghost's frenzied barking grew louder. The side door to the garage. If she could reach it, she could get Ghost—

"Hannah!" Pike's voice rang through the house.

He was right behind her, too close. Already running down the stairs. Almost on top of her. "I'm coming for you, you little slut—!"

She fumbled for the doorknob and jerked open the door. She threw herself through the doorway, took a step, and fell into empty space.

Her knees buckled and her feet struck uneven floor. The impact jarred her from the soles of her feet up through her spine.

She nearly pitched face-first down the stairs.

She skidded, stumbling, falling. Her hands flailed, scrabbling for purchase. Her bad hand banged against the wall. Her good hand closed around something round and smooth. A railing. She jerked herself to a stop almost halfway down the narrow wooden staircase.

Her ankles hurt. Her knees stung. She'd wrenched something in her belly. She barely registered any of it.

The smell hit her first. The scent of earth and damp concrete and musty old things like air from a tomb. Like stale ghosts escaping.

Horror filled her.

In her panic, she'd opened the wrong door. She wasn't in the garage.

Hannah was back in the basement.

17

HANNAH
DAY TWENTY-ONE

A scream crawled up Hannah's throat.

This was a different basement.

It didn't matter. In her nerve-shredded terror, it was the same.

A creak above her. His heavy stomping boots. She could feel him like a cold draft sifting up through the floorboards, the prickle of dread at the base of her skull.

A wave of darkness threatening to overtake her.

The last three weeks evaporated in a blink. The past came roaring back. She was in the basement again. The same basement she'd awakened to every day for five endless years.

Her prison. The trap that had caught her, snatched her from her life, from her family, from the outside world. It had swallowed her up like a grave.

Blinding fear took over. Her only thought was to *hide*.

Gripping the railing for balance, barely able to see through her terror, she fled down the remaining steps.

Down, down to the basement.

Down to the pit of her worst nightmares.

Two narrow windows offered the dimmest light. The floor

was dirt. A stench of worms and rot. Cobwebs and rough stone walls. Everything cold and damp.

Thick dusty hand-hewn beams crossed the low ceiling. A huge hulking furnace in the far corner.

Stacks and stacks of cardboard boxes taller than her head. Rickety old shelves filled with cloudy jars, rusting metal tools, knickknacks and junk.

On the other side of the basement, she glimpsed a pair of slanted doors like in the *The Wizard of Oz*. Bilco doors, but too high for her to reach.

Her gaze snagged the furnace in the corner. It was set back in an alcove steeped in shadows.

Behind the furnace, deep in the alcove, was a crawl space. Not two feet high, it went too far back to see the rear wall.

It was darkness and cobwebs. Dirt and rotting beams.

A hiding spot.

Pike's boots clomped on the basement stairs.

Limping, she shuffled across the dirt floor to the furnace. She flattened herself against the stone wall and inched past the narrow space between the wall and the furnace, holding her breath, sucking in her still-swollen belly, imagining centipedes and spiders dropping into her hair, onto her face.

The stink of grease and dirt invaded her nostrils. She inched past pipes and wires and dim metal shapes until she reached the crawl space at the bottom of the wall.

She couldn't see it, could only feel it with her fingers.

She crouched, turning her knees sideways so she could get low enough. She squeezed herself flat and dropped onto her belly. Using her elbows on the hard dirt, she wriggled forward, easing her body into the shallow crawl space.

Her sweatshirt snagged on something and she reached back to tug it free. Her arm could barely slide in next to her torso. She squished herself as deep into the confining space as she could go.

She could hardly move. The dirt pressed against her stomach, legs, chest, and face. The weight of the entire house bore down on her.

Footsteps in the dirt. Slow and halting, but still coming, still relentless.

They stopped a few feet from the furnace.

"Well, well," Pike said. "Here we are again."

She held her breath. A whiff of iron. The coppery stench of blood in the back of her throat.

"You shot me, you know. Just a graze. Pretty pathetic, really. That hair spray, though." He swore vehemently. "You nearly blinded me, little mouse. My eyes are still smarting. I bet you're proud of that. I bet you think fighting back makes you special, don't you?"

Horror surged through her veins. She squeezed her eyes shut.

"Well, you're not special. You're nothing. You've always been nothing. I never should have left you alive this long."

Dust clogged her nostrils and irritated her throat with every shallow breath. It took everything she had not to sneeze. Her eyes watered.

"Come out!" His voice hardened. "You think I won't find you? You think there's anywhere you can go in this whole doomed world where I can't get to you? There's nowhere to run. Nowhere for you to hide."

Her entire body trembled. Darkness shimmered in front of her eyes, threatening to take her under again. There was nothing to count, nothing to anchor herself to.

"Your soldier is dead, you know."

Grief mingled with the fear. She hadn't let herself think those thoughts. Now they came crashing down on her.

Liam, the loner haunted by loss and secrets. Liam, the brave, competent soldier. Liam, who'd chosen to save her, who'd risked his life for hers.

"I killed him. I'm sure you know that. He didn't need to die. He came after you. He came between us. Stuck his nose in business that didn't belong to him."

She bit down on a sob.

"I wonder if he regretted helping you as he took his last breaths. What do you think? I think he did. Of course, he didn't tell me." Pike chuckled. "He didn't say much of anything, actually."

Maybe he was lying. Maybe it was a ploy to get a rise out of her. To get her to give in to despair and come out. It was working. Despair tugged at her, threatened to overwhelm her.

It didn't feel like he was lying. He was here and Liam wasn't.

"How about this. I'll offer you a deal." He paused. "Give me my child and I'll let you live."

She didn't move. Didn't breathe. Her heart forgot how to beat.

"Don't think I didn't notice underneath that baggy sweatshirt. The baby. You had it."

A part of her had been desperate to believe that he wouldn't realize she'd had the baby. That he wouldn't even think to look for her. How wrong she'd been.

"The last one was a boy. I wonder...did you give me a son...or a daughter?"

She could hide here. For hours. Days, even. He would never find her. Even if he did, he couldn't reach her. She was safe from him.

Charlotte wasn't.

Her baby. Her child. Her responsibility.

In her fear, she'd fled instead of fighting. Maybe hiding would keep her alive, but it wouldn't protect her child.

No one could protect Charlotte. No one but Hannah.

"Stay here and hide like the little mouse that you are, Hannah," Pike continued. "You're scared and meek, aren't you? Just like you've always been. A few weeks under the sun won't change who you are. That's why I picked you!"

She hated her quivering, traitorous heart. Despised the fear clamping down on her like a vise, the panic that blurred her thoughts and muddied her resolve.

She'd tried to fight back. She'd thought she was getting better. Stronger.

What if she wasn't? What if she'd already failed?

18

HANNAH
DAY TWENTY-ONE

"I know you," Pike said. "I *know* you! Better than anyone. Better than Soldier Boy. Better than your husband. Better than your son...Milo."

At the mention of her son's name, she sucked in a sharp breath.

She felt Pike perk up. Felt his attention drawn toward her like a magnet. "Ah. You didn't like that, did you?"

She bit her tongue until she tasted blood.

"Sweet little Milo, with those dark eyes and dark curls. He'll be quite the ladies' man, if he ever grows up."

She could sense that he was moving by the sound of his voice growing distant, his dragging footsteps.

"I can kill every single thing you love, Hannah. I don't have to touch you to hurt you. Your Soldier Boy is already dead. That damn dog is next on my list."

A soft cry filtered through the floorboards. The distinctive wail of a newborn.

Even in the basement, even over Ghost's relentless barking, the sound was unmistakable.

Her heart stuttered in her chest. A terror like she'd never felt took hold of her.

"Ah! There it is," Pike said. "You know, maybe I'll leave you here to rot. Maybe I'll kill your child first, then come back for you. Maybe you should die knowing its blood is on your hands. Is that it? Or maybe...I'll take it to Fall Creek. I've been there all this time, you know. Living and working right alongside Noah. Watching Milo grow up. He's even had dinner at my mother's house. Did you know that?"

Anger sprouted in her chest. Rage mingled with the fear and grief and dread. This man had stolen everything from her. From her family. From her son. Her children.

Milo and Charlotte. The two chambers of her heart, beating in tandem.

She'd stayed alive for five torturous years for her son. For her daughter, she'd come back to life.

She hadn't escaped her basement prison for this. She hadn't bled and fought and clawed her way out for this.

Not to cower in the dark. Not to be controlled by fear. Not to let a man destroy everything she loved.

And that's all he was, in the end. A man. Flesh and blood. Not an all-powerful demon who couldn't be vanquished.

She'd made him bleed. She could do it again.

"Last chance, Hannah."

His limping footsteps faded. He was heading for the stairs. Headed for Ghost—and for Charlotte.

Hannah's heart nearly burst inside her chest. The ceiling of the crawl space pressed down on her, a thousand tons pushing her down. Willing her to stay in place, to stay trapped.

She moved anyway.

Hannah inched backward. Slowly, painstakingly. Dirt and

dust stung her nose, itching her throat, crumbling against her lips. Concrete scraped against her side and back.

She shoved and crawled and fought her way out of the confined space, feet first. In the narrow alcove between the furnace and the wall, she wriggled to her knees, then used the wall to clamber to her feet.

She was covered in dirt, cobwebs snarled in her hair. She didn't bother to wipe them away.

Urgency gripped her. She had to get to Pike before he reached the top of those stairs. She had to stop him.

She wasn't running anymore. She was coming to him.

Despite the fear. Despite her deformed, crippled hand.

She would fight, even if she was all alone. She would protect the ones she loved with every drop of blood that remained in her body.

"Pike!" she shouted. Her voice felt gritty, gravel in her throat. She pushed and shoved against the tangle of wires and pipes. Sharp things scraped and poked at her. She barely noticed. "I'm right here!"

She stepped out from behind the alcove.

Dim light from the narrow windows cast the room in filmy shadows. She was used to the dark. She could see just fine.

Pike was poised halfway up the stairs, one hand on the railing, one holding the kitchen knife. He stopped at the sound of her voice.

He turned toward her, a startled look on his face. He hadn't expected her to come out.

She took a step toward Pike. Her legs trembled but did not give out on her. She took another step. "Here I am."

An eager gleam came into his eyes. That look of cruel pleasure she remembered so clearly when he'd broken her fingers. When he'd hurt her.

She did not cower from the memory. She pushed into it. She focused on his squinty, reddened, watery eyes, on the trail of red staining his shoulder.

She'd done those things. She'd hurt him.

Just a man.

She remembered who she was now. She remembered what she'd forgotten.

Hannah shoved her hands inside her sweatshirt front pocket, lifted her chin, and walked toward him. "I'm the one you want."

He hobbled down the stairs toward her. His gait uneven. Slower than she'd expected. More blood streaked his leg. A large scarlet blotch stained the right side of his winter coat.

Maybe she'd shot him two or three times. Or maybe Liam had gotten in a good hit. Either way, Pike was wounded and hurting. More than she'd thought.

He stopped at the bottom of the stairs. "Take your hand out of your pocket. No funny business, now."

She stopped a foot away from him. Well within range of his knife. It glinted in the pale light. He held it low and loose. He wasn't afraid of her. He wanted to take his time.

She heard her baby crying. Heard Ghost barking. Her own ragged breathing.

She tore her gaze from the blade and trained her eyes on his. She removed her right hand, opened her fingers, showed him she was harmless.

"I'm the one you want," she said. "Take me instead."

Pike leered at her. "Oh, I will. I've dreamed of this moment. Haven't you? I know you have. I know you've been thinking about it just as much as I have."

Her left hand remained inside her sweatshirt pocket. In her blind panic, she had forgotten it, just as she'd forgotten herself. She remembered now.

He leaned in close. His breath in her face, red mouth grinning. "You know, I'll take it anyway. Girl or boy, it's mine. It belongs to me. Just like you. Just like—"

Her deformed fingers closed over the handle of the pocketknife. Painfully, awkwardly, but they closed. Twisted, gnarled fingers, broken again and again.

They worked enough. They worked for this.

She withdrew the knife, flicking it open with an agonizing twist of her thumb.

He didn't even glance down. He feared nothing from the thing he'd already broken.

With her bad hand, Hannah stabbed Pike in his stomach.

19

HANNAH
DAY TWENTY-ONE

The four-inch blade angled up and sank through Pike's coat into his stomach to the hilt. Blood gushed over Hannah's misshapen fingers. Her hand slipped from the handle.

Pike let out a startled gasp. He stared down at the knife stuck in his stomach, mouth gaping.

Before he could regain his senses, she pushed him. He stumbled back against the post at the bottom of the staircase and collapsed to his knees. The kitchen knife slid from his grasp and clattered to the concrete.

Hannah bolted up the stairs. Her feet pounded the wood treads. Her hand grasped the railing and hauled her upward, toward the door, toward freedom.

Below her, Pike let out a groan of pain and outrage.

At the top of the stairs, she opened the basement door. One hand on the door handle, she paused on the top step.

She turned and looked back at him. "You're going to die here in this basement."

He stared up at her. His face contorted, half grimace, half leer. That red slash of a mouth that had once so terrified her. "You think you can get away from me...little mouse? You think there's... anything *you* could do to me?"

Hannah said nothing.

Pike staggered to his feet. He was breathing hard, a stain of dark blood spreading rapidly over his coat. With quavering hands, he pulled out the pocketknife and tossed it away. He clutched at his bloody stomach, grievously wounded. "You...can't kill me."

Hannah gave a grim smile. "Who said it would be me?"

She took a step into the hallway. Wiped her bloody hands on her sweatpants and seized the handle to the garage door. She opened it wide.

She didn't have to tell Ghost what to do. He already knew.

The Great Pyrenees burst through the doorway, crossed the short hall in a single bound, and plunged down the stairs.

He charged at Pike, one hundred and forty pounds of solid muscle, gleaming fangs, and relentless fury.

Pike blanched. His face went bone white. "Stay! Go back! Stop! Obey, you stupid—!"

He never got a chance to finish his sentence. He barely had time to raise his hands in self-defense before the great dog was on him.

With a savage snarl, Ghost leapt from halfway up the staircase and pounced on Pike.

Pike toppled backward, Ghost on top of him, teeth bared, snarling and snapping. They landed with a crash. Pike screamed, flailing wildly.

The dog didn't hesitate. Ghost lunged in. His sharp teeth ripped through the coat at Pike's neck, shredding fabric like tissue paper. He closed his powerful jaws over Pike's jugular.

Pike let out an unearthly howl that cut off abruptly in a wet gurgle as Ghost ripped his throat out.

Hannah sagged against the wall, listening to Ghost's jaws

tearing and slashing, listening to the terrible sounds of a man dying in agony.

In only moments, the anguished, gurgling moans went quiet.

There was nothing but the silence. The house still and waiting. The walls watching.

Hannah breathed in and out. Her heart thudded in her chest. She stared down at her bloodied hand for a moment like it didn't belong to her.

Alive. She was alive.

Pike, her nemesis, her monster, was finally dead.

Ghost—beautiful, brave Ghost—had meted out justice for them both.

20

HANNAH
DAY TWENTY-ONE

Ghost's nails scrabbled across the concrete floor. He padded up the steps, limping slightly. A wet, blood-drenched muzzle pressed into Hannah's bad hand.

Though it hurt, she forced her deformed fingers to move. She buried them in Ghost's thick white fur.

Her legs turned to water and she sank to the floor in the alcove between the basement and garage doors. She leaned her head against the wall.

Minutes passed. It could have been hours. She breathed, just breathed.

Upstairs, her daughter had stopped crying. She must have fallen back asleep.

She was safe. Hannah had kept her safe. Hannah and Ghost, together.

Ghost did not move from her side. With a soft whine, he flopped across her legs, a hundred and forty pounds of unconditional love and unfailing courage.

Her heart swelled. She thought it might explode right out of her chest. She petted him with both trembling hands. She wrapped her arms around Ghost's neck and nestled her cheek against his giant head. "I love you, you know that, right? You are the best dog in the whole wide world!"

Ghost raised his muzzle and chuffed softly, as if the compliment was as obvious as the nose on his face.

"I promise, when the world goes back to normal, if it ever does, I owe you a wheelbarrow full of beef jerky. You'll be in beef jerky heaven."

Ghost pressed his head against her chest and thumped his tail.

Upstairs, Charlotte whimpered softly.

Hannah pushed gently on Ghost. "Let's go get her."

Ghost scrambled off her legs. She pulled herself unsteadily to her feet. He stayed close as she made her way from the kitchen to the living room and then to the staircase.

She ascended the stairs, Ghost beside her. Not ahead or behind her, but right at her side. He leaned against her, providing steady support, strength, and comfort. Just like he always did. Somehow, he sensed just what she needed, and when.

With each step, she felt herself growing lighter. The darkness shedding like a snakeskin. Felt the strength returning to her limbs, vigor to her soul.

Hannah rushed down the hallway, entered the purple room, and fell to her knees in front of the dresser. She had blood on her hands, but she didn't care. She opened the drawer, picked up her baby, and cradled her against her chest.

Smelling her mother's scent, Charlotte began crying in earnest.

"I know, I know," Hannah crooned. "I'm right here. I'm here and I will never leave you. I promise, okay? I promise. I'm right here."

Ghost padded over and touched his nose to Charlotte's cheek.

He sniffed her from head to toe as if checking to make sure she was okay. Seemingly satisfied, he gave a low chuff of approval.

"She's yours now, too," Hannah said softly.

Ghost cocked his head, pricked his ears, and gave her a look, as if he found that fact quite obvious. He chuffed again and took up a position in the doorway.

He sat tall and alert, keeping watch—a handsome prince of a dog intent on guarding his little flock. His plumed tail thumped the floor in a slow, contented rhythm.

Hannah sat next to the dresser, leaned against the foot of the bed, and rocked Charlotte. The baby's cries subsided. Safe in her mother's arms, her tiny scrunched face relaxed, and she drifted back into sleep.

Hannah felt the tug on her own eyelids, her limbs suddenly heavy.

She felt tired, so tired. Her body and mind exhausted to the core. But she couldn't allow herself to rest. Not yet.

With Charlotte still in her arms, she clambered awkwardly to her feet. She couldn't bear to put her down.

Ghost rose and gave an anxious whine. She glanced at him. He turned toward the doorway and chuffed.

"I know, boy. I know."

She followed him out of the room, down the stairs, and into the living room. Ghost bounded to the front door and gave a low, throaty growl.

Outside, the snow still sheeted from the iron-gray sky. The wind howled around the corners of the house. Fingers of icy cold slipped through the seams in the windows.

Hannah's chest tightened. She felt a sob rising in her throat and swallowed it back. If she started weeping, she might never stop. "You're looking for him, aren't you?"

He whined again, high and plaintive.

She looked down at Charlotte nestled peacefully in her arms. The crooked knit hat was tugged over her soft, fragile skull. "Do you think he's still alive? I want him to be. That doesn't mean he is."

Ghost scratched at the door and looked back at her imploringly.

"If anyone could still be alive out there, it would be him."

The dog went to her, poked his nose against her palm, then circled back to the door. His tail swished back and forth. He pressed his muzzle against the door handle.

"You want to go out there. You want to go find him."

Ghost gave a low chuff of assent.

"It'll be dangerous. It's deadly out there, Ghost. I can't—" She sucked in a breath, her eyes stinging, and tightened her hold on Charlotte. "I can't lose you, too."

Ghost rose onto his hind legs and pressed his front paws against the door. He was taller than she was. Strong and beautiful and courageous.

She bit her lower lip but nodded slowly. She raised her chin. "Then I guess we'll both have to be brave."

Ghost glanced back at her, a question in his beautiful brown eyes.

"You are so brave. So good and brave. I have one more request of you, my friend."

Ghost waited expectantly.

"If he's alive, find him and bring him back." Hannah reached for the door handle. "Find Liam."

21

LIAM
DAY TWENTY-ONE

Liam was dead.
  Or, nearly.

He had fought in wars. Assassinated dozens of men. Leapt out of choppers and airplanes. Survived bombs, shrapnel, and ambush attempts.

Hell, he'd even survived a plane falling from the sky in downtown Chicago.

Nothing had ever felt like this.

He was paralyzed. Frostbite and hypothermia took hold of his body and mind. It didn't matter how strong, how skilled, or how fierce he was—nature was stronger, fiercer.

Not only could he not feel or move his legs, his hands were growing stiff and numb. The frozen ground beneath his butt sapped the warmth from his body. Snow matted his hair. His face felt scalded.

He knew maintaining circulation in his extremities was critical to preventing frostbite. He couldn't do anything about his lower body, but he twitched and wrinkled his face, rubbing his ears, cheeks, and nose with his hands. He wiggled his fingers inside his gloves, squeezed his hands into fists, windmilled his arms.

He was losing critical water through every intake of cold, dry air, which had to be humidified by the body to be used effectively. It felt like the cells lining his respiratory tract were freezing with each ragged breath.

The cold crept into his mind, infiltrated his brain. His thoughts began to slow, becoming jumbled and disjointed.

His nightmares stalked him, images of his past haunting him—Jessa and Lincoln and the babe he'd left behind, his namesake. His nephew.

Thoughts of Hannah slipped in and out of memories of Jessa. He saw them both—Jessa's warm brown skin and generous smile, Hannah's delicate freckled face and those green eyes shining like gemstones, beckoning to him, whispering an answer he desperately needed, but no longer remembered the question to.

Sometimes, he no longer knew what was past or present. Where he was or why. Who he'd been chasing, who he needed to get back to.

Time drifted, and after a while—a minute, an hour, a day—he didn't feel cold anymore. He didn't feel much of anything.

He could just sit here and rest. Wait for Jessa or Lincoln to come for him.

I'm not coming for you, Jessa whispered in his mind. *No one is coming for you.*

His eyes stung as if ash had been sprinkled into his eyeballs. Blinking was getting difficult. His eyelashes were sticking together. Soon, his eyelids would be iced shut.

He would be blind as well as paralyzed.

You have to get up, Jessa said in her strong, capable voice. *You need to get up now.*

If he didn't get his butt up and start moving, he would die

here. He didn't fear his own death. He'd never feared death. He did fear what he would leave behind.

Hannah and Charlotte would be on their own. And that was unacceptable.

You have to go. You have to go to Hannah.

He forced himself to sit up straighter. His back scraped against the tree trunk. Snowflakes tumbled from his head and shoulders.

I'm already gone, Jessa said. *You aren't yet.*

Don't leave me, he thought. *I need you.*

No, Jessa responded, her voice already growing dim and distant. *You don't.*

He knew he'd never hear her voice in his head again. Just as he knew that she was right.

It was Hannah he needed now. Hannah he needed to get to.

It wasn't just a mission anymore. Hadn't been for a long time. His frozen heart thawing painfully, achingly slow, but thawing all the same.

He cared for her. He cared for Charlotte. He had to get back to them. *Wanted* to get back to them, with every beat of his heart.

He would crawl to her if he had to.

With a pained grunt, he forced himself to move. He sank onto his side and rolled onto his belly, awkwardly forcing the AR-15 to his back. He began to low crawl up the steep slope.

It felt like attempting to scale the back of a frozen wave. He used his forearms to pull himself along, arm over arm. Snow in his face, his mouth, his arms grasping for the next branch, the next slim trunk poking from the snow, the next tangle of roots buried in the powder.

He dragged himself upward, inch by inch, foot by exhausting foot.

His hair had frozen into brittle tendrils. His hands were snow-burned, his cheeks scalded. His legs and arms felt like deadweights—the blood freezing to sludge in his veins. His toes burned.

His toes. Burning. Hurting.

He tried to move them. They were numb. Both of his feet were numb. Simultaneously, they burned like he'd pressed them against a hot stovetop.

If he were truly paralyzed, he wouldn't feel anything. Nothing at all.

He choked in a breath that seared his lungs.

The memory came to him in fractured pieces. This had happened before, years ago in Afghanistan after a mission. His crushed discs shifted, grinding, pinching a critical nerve that had severed the feeling in his lower half for hours.

His feet tingled painfully like they were being pierced with needles. It hurt like hell. The feeling spread slowly up his legs—so did the pain. Electric jolts seared his spine, scalding his nerves.

But he could feel. He could move his legs.

Relief washed through him—replaced just as quickly by nerve-shredding fear.

Hannah. He had to get to Hannah.

He looked up. Just above his head, a thick branch protruded from a tree trunk. He reached up and grabbed hold of it. His stiff hands slipped a few times, but he finally got a good grip and pulled himself to his feet.

He slid his foot forward, straining to place the heel down, then the toe, every step slow, brutal, strenuous. He leaned into the incline, legs aching, muscles burning, pain burrowing deep.

White-hot electric pain shot up his spine. He cried out. Sucked in a sharp breath that seared his throat and lungs.

He needed to manage the pain, or it would overwhelm him, send him into shock.

He'd dealt with pain like this before. He knew what to do.

He analyzed the pain, imagining it like a white ball of fire at the base of his spine. He traced it through his body—a fiery trail of nerves, muscles, bones, and tendons.

He created a clear image of the pain in its entirety. Then he placed it in a mental box and sealed it away. He locked it down.

It partially worked. His thoughts were too slow and ragged. The cold slowed his mind, his reflexes, everything.

If you can't think, you can't lock it down. An old Army Ranger buddy had told him that.

Still, it was enough. It had to be enough. Failure was not an option.

His heart was pumping so fast that he felt his temples begin to throb. The incredible exertion was causing him to sweat, his body clammy beneath layers of clothing.

Once he was damp, the frigid cold would take him that much faster.

If he stopped, he died.

Finally, he reached the top of the ravine and collapsed. He needed to catch his breath and regain his strength. He lay back, gasping searing breaths, willing his body to move, to keep going.

He struggled back to his feet and started toward the woods, searching for the tracks that he and Pike had left.

He had no idea where he was, no way to orient himself in the whiteout conditions. People could freeze to death five feet from their house—five feet from safety that they couldn't see, hear, feel, or sense in a blinding snowstorm.

He plodded ahead. He resisted the urge to shuffle forward with his hands outstretched. It was the opposite of absolute black—sheer blinding whiteness.

He stumbled forward in the snow, boots sinking deep, staggering from tree to tree. Red droplets snagged his gaze. He'd nearly walked right over them before seeing them. A trail of blood splatters beside two sets of tracks nearly filled in, smoothed over and almost erased by the brutal wind.

Nearly, but not quite. If he squinted, he could just make them out.

He followed the tracks, never wavering, his years of training kicking in. He had no idea how far his legs would hold him, how long until his body temperature dipped to critical levels.

If it were only his survival to consider, he would stop now and use the last of his strength to create a snow shelter to block the merciless wind and optimize his own body heat.

It would save him from freezing to death. He could safely wait out the snowstorm.

But he could not delay any longer. The monster was after Hannah. He had to stop it. He had to get back to her.

He yelled Hannah's name as loud as he could. His mouth formed the shapes to make the correct sounds, but he heard nothing.

He shouted again. The sound was so utterly obliterated by the wind that he didn't know whether he'd made a sound at all.

He was a soldier. He was trained for this. Trained to survive in any conditions, anywhere.

That was who he was. It was bred into every fiber of his being.

He kept moving. Every step slow and halting, requiring tremendous effort and concentration. His spine was on fire, his legs like wooden blocks separated from his own body.

He was caught in a snow globe being shaken violently by an unseen giant hand. Snow everywhere he looked. In every direction. Until he was unsure what was ground or sky, left or right.

Still, he maintained a dull awareness of his surroundings. The howling wind. The bending, creaking trees—white pine, sugar maple, red oak, hemlock. The relentless snow.

Every few yards, he stopped to listen. It was a long-engrained habit, but he heard nothing. Saw nothing—

Between the trees, something moved.

He balanced himself against the slim trunk of an aspen tree and fumbled for his weapon. His hands felt like frozen blocks of ice. How many rounds did he have left? Five? Ten? He couldn't remember. He had his Glock but wasn't sure if he could even squeeze the trigger anymore.

He was in no shape to defend himself effectively. Even he knew that.

The shape moved again. Darting from tree to tree. So blurry and indistinct, he might be imagining it.

It was no man, no human. A ghost maybe.

It was Lincoln, returning for vengeance. His eyes accusing. *How could you leave me? How could you let her die?*

Liam blinked.

Not Lincoln. His twin was dead and gone.

His ghost existed only in Liam's mind, not out here in this harsh winter landscape. Not in the snow and cold.

Jessa. But not her, either. She had left him. She wasn't coming back. Not even her voice. He knew this and accepted it.

A white shape against a wall of blinding whiteness. A white thing leaping through snowbanks, kicking up sprays of snow.

The blurry figure gradually took shape as it drew nearer. Liam could barely make out the length of the body, the regal head, the long-plumed tail.

Relief washed through his veins. Even in his delirious state, he knew who it was.

Ghost was coming for him. A great fluffy angel bounding through the snow.

The dog dashed up to him, barking urgently. He pranced

around Liam in enthusiastic circles. Had he been barking all this time, and Liam had never heard it, never registered it?

He forced his bleary mind to focus. He buried his numb hand in Ghost's ruff and held on tight.

"Lead me to our girl," he said, his voice raw. "Take me to Hannah."

22

HANNAH
DAY TWENTY-TWO

A soft but persistent sound penetrated Hannah's dream. Her eyes snapped open.

It felt like hours had passed since Ghost had dashed out into the blizzard in search of Liam. She'd tried to remain awake, but exhaustion had finally lulled her into sleep.

She lay on the couch in Liam's customary spot. The Ruger .45 was reloaded and resting on the floor beside the couch within easy reach.

Charlotte slept on her chest, a tiny heater warming Hannah's entire body. The house was completely dark but for the low fire barely flickering in the fireplace.

She stilled her breathing and strained her ears.

The sound came again. A low, distant bark.

She sat up so fast that Charlotte gave a whimper of protest. She shushed the infant and set her gently in her drawer bassinet. Hannah had brought it back downstairs and placed it near the fire to keep her warm—and close by.

She grabbed the gun with her good hand, following Liam's

training. She went to the door and pressed her ear against it, listening.

Another bark. This one slightly louder.

She knew that bark. Knew it like she knew her own name.

Hope surged in her chest. Maybe it was futile, maybe it was pointless, but she hoped anyway. With her whole broken heart.

Be alive. Please be alive, she prayed, mouthing the words fervently. *Bring him back to me.*

She fumbled for the lock, kicked aside the door stopper, and threw open the front door.

The wind grabbed the door. She had to hold it tight to keep it from slamming open as snow and wind and cold gusted in.

The blast of freezing air slapped her in the face. Snowflakes drove into her face and clotted her eyelashes and eyebrows.

She ignored it all. She shielded her eyes with her bad hand and peered into the snowy darkness.

A shadow moved in the distance. Maybe two shadows.

"Here!" she screamed at the top of her lungs. "Come here!"

She remembered the whistle Liam had given her, tucked beneath her sweatshirt. She pulled it out and blew as hard as she could.

An answering bark from Ghost.

She whistled again and shouted. The cold seared her lungs. She didn't care. She waved frantically. "Come on! You're almost here!"

Ten yards away, two figures emerged from the darkness.

Ghost slogged through the snow, head down, ears back, powerful legs straining with every plodding step. Liam staggered beside him. His back was bent, shoulders hunched, one hand buried in the fur along Ghost's spine. The dog was practically dragging him.

But he was alive. Liam Coleman was alive.

Hannah ran out into the snow. The sudden shock of cold felt like plunging into a frozen lake. She sank to her knees. She wore only socks, but she didn't care.

Relief surged through her veins. She could've wept with joy.

She dashed to Liam, grabbed him, and slung his arm across her shoulder. He was so heavy. And so, so cold. His face was ashen beneath the scarf wrapped around the lower half of his head. He looked half-dead.

Concern flared through her. She had to get him inside. She had to get him warm.

Luckily, he was still on his feet. Otherwise, she'd never be able to drag his weight inside. "Come on! You're almost there!"

"J-Jessa?" Liam mumbled.

Her lungs constricted. He couldn't see her. His eyelids were glued shut from ice and snow. He was hallucinating.

"It's me, Liam. Come on. It's me."

She staggered forward. One trembling step in front of the other. Snow scalded her feet. The snow crusted to Liam's coat froze her neck and shoulders.

Somehow, she and Ghost got him into the house. Liam stumbled inside. Hannah couldn't hold his weight anymore, and he collapsed to his knees just inside the doorway. Ghost slipped inside, and she shut and locked the door.

She scratched Ghost beneath the chin. "Good boy! I knew you could do it. There's fresh water and food waiting for you in the kitchen. I'll stoke the fire in a minute and get you both warm."

Ghost shook himself, spraying snow all over Hannah. Chunks of ice and snow still clung to his coat.

At least he had thick, insulating fur. He was born for this, his ancestors bred to withstand below freezing temperatures in the Pyrenees mountains.

He'd be fine. Liam wouldn't.

Liam needed her.

"J-Jessa," Liam mumbled. "I-I'm sorry. I-I'm s-so sorry."

He swayed on his knees. He looked like he was about to pass out.

"I need you to help, Liam," Hannah said firmly. "I need to get you to the mattress. You're almost there. Let's go."

Hannah got hold of him beneath his arms and dragged him to the purple mattress in front of the fire. It took every ounce of strength she had in her and then some.

With a grunt, she rolled him onto his back. The man felt like he weighed half a ton.

Worse, every inch of him felt frozen solid. He was shivering violently. His lips were blue. Patches of his face were reddened, the tip of his nose white with frostbite.

Urgency gripped her. Liam was hypothermic. He was alive now, but if she didn't act quickly, he wouldn't be for long.

Only three weeks ago, Liam had found her weak and shivering in the middle of Manistee National Forest. He'd taken care of her. Now, it was her turn to take care of him.

The fire had gotten too low while she'd slept. She added a few logs and stoked the fire. Flames spit toward the flue. Sparks whirled.

The heat warmed her. It would warm Liam, too, but she had to get him out of those clothes.

As swiftly as she could, she unlaced his boots. It was difficult with only a hand and a half. She gritted her teeth in frustration as she yanked off each boot and stripped both pairs of his socks. The outer wool sock was damp, but the Ziploc baggies had kept his feet dry, thank goodness. Still, they were almost as hard to remove as his gloves.

"Sorry," she whispered as she jostled and tugged at his upper body to get his coat off. He was practically dead weight. "Work with me, here!"

He yanked his arm out of her grasp and flailed wildly. She ducked. He nearly punched her in the face.

"No!" he cried. "Get away f-from me! J-Jessa, I'm coming! I'll c-come for you!"

He was delirious, hallucinating. A sign of severe hypothermia.

She'd grown up in the Upper Peninsula. She knew what hypothermia and frostbite looked like. She knew what to do. She had to warm Liam's torso and get his core body temperature up without sending him into rewarming shock.

There was no warm bath to stick him in, which was the best method but also the most dangerous. Applying heat directly to the skin was also a bad idea. So was massage, even though it seemed counterintuitive. Massaging the extremities could circulate the colder blood from near the skin to the core, shocking the body.

Instead, she needed to get him in a hypothermic wrap. A hypothermic wrap covered every part of the body with as few open spaces as possible. A sleeping bag and multiple blankets should do it.

But first, she needed him out of the rest of his clothes. He could hurt her if he wanted. Even if he didn't mean to. He was strong and trained to kill. She'd seen him do it more than once.

She stared down at him, her hands on her hips. "Liam Coleman, take your clothes off, right now!"

He flinched, as if jolted out of his fugue. "J-Jessa—"

"This is Jessa." A part of her hated herself for the lie. A bigger part was willing to do whatever was necessary to keep him alive. If he'd listen to Jessa, so be it. He could hate her later. "I'm Jessa. And I'm trying to save your life. For Pete's sake, take off your damn clothes!"

He responded immediately. Obediently, he fumbled for his

sweatshirt. She knelt beside him and helped. She yanked his arm out of the left sweatshirt sleeve, then the right. He was able to lift himself enough to pull off his long-sleeved layers.

She wondered briefly who this Jessa was; how it was that Liam obeyed her so quickly and completely. She'd never known him to be compliant. Not in the least.

Jessa was someone he clearly cared about. Someone he loved.

She swallowed. "Now, your pants."

His fingers were too numb to undo his belt and other things. Her face burning, Hannah did it for him. She wasn't embarrassed for him, but for herself. She didn't even know why.

Ghost sat in front of the fireplace lintel, warming himself. He watched them, his head cocked in bemusement.

"I know it's weird," Hannah said as she pulled down Liam's pants. "Believe me, I know."

She grabbed the blankets from the couch and spread them across his naked, prone body. She didn't have a sleeping bag to put him inside; hers had been left behind with her backpack in the library.

"I-I have to c-confess," Liam mumbled. His beautiful gray-blue eyes were vacant, distant, staring off into some other place, with some other person. "I-I left him. I left him b-behind."

"You can confess later," Hannah said briskly. "Right now, you just need to focus on staying alive."

She pressed the palm of her hand to his bare shoulder, his broad chest. Some part of her registered how well formed he was, the latent strength in those ropy muscles.

His upper torso was etched in scars. Scratches and bruises engraved his flesh. His was the body of a soldier, a warrior.

Her heartbeat quickened. Someday, she wanted to ask him the origin of each battle scar, but that day was not today.

His skin still felt like ice. Not even human.

Worry twisted in her belly. She could warm up some water bottles and put them beneath his armpits and against his groin. She could try to get him to drink something warm and sweet, but he was too out of it to get much down. She feared that wouldn't be enough.

He balanced on the brink of unconsciousness. Maybe on the brink of death.

She needed to bring him back. She needed to do more.

This man had protected her, saved her, taken care of her. Strong, gruff, and reticent, but never unkind. Always thinking of her first—her protection, her safety, her comfort.

No one had taken care of him.

Not anymore. She was here. She would take care of him.

This time, she would save him.

Hannah settled back on her heels, bit her lower lip, and scanned the room, searching desperately for something that would help, for the answers she needed.

There was nothing. Nothing but herself.

"You aren't going to die on me," she whispered. "I won't let you."

The fire crackled. A log popped and spit. Heat radiated through the room.

Ghost looked at her. His tail thumped. Charlotte slept soundly in her drawer. They were warm. They were safe.

She rose to her feet. She lifted her arms and pulled off her sweatshirt. She let it fall to the floor. She removed her two long-sleeved thermal shirts and the tank top beneath it.

She tugged down her sweatpants and wriggled out of her still-damp wool socks. She stood for a moment, naked, feeling vulnerable and exposed.

She had been naked in front of Liam before. He'd helped her give birth. He'd saved her life. He'd saved her daughter's life.

There was nothing untoward in this act. Nothing wrong. Not with her nakedness. Not with what she was about to do.

There was no hesitation in her when she moved toward the mattress. No doubt in her mind. She lifted the blankets and slid beneath the covers. She wrapped the blankets around the two of them, tucking the ends beneath their feet.

She fitted her soft body to his strong, muscled one, wrapping her thin arms around his, folding her legs over his thighs. She pressed herself against him, willed the warmth of her own body into his, her vitality, her life force.

She willed him to live with every stubborn, ferocious beat of her heart.

Liam's eyelids fluttered open. He turned his head and looked at her.

He said, "Hannah."

23

NOAH
DAY TWENTY-THREE

"What's the news?" Noah asked.

He'd radioed Dave Farris for his daily ham radio update, but Dave had requested an in-person meeting. The news must be serious.

Noah had taken an hour off from his duties to grab lunch out of a brown paper bag and visit Dave's rural property just north of Fall Creek. Milo liked Dave, so Noah decided to give Quinn a break and take his son with him.

Dave's fifteen-acre property boasted a massive forty-foot antenna that he'd built a decade ago for his favorite hobby. His office behind the garage featured a big desk and shelves filled with machines bristling with wires, knobs, and doohickeys.

Even though Rosamond had given Dave a house in Winter Haven, he had a generator for his garage and pretty much lived here—only eating, showering, and sleeping at the new house.

Dave swiveled in his office chair, smiled grimly, and offered Noah a salute. "Hey, Chief Sheridan! It's been a few days."

Noah still wasn't used to the moniker. It had been bestowed

on him only a week ago when Chief Briggs had abruptly absconded from his duties.

Chief Briggs was a dour bulldog of a man who'd resisted the out-of-the box thinking and rapid-fire decisions required to effectively respond to the EMP crisis. It was better for Fall Creek that he'd abandoned his post to protect his grown son and daughter-in-law in St. Joe, a nearby town.

Noah wouldn't abandon Fall Creek. He hadn't asked for the responsibility, hadn't wanted it, but once he'd accepted the mantle, he'd grown into it.

He straightened his shoulders, standing a little taller. "That last blizzard was nuts, wasn't it? Just when we thought we'd catch a break."

"Which one?" Dave grumbled. "There's been so many I think I've lost count. It's like the geomagnetic fields have shifted, and we're actually in Antarctica instead of Michigan. Sheesh."

"I know the feeling." Noah settled into the creased leather office chair beside Dave. He motioned to a narrow table in the corner for Milo. "Set up your stuff over there, buddy."

Noah had brought a backpack with an art pad and colored pencils for Milo. Since Quinn was a bit of an artist, Milo was suddenly interested in drawing.

For lunch, he'd packed a peanut butter and honey sandwich and Ritz crackers to dip in packets of applesauce. They were now officially out of cheese.

Once spring hit, Rosamond had assured them that the town would strike trade deals with local farmers to produce cheese, milk, and eggs. For the rest of winter, they'd just have to make do.

But Fall Creek was doing just fine, especially considering the state of the rest of the country. Thanks to Dave, the town council received regular updates on the cascading collapse of pretty much everything.

Dave offered Milo and then Noah an opened bag of Doritos. "Sorry I don't have higher-class delicacies on hand to offer my guests. It's been slim pickings lately."

In his early sixties, Dave was a loud, boisterous white man who loved fishing, his ham radio, and sports cars. He served on the town council and owned Fall Creek Inn.

Rosamond had given him one of the houses in Winter Haven, which he'd generously shared with three of his long-time friends and their families. The Winter Haven homes started at five thousand square feet—there was plenty of room.

Noah took a handful of chips. "How's the Inn doing?"

Dave made a face. "I'll say this for those militia guys. They've brought me enough gas to keep the Inn's ancient generators running. Right now, the Inn's almost nicer than Winter Haven, since the solar panels are currently covered in snow."

Dave had opened up the fifty-room inn to Fall Creek's most vulnerable elderly and sickly—those with cancer, lupus, and other debilitating illnesses. Dave had offered a few rooms for volunteers and their families if they took care of the place and checked up on the new residents.

Dave Farris's generosity was saving lives. And he wasn't the only one.

A couple of dozen reserve officers were volunteering their time to take care of trash, help with sanitation, and other pressing needs. Annette King, the former Fall Creek High School principal, and the pediatric nurse, Shen Lee, both worked tirelessly along with several townspeople to run the shelter at the school for those who didn't have fireplaces or woodstoves in their homes.

Noah had never been prouder of his town.

"Fall Creek owes you a great debt. I hope we can pay you what we owe you someday."

Dave shrugged dismissively. "Right now, cash is useful for one thing—wiping my hiney."

"These days, that's no small thing."

"You aren't kidding." Dave leaned forward in his seat and winked at Milo, who was half-listening to them as he drew. "I'm rationing toilet paper like there's no tomorrow."

Milo giggled.

"Oh sure, laugh it up," Dave said, grinning. "It's all fun and games until we run out."

"Imagine what the history books will say about us," Noah said.

Dave raised his pointer finger in the air like he was giving a pretentious, self-important college lecture. "And then the toilet paper wars commenced..."

They all had a good chuckle. They needed it desperately.

"You good, buddy?" Noah asked when they'd regained control of themselves. "The grown-ups need to talk now."

Milo gave him a thumb's up. "Got it, Dad."

Noah and Dave turned to the ham radio and lowered their voices while Milo went back to his superhero drawings.

"Any updates on the rescue team?" Dave asked.

"They've found seven or eight residents of Fall Creek. A couple stuck in St. Joe that needed to get to Dowagiac. That's all."

Bishop, Reynoso, Perez, and a few others had been gone for two days. They were checking one more town—Watervliet—before calling it quits and heading back to Fall Creek for good.

Rosamond had sent them out on a goodwill rescue mission ostensibly for all of Fall Creek, but in reality, she was searching for her son, Gavin Pike. He'd vanished the day of the EMP and never returned home.

Dave lowered his voice even further. "So Bishop doesn't know about the Crossway community pantry?"

Noah's gut tightened. He glanced at Milo. "No, Bishop doesn't know."

"I imagine he won't take it well."

Noah dreaded having to tell him. As police chief, he'd have to deal with it, just like he had to deal with every other unsavory aspect of this job. As Bishop's friend, it was going to royally suck.

"What do you think he's gonna do?"

"Nothing. He's going to accept it like everyone else."

Dave pursed his lips. He studied Noah, hesitating for a moment before speaking. "It does seem a little...strict."

Noah was tired of talking about it, tired of the complaining. "It's simply about consolidating the supplies so it's easier to keep track of everything."

"It doesn't have anything to do with those people getting killed at Winter Haven? Or with certain parties wanting to exert undue control?"

Noah blew out a frustrated breath. "Did you ask me here to berate me, too, Dave?"

Dave rolled back in his chair and raised his hands in a conciliatory gesture. "Hey man, I'm as laid back as they come. Just sharing some concerns. As a friend."

"I know. You're concerned. Everyone is concerned. They've made that abundantly clear. So have most of the town council."

"Hey, can you blame the council for getting upset when the superintendent makes unilateral decisions without consulting anyone? We haven't had a town hall or council meeting in a week."

"She's busy keeping this town from falling apart, Dave."

"I'm just saying, the only people who've got the food now are the militia. A bunch of strangers with guns. People aren't happy, man. I know that bothers you, too."

Of course it did. But concessions had to be made to keep the peace. To protect the town. Noah was tired of defending himself, tired of defending the superintendent.

People didn't get it. They didn't want to get it.

He didn't feel like arguing with Dave Farris. He needed Dave's help.

"Your point is noted." Noah sighed. "Can we just talk about what you asked me here for? I've got to get back out there."

"Sure, sure. Of course." Dave wheeled to face the wall of ham radio gear. "Honestly, it's pretty bad out there. We've been damn lucky."

"Tell me what you've heard."

"Like I told the council, I've made contact with most of the towns and villages within a hundred-mile radius. Thank goodness for rural radio buffs. Several of the gangs from Benton Harbor have abandoned the city and started attacking nearby neighborhoods. Most of Detroit has dissolved into gang wars."

"Those gangs spreading out anywhere near us?"

"Not yet. But the reports about vicious attacks on nearby towns keep coming in. They do snatch-and-grabs. Hit one part of a town, then they're gone before the town can muster a defense. Several days later, another neighborhood gets hit. Anyone resists, they get shot in the head, execution-style."

"Any details on them?"

"Not much. They wear all black, with either black ski masks or grease paint on their faces. They've got semi-automatics and know how to use them. The only good news is since the attack on Niles, they seem to be moving away, not closer. Looks like they're preying on the outskirts of Kalamazoo. The last report was from Paw Paw, forty miles northeast of here. Granted, not every town is in radio communication, though."

Noah rubbed his face, scratched at his prickly jaw. He nearly had a full beard now. "Any other good news?"

"Some of the towns are working together to form a roaming security team. Volunteer police officers, fire fighters, military, and former military. If any one of the towns are attacked, they radio the team to defend them."

"If they get there in time."

"Yes, there's that. Wouldn't have helped much during all these blizzards."

"Even in good weather, travel is slow and arduous. A lot of destruction and violence can happen in thirty minutes."

"I hear you. But it's got to be better than nothing." Dave stuffed the last handful of broken Dorito chips in his mouth, balled up the bag, and tossed it in the trash can beneath the desk. He looked around for a napkin, didn't see one, and wiped his hands on his pant legs. "I wish Fall Creek would join."

Noah snorted. "I don't see Rosamond Sinclair going for that."

"No, I suppose not. She always likes to blaze her own trail. And she won't be too keen on sharing her militia posse, I'm sure."

Noah gave a noncommittal grunt. "Anything else?"

"Some of the beachfront cities are doing okay. South Haven, Saugatuck, and Holland. They're figuring out how to do ice fishing."

"We've got folks getting some fish from Lake Chapin and Fall Creek."

"Good thing. I'm jonesing for some fried fish. Some bluegill, walleye, and smallmouth bass. I've seen Julian down by the river across from the Inn a few times. I wonder if he's caught anything good."

At the mention of Julian, Noah stiffened. They'd barely spoken in ten days, since Rosamond had appointed Noah chief of police instead of her own son.

Noah didn't know how to cross that void. Julian had always

had a capacity to be vindictive and spiteful. He'd never turned that rancor on Noah—until now.

Noah wanted to think that Julian would get over it. That he'd see that Noah was good at his job, good for Fall Creek. That he'd come around and things would go back to normal.

Some part of him whispered that normal was never returning —not for the country, not for Fall Creek, and not for him and Julian.

Sometimes, it felt like the only thing keeping the sky from crashing down was Noah's own two hands—like Atlas balancing the weight of the world on his back, spine bent, straining and struggling to keep it all afloat.

"Anything bigger? Any reports on who unleashed the EMP?"

"So far, just chatter and rumors. Our nuclear missile defense system was attacked by sophisticated hackers. They must have had help from the inside. Our national security was compromised. They brought the system down just long enough for the nukes to strike."

"Who's 'they?'"

"Don't know yet. I've got a friend out of Washington who says the military is gearing up for something big. The government is being very tightlipped about everything. All I know is, at first they thought it was China. Now, the rumor is whoever is behind it tried to set China up."

"China doesn't make sense. They hate us, but they need us to buy all their junk products. They purchase all our debt for political leverage and control. They want us subservient, not destroyed."

"True. North Korea would obliterate us if they could. Iran hates us. Maybe Russia? Maybe we won't know until the president nukes 'em to kingdom come."

Noah sighed. "I sure hope so. Even if it doesn't change

anything on the ground for us, it matters. Knowing America got her vengeance."

"Hell yes," Dave said, pumping his fist. "America isn't gonna lie down and take it. Not ever."

Milo jumped to his feet. He made gun-shapes with his hands and pretended to fire over Noah and Dave's heads. "We're gonna get the bad guys. They can't beat us!"

"I sure hope so, kid," Dave said with a tired sigh. "We can still hope."

24

QUINN
DAY TWENTY-THREE

Bathing in the apocalypse royally sucked. Quinn had loved showers as much as the next girl. Now, they were a pain in the butt.

Gran and Gramps had always talked about installing a cool gravity-fed shower system in case the turds hit the fan, but they'd never had the money in their tight budget. They had an outdoor solar shower—basically a big black bag that they filled with water and heated in the sun—but Quinn had zero interest in using it in ten-degree weather.

For now, Gran and Quinn washed themselves using an antiquated towel, soap, and hot water system. They boiled water that Quinn had pumped from the well in a large pot on the wood stove.

When the water started steaming and forming small bubbles, Quinn took the pot from the stove, carted it into the bathroom, and set it on the counter.

She stripped out of her dirty clothes, then carefully dipped a hand towel in the water and allowed it to wick up the hot water without becoming completely soaked.

She used the hot, wet towel with a bar of hand soap to wipe down and disinfect her arms and torso, back and legs, feet and armpits, then private parts last.

The towel never stayed hot for long, no matter how many times she re-dipped it. By the end, she was shivering and dancing to warm herself in the chilly air. She dressed as quickly as she could.

Quinn studied herself in the mirror. Her black roots were showing. The vibrant blue hair that she'd maintained for years was quickly fading. It was funny how quickly priorities changed. She didn't care much about makeup or hair dye anymore.

Blue was her favorite color, but that wasn't the real reason why she'd kept it dyed. She stared at the black roots until her eyes blurred.

With her dark hair, everyone used to say how much she looked like Octavia Riley. Her meth-head mother was the last person she'd wanted to resemble.

Now Octavia was dead. Now it didn't matter.

She didn't miss her mother. She told herself she didn't. What she missed was the mother she was supposed to be.

It still felt like a hole in her heart that would never heal. Even the scar tissue hurt when she pressed on it.

Gran knocked on the door. "You still alive in there?"

Quinn cleared her throat to get rid of the sudden lump of emotion. She rubbed her eyes fiercely and opened the door. "That didn't even take ten minutes."

"Coulda fooled me." Gran was dressed in jean overalls, winter boots, and a bulky knit sweater over a few long-sleeved shirts. Wrinkles crisscrossed her weathered face. She was in her late seventies, but her blue eyes were still as sharp and intelligent as ever.

Loki snaked between Gran's legs and jumped on the toilet

seat lid. Odin and Thor followed right behind him. The cats followed Gran around like her own personal entourage.

"You feel all clean again?" Gran eyed the pot on the bathroom counter. "You certainly used enough water."

She scratched Loki behind the ears. "Yeah, except I haven't washed my hair in five days. My scalp is all greasy, and I feel gross."

They were only washing their hair once a week now. Apparently, that was how things used to be before everyone had running water and fancy bathrooms.

Gran thought it was fine; it bugged the heck out of Quinn.

"We can always shave your hair off," Gran said with an evil cackle. "That'll do away with the lice issue."

"Baby steps, Gran," Quinn said. "And I do *not* have lice."

"I have something for that itchy feeling." Gran leaned her cane against the wall and shuffled past Quinn. She rummaged around in a cabinet beneath the bathroom sink and pulled out a bottle of baby powder.

Quinn glared at it like it might bite her. "What's that for?"

"Rub it on your scalp. It's like dry shampoo. It will help the itching to go away in between hair washes."

"I ran out of shampoo and conditioner," Quinn said. "I searched the storage room in the basement but didn't see where you hid them."

Gran grinned. "That's because there isn't any."

Quinn stared at her. "That's not funny."

"It's not a joke. Shampoo strips your hair of its natural oils. You don't really need it."

Quinn made a face. "Don't tell me you haven't really been washing your hair all this time. Is that where that funny smell comes from?"

"Watch that sass, smarty-pants." Gran bent beneath the sink again and came up with a box of baking soda. "Use this."

"Doesn't that belong in the kitchen?"

"It exfoliates your scalp and helps get rid of build-up. Mix baking soda, water, and a few drops of lavender essential oil in an empty shampoo bottle and shake to make a paste, and there you go. Homemade shampoo."

"I'd prefer my Pantene Pro-V, thank you very much."

"We'd prefer a lot of things. This is the world we got."

"Thanks for nothing," Quinn muttered. Her scalp was itching so bad, she was willing to try anything. She thrust out her hand. "Oh, fine. I'll take it."

"Don't knock it until you try it, girl. It's very useful. You can also use baking soda to make a great toothpaste, too."

Quinn groaned. "Don't tell me we're going to be making our own toothpaste from now on."

"We sure are."

"Is that why we have so much of this stuff stored downstairs?"

There had to be ten pounds of baking soda stored in Gran's secret storage room hidden in the basement. Maybe more.

"It's got a three-year shelf life and works great for dozens of uses other than baking. It provides relief for bug bites, rashes, inflammation, and itching. You can make mouthwash or mix it with cornstarch for deodorant. It's as close to a miracle product as we're going to get."

"Gross."

"When the fecal matter hits the oscillator, what matters is whether it works. The cheaper it is, the more versatile, and the easier to store, the better."

"Yeah, yeah I know." She did. She understood and appreciated everything Gran and Gramps had done to prepare for a disaster like this.

Baking soda shampoo and toothpaste. Two more things to add to the "Reasons the Apocalypse Sucks" column.

At least they had a way to make what they needed. There was that. She couldn't imagine life without a way to clean your hair and teeth.

Gran met her gaze in the mirror, her expression suddenly serious. "Noah told me what happened at Winter Haven. Did you think I wouldn't hear about it?"

Her cheeks went red. "Traitor," she muttered.

Gran clucked her tongue. "Don't blame Noah. I don't like what I heard about you attacking that fool soldier. Not one bit."

"They're not even real soldiers."

Gran narrowed her white brows. "Their guns real?"

"Yes." Quinn heaved a sigh. "I know, Gran. I know. I was all set on being careful and being patient, just like you said. But when that jerkwad Desoto started pushing Milo around, I just lost it. He was choking a little kid, Gran. I had to do something."

Gran clucked her tongue again. "You got your grandfather's fire in your blood."

"I'm not being stupid, I promise."

"You created an enemy, is what you did. That big ape isn't going to forget you."

A chill ran up her spine. She remembered the way Desoto had looked at her, like he wanted to strangle her right then and there. "I know."

Gran pressed her lips together. "Maybe you need the shotgun with you."

Quinn had her own .22 rifle for shooting small game. She'd kept it close by whenever she was in the house but didn't usually take it out with her. It wasn't like it could take on one of the militia's AK-47s.

Quinn's gaze dropped to Gran's Mossberg 500 leaning against

the hallway wall just outside the bathroom. Gran took it everywhere with her. It even went into bed with her so she could grab it easily in the middle of the night.

"You need it, Gran. If someone tries to break in when I'm gone, you've gotta protect yourself."

Gran gripped her cane and leaned on it heavily. She suddenly looked tired—and older. "Just be careful. You're the only kin I got left."

Quinn forced a grin. "There's always the cats to keep you company."

"I'm serious, girl."

Quinn's chest tightened. In this world, being careful didn't make you safe. "I know."

25

LIAM
DAY TWENTY-FOUR

Liam woke up gasping.

His body was drenched in a cold sweat, memories of combat bombarding him. Men yelling, grunting, screaming. Explosions rocking him to the core. Tracers and rockets flying overhead. Slugs striking, dust so thick, he could taste it.

Adrenaline drenched his synapses, shutting out the fear, the mayhem, the sensory overload, and forcing himself to focus on the mission: identifying targets, firing, reloading, staying alive.

He shot straight up. He didn't know where or when he was. Anxiety thrummed through him. He scrambled for a gun, a weapon.

"Here, it's right here."

Something was shoved into his hands. The Glock. He closed his fingers around the shape of it, as familiar as his own hands.

The nightmare faded slowly, his heart still thudding hard. Sweat drying on his skin.

Blinking, he looked around, taking in his surroundings. The gunshots and explosions dimmed. The smoke and fire and screaming, gone. The stink and heat and sweat and panic vanished.

He was back in the house, in the living room. He sat on the purple princess mattress, with his lower half covered in a pile of mismatched blankets. The fireplace at his back. The couch pushed against the wall. The windows covered.

Ghost was stretched out along the other side of the fireplace. His muzzle rested on his paws, his brown eyes alert and pinned on Liam.

Next to him, little Charlotte slept peacefully inside her dresser drawer.

Hannah knelt beside the mattress. Her new, shorter hair hung loose around her shoulders. Concern lined her beautiful face. "I reloaded it. I thought you would want me to."

Hannah and Charlotte Rose were alive. They were safe.

A giant hand released his chest.

He racked back the slide of the Glock and checked the chamber. A .124-grain jacketed hollow point round gleamed up at him.

He set the pistol down on the mattress beside him and released a slow breath.

"How do you feel?" Hannah asked.

The tips of his fingers and toes felt scalded. His whole body ached. The pain in his lower back throbbed dully. He felt utterly drained. "Like I've been run over by a Mack truck."

Her lips twitched. "That good, huh?"

"Just about."

"We ran out of firewood. I burned the end tables you chopped. And the bookcase and coffee table. We're on the kitchen table, now. I had to chop that one myself."

He glanced at the hunks of wood popping and spitting in the fireplace. The blaze was warm and inviting. "You did good."

She beamed. "I thought it might break my arms, but I did it."

She rose and hurried to a pot heating near the fire. She drew it out and ladled soup into a bowl with a spoon she'd conjured from somewhere. She came back to him, careful not to slosh the soup, and handed him the bowl.

"I was hoping you would wake up soon. You need something warm in you."

He sipped it carefully. It was hot but felt deliciously soothing sliding down his throat. Suddenly, he was ravenous. His empty stomach gnawed at him like he hadn't eaten for a week.

He slurped up several more bites before pausing. "How long was I out?"

"Three days."

He winced. "Three days?"

"It was touch and go for a while." She nibbled on her lower lip. "I thought—I thought you wouldn't make it."

"I'm hard to kill."

"Yeah, well." She looked away. Her cheeks reddened. "We were worried."

Ghost thumped his tail in agreement. He panted, his black jowls stretching back like he was grinning.

"Ghost found me. In that blizzard..."

"He knew you were still out there. He believed he would find you. And he did."

His chest tightened. "Good thing."

"Finish your soup. I'll get some tea going. We're running low on supplies, but we still have some honey in the pantry. You need more calories in you."

He reached out and seized her hand. "Wait."

Her palm was soft and warm. He didn't want to let go. He felt heat rising in his face. "Pike. We fought in the woods. I wounded him. Shot him at least once, maybe twice. He got away. I was sure he was coming here. I hoped he died on the way. Maybe he did. I thought..."

Hannah didn't pull her hand away. "He did. He did come here."

Liam's heart stopped cold. Ice ran through his veins. "What happened?"

Her eyes were so dark, as though the pupils had eaten the emerald green of her irises. "He came in through the garage. He trapped Ghost inside. I couldn't get to Ghost. Pike came for me and Charlotte. I got the .45. I shot at Pike until the ammo ran out. I hit him once, but in the shoulder. My hands were shaking so hard, it was a miracle I hit him at all."

Liam's heart thudded hard in his chest. He squeezed her hand and didn't let go.

She told him the rest. Haltingly, with several starts and stops, but her gaze never wavered from his. Her eyes shadowed with pain, with loss—but also triumph.

With every word she spoke, his rage grew—but also his pride. He was proud of her. Proud of how she'd fought like a wild thing to protect herself and her child.

She looked nothing like the frightened woman he'd discovered cowering in the woods. She was a completely different person.

"We killed him," she said. "Ghost and me. We did it together."

Ghost raised his muzzle and pricked his ears, like he knew they were talking about him. He gave a loud, self-satisfied chuff.

"Good job, boy," Liam said gruffly, emotion thickening his throat. "Both of you."

"He's still down there."

"Leave him to rot."

Hannah's mouth twitched. "I thought you might say that."

Beside the dog, Charlotte shifted. She flung her tiny arms out like a starfish and whimpered.

Before Hannah could go to her, Ghost nosed her gently, like a mother might stroke her baby's back. Charlotte opened her heavy-lidded eyes for a moment, gave a contented gurgle, and promptly fell back asleep.

"She smiled," Liam said.

"At this age, it's just gas."

"I don't believe that."

"Believe what you want to."

"She did. I saw it."

Hannah suppressed a smile. She rose to her feet. "You need sustenance. I'll get you that tea."

"I can get it." Liam swept the blankets aside and started to get up. His muscles were too weak. His legs quivered like Jell-O beneath his weight.

"Sit down," Hannah ordered. There was no hesitation in her voice, no equivocation. It was a command.

He sank back onto the mattress. "I'm fine."

Hannah fisted her hands on her hips. "You're recovering from hypothermia. You're injured, and you almost died. You don't have to do every single thing yourself."

Liam only grunted.

"You're as stubborn as a toddler."

Ghost chuffed in amusement.

Liam glared at him. "What are you looking at?"

Ghost just thumped his tail.

"Traitor," Liam grumbled. "I thought you were on my side."

"He's on all our sides," Hannah said. "But mine more."

"I suppose that's only fair."

He glanced down. He realized suddenly that he was completely nude. Not just his upper half, but everywhere. Naked as the day he was born.

Embarrassment flushed through him. He seized the nearest blanket and wrapped it around his waist. "What the hell happened to my clothes?"

"Your boots are by the fire. I stuffed them with old newspaper I found in the office to help them dry faster. As for your clothes—" She gestured at the sofa. "They're hand-scrubbed, washed, and folded on the couch for whenever you're ready."

"I'm—you took them off—you—" he sputtered.

Her eyes narrowed. "Who do you think took care of everything the last three days?"

His face burned at the thought of how she'd seen him. The bodily functions she'd cleaned up. It made him feel weak and helpless and vulnerable.

He hated that feeling above all else.

Her expression softened. "Liam. You did the same for me."

"It's not the same."

"Of course it is."

She was right. He still didn't have to like it.

A hint of mischief gleamed in her eyes. "Besides, I kind of like you like this."

"Naked?"

Now it was her turn to blush. "All flustered and discombobulated. It's a refreshing change."

He snorted. "Can I have my clothes now?"

"In a minute. You should get cleaned up first. You've got blood caked on you. And you're dirty. Frankly, you stink."

That tugged a tight smile out of him. "You should've seen me in Iraq."

"I can imagine."

Liam eyed the couch. Across the room suddenly felt like a mile. "Hand me my boxers, at least. Give a man some dignity."

Hannah gave him a little smirk but handed him the folded pair of boxers. She went back into the kitchen—ostensibly to give him a moment of privacy. He dressed quickly, and she returned a minute later with steaming tea so thick with honey that he could eat it with a spoon.

Her belly was still a bit swollen from childbirth, but she moved differently. She had an effortless grace, a confidence she didn't have before. He felt drawn to her.

She headed back into the kitchen and came back lugging a large bowl of water. She placed it by the fire to warm. She set a towel and a stack of clean washcloths beside it.

"I can clean myself."

"I know that. You shouldn't be on your feet quite yet. Once you're up, you won't rest. You pace around here like a caged lion. Take another day to recover."

He couldn't drag his gaze from her. Her skin seemed to shimmer in the firelight. The warm light highlighted her cheekbones, the delicate slope of her nose, her small stubborn chin. The way her green eyes shone.

"You've suffered for everyone else. You served your country. You gave your body, your mind, risked your life." She gave him a small smile. "Let someone else help you for once. Let me help you."

He couldn't say no to her. He'd always been worthless at denying a beautiful woman anything. Especially a woman like Hannah.

Grudgingly, he nodded.

"Trust me," she said.

He did. God help him, but he did.

26

LIAM
DAY TWENTY-FIVE

Hannah washed Liam.
    She dipped the washcloth in the water, wrung it out, and began wiping his back. The water was hot but not scalding. She washed away the dirt, grime, and dried blood. Her small, warm hands were firm but gentle as she brushed his bare shoulders, his back, his chest.

Her fingers did not flinch away when they moved over his cuts, scrapes, and scars. His war-damaged skin.

For several minutes, she worked in silence. Neither of them spoke.

Ghost panted softly. The fire crackled and popped. The heat and the flickering firelight made the room warm and cozy.

Her nearness was a little unnerving, but also comforting. It was intimate in a way that he couldn't remember ever experiencing before. It felt good. It felt right.

"Can I ask you something?" Hannah asked.

"Of course."

Her words were hesitant, cautious. "When you were delirious, you said things."

Liam went still. "What?"

"You were talking to someone. Someone named Jessa."

He closed his eyes. Firelight danced behind his eyelids.

"You can talk to me, you know. You don't have to, but I'm here. I'm listening."

She traced a bullet scar on his lower back. She touched him with a tenderness that almost made him weep for reasons he couldn't name or explain.

He'd been strong for so long. Tough and hard. He felt anything but tough now.

His defenses were down. She'd disarmed him completely.

He felt like he was shattering, piece by broken piece.

Hannah had trusted him with her broken pieces. Maybe he could do the same.

"Something happened," he said haltingly. "In Chicago."

She sat back and shifted on the mattress so that she faced him, her gaze on his, her expression warm, compassionate, and open.

"I had a brother named Lincoln. My twin. His wife was named Jessa. I—" He swallowed. "She was my sister-in-law. She was pregnant with their first child. I flew to Chicago to see them. My brother's PTSD was getting worse. She was worried about him. She said he needed me, that I was the only one who could reach him. It was Christmas Eve. They'd just picked me up when the EMP happened. We were in downtown Chicago, and the car just stopped. The stoplights, everyone's phones, everything. We crashed into the car ahead of us. It wasn't bad—no one was hurt—but Jessa's seatbelt was jammed. Lincoln and I got out of the car. We just stood there. I thought we had time. I didn't think...I didn't know.

"The planes—they stopped working, too. We watched one crash. Then another one appeared between the buildings. It was huge and so low. Gliding straight toward us. There wasn't any time. I shouted for Lincoln to run, but his PTSD kicked in, and he froze. He wouldn't move. He went into this trance—he didn't know where he was or what was happening. Jessa was still trapped in the car. The seatbelt wouldn't budge. The plane was still coming. I ran out of time. I had to choose. Lincoln or Jessa."

He sucked in a sharp breath. "God help me, I chose Jessa. Jessa and the baby. I knew what Lincoln would have wanted. He'd have killed me if I'd saved him and let her die. It felt like ripping my own heart out of my chest to leave him. But I did. I had to.

"I cut Jessa free and we ran. She couldn't run as fast, since she was nine months pregnant. The plane came down behind us. Without the engines, it was nearly silent. This great harbinger of death sailing over us, coming down on top of our heads. We managed to take shelter in a bank. I pushed Jessa ahead of me, shouted at her to get behind something. She went in. I was just behind her.

"I saw the plane come down. The wings hitting buildings and shearing off like they were made of paper. The fuselage exploding. Huge chunks of shrapnel as large as cars blasting in all directions, smashing cars and buildings, punching through steel and glass and brick. I dove for cover. I got up as soon as I could, searching for Jessa, screaming for her. There was so much dust and smoke. Everything was burning. I found her at the back of the bank. At first, I thought she was okay. I thought we'd made it."

He paused. A lump rose in his throat. His eyes burned.

Hannah didn't push him. She waited.

After a moment, he regained his composure and continued. "A big chunk of shrapnel had shredded her thigh and hit her femoral artery. I put a tourniquet on it, but it wasn't enough. She was bleeding out. We were two miles from a hospital. Two miles of hell. No cars working. People running, yelling, and screaming. I carried her most of the way. We—we didn't make it. She begged me to stop. She said she needed a rest. We both knew better. She was thinking of the baby, not herself. She knew what was coming. I knew, too, but I wasn't willing to admit it to myself yet. It was too terrible, too awful.

"We found a hotel that would take us in. I paid cash. One of the staff members gave us a hotel room. Her name was Prisha Hunjan, and she helped us. She did everything she could. Jessa—she was so brave. Braver than me. She told me she was dying. She was a doctor; she could feel what was happening. The baby could only live in her womb for a couple of minutes after she died. It's why she refused to go the rest of the way to the hospital. It'd take too long to get help. She would die, and the baby would die. She was determined not to let that happen."

He wiped fiercely at his eyes. "She told me everything I needed to do. Step by step. She was dying and she still had the presence of mind to tell me how to cut her open. She—she died there, in that hotel room. There wasn't a damn thing I could do to stop it. I couldn't mourn for her. I had two minutes to get that baby out or my nephew died. I had no choice; I did it. I sliced her belly open. Pried open her insides and pulled out Jessa and Lincoln's son. It sounds easy to say it, but it was the hardest thing I've ever done. Slice a quarter inch too deep and I'd accidentally kill the baby. Every cut had to be precise. And every second was a second he was losing oxygen..."

Liam shuddered at the memory.

"You saved him," Hannah said softly. "Like you saved Charlotte."

Liam nodded heavily. His hands twisted in his lap, his fingers balled into fists. "That's not the end. That's not all. Jessa's parents lived in Chicago. Jessa had asked me to take her son to them. Prisha helped me clean the baby up and use strips of a sheet to make a carrier. I walked to their place. I barely remember it.

Jessa's parents were there. Mr. and Mrs. Brooks. They took the baby. I told them to get out of Chicago. They had a classic car that still worked and family that owned a farm in Tuscola, a small town somewhere in Illinois. I wished them luck and I...I left."

"That hat that you gave to Charlotte...you made it for your nephew."

"I did. He wore it from the hotel to Jessa's parents. It fell off in the snow. When I saw it again, I couldn't bear to take it back. I—I needed something to remember him. I just...I needed it."

"Oh, Liam," Hannah said. "I'm so sorry."

"They named him after me. They named him Liam."

The tears came then. He didn't try to stop them. Sorrow broke over him in waves.

Hannah slid closer to him. She slipped her thin arms around his chest and held him. She didn't say anything. She just held him.

"I left him there. How could I have left him? I should have escorted the Brooks to Tuscola. I should've made sure they were safe. I could've done it. It's what I do. It's who I *am*."

"It was too painful," Hannah said.

It had nearly broken him to leave that child behind. His heart had already shattered into a million pieces at the loss of Lincoln and Jessa. As much as he'd loved his nephew, his heart hadn't been able to bear any more loss.

Once again, he'd chosen isolation over love. Loneliness instead of connection.

Running away had always been his solution to life's problems. It was no solution at all.

"It wasn't the first time," he said.

He kept going. He had to. He had to get it all out. It was like a poison eating him from the inside out. If he didn't do it now, he never would.

"I loved my brother. I loved Jessa." He clenched his jaw. "I loved her from the moment I first laid eyes on her. I couldn't help it. She chose Lincoln. I never resented her for that. Never. But I couldn't stop loving her, either."

He felt hollowed out. All that love with nowhere to go but inward to scrape out an ever-widening hole in the center of himself.

"I let that keep me away from both of them. I let it come between us like a wall I couldn't scale. For four years, I didn't see my brother. I didn't see her. I lived alone, stewing in my own misery. It was wrong. I was so wrong."

Hannah squeezed his shoulders. He let himself melt into her. She was warmth and softness and comfort, all the things he hadn't believed he'd deserved.

"We need each other," she said. "None of us can do this alone."

They were two wounded people. So different and so much the same. Both of them survivors. Both of them suffering from trauma and loss. Mirrors to each other's suffering and struggles.

But she couldn't save him. Just like he couldn't save her. Not really. The hard work had to be done yourself.

But that didn't mean you had to make the journey alone.

He realized then that it wasn't humanity he had given up on. He had given up on himself. He'd given up on a chance for a life of meaning, of human connection, of love.

No matter the lies he'd told himself, he understood the truth now.

Love brought pain. It brought suffering. It was worth it.

He pulled away from her. Their faces were inches apart.

His heart swelled, filling with emotions he couldn't name. The things he'd tried to deny even to himself. He couldn't deny them anymore. He didn't want to.

His world had been dark and meaningless. But Hannah had given it meaning. Hannah had given him hope.

He reached his hand up and brushed a strand of hair behind her ear. He could have kissed her. He longed to.

Charlotte let out a loud cry.

Hannah smiled at him. His whole chest cracked open.

"Duty calls," she said softly. She climbed to her feet and went to the baby.

Liam couldn't take his eyes off her. Once again, he'd fallen for a woman he could never have. He'd fallen completely, utterly, and wholeheartedly.

Liam was in love with Hannah Sheridan.

27

HANNAH
DAY TWENTY-SEVEN

The sun shone bright in the blue sky. The air was crisp and almost warm compared to the previous weeks, somewhere shy of thirty degrees.

Hannah had taken Ghost for a walk. Rather, Ghost was taking her for one.

They were walking down the main street along the snow-covered sidewalk, shuttered and graffitied businesses on every side. The streets were empty.

Earlier, she'd met a few neighbors who'd dared to venture outside their homes. They were rural, small-town folks. Hardy and tough. But everyone was scared, tired.

They just wanted things to go back to the way they were before. But it wasn't going back. Nothing would ever be the same.

In this world, anyone could be a threat. No matter how innocuous they first appeared.

Ghost frolicked ahead of her. He snapped at the snowballs she tossed him. He buried his muzzle in the powder and snorted happily as he pranced through snowdrifts, his regal plumed tail streaming behind him like a flag snapping in the breeze.

As warm and cozy as the house was, she'd needed a break. She needed to get outside.

Liam was on his feet again, but his bout with hypothermia and his back injury had taken a lot out of him. He'd endured too much.

He wasn't a robot, much as he wanted to pretend he was. His body weakened, just like anyone's. It could fail. It could break.

She'd left Liam resting with Charlotte snuggled on his broad chest, his hand resting protectively across her back. The sight of them together had done something to her, warming her and squeezing her heart at the same time.

It had been two days since Liam had opened up to her about his past, since he'd revealed his most damaged parts.

Every broken heart fractured differently. She knew the pattern of her own cracks. Now she knew his, too.

She felt honored to be trusted with his secrets, his fears, and his vulnerabilities. Just as she'd trusted him. She would not betray that trust, not for anything.

It was a strange thing to step inside another person's loneliness. It was like entering a darkened cave, feeling along the walls, bumping into sharp edges, learning the contours of a foreign yet familiar place.

She knew his pain. Recognized herself in him, inside that dark cave of loss, regret, and grief. They were making their way out of it, slowly, halting and tentative, but together.

These precious moments of peace and calm felt stolen. Like Hannah, Liam, and Charlotte were caught in a translucent bubble floating outside of time.

But they weren't. No matter how much she cared about Liam. No matter how much they both needed this to recover physically and emotionally, to heal.

Time was passing. The broken world was turning, becoming even more broken with each day, each hour.

She thought of Milo with a pang. She had a responsibility and a goal she could not lose sight of, not even for a moment.

She needed to reunite with her son and husband. Her entire family whole and together.

She needed to go home.

The rumble of engines drew Hannah's attention.

In the eerie silence of the new post-EMP world, the engine noise seemed deafening. It cut through the quiet like a knife through butter.

Her heartrate accelerated. Instinctively, she slunk back into the shadows beneath the awning of a hair salon. She didn't want to be seen. It was best to avoid even the possibility of trouble.

Her good hand went for a weapon. Liam had retrieved her pocketknife from the basement. It was tucked into her pants' pocket; her .45 snug in her coat pocket—locked, loaded, and ready to fire.

The rumbling engines grew louder, closer.

She strained her ears, trying to parse where the sounds were coming from. She shielded her eyes with her bad hand, her good hand stuffed in her pocket, her fingers closing around the .45's grip.

Down the street about thirty yards, three trucks turned the corner and rumbled toward her.

She felt for the door at her back with her bad hand and tried to pull it open. It was locked. Unlike the other shops and cafés on this street, the hair salon's windows and doors were still intact.

Adrenaline shot through her. Her palms went damp inside her gloves.

It was too late to make a run for it. Sudden movement would draw their eyes. Hopefully, the deep shadows would provide enough concealment, and they'd just drive on by.

"Ghost!" she whispered urgently. "Come here!"

Sensing the tension in her voice, Ghost stopped nosing the snowdrift half-covering a fire hydrant and loped back to her.

She pushed on his back. "Sit. Stay with me."

Obediently, he sat. He watched the trucks approaching, his gaze alert and wary. So did Hannah.

The trucks were old and rickety, made sometime in the 1970s. One was white, one black. The third one was probably some version of beige, but it was too coated in dirt and grime to tell.

They were outfitted with snow tires and drove slowly, maybe ten miles an hour. As the first truck drew even with her hiding spot, she noticed something was spray-painted along the sides of each truck.

Hannah squinted against the bright sunlight as she read the hastily scrawled words: "Fall Creek Police Department."

Blood rushed in her ears. A wave of vertigo washed through her. Her legs went weak and watery. She leaned against the glass door of the salon, steadying her nerves.

She'd read it wrong. She'd read what she wanted to see, not what was really there.

The first truck passed. She focused her gaze on the second truck. The white one. The spray-painted letters large, black, and crystal clear.

She stood frozen with indecision.

Hope bloomed in her chest, warring with caution. Hope won.

Hannah dashed into the street. Her heart hammering against her ribs, her breath caught in her throat like a prayer.

She raised her arms, pistol still in her right hand, and waved wildly. "Stop! Please stop!"

The white F150 slammed on its brakes. The tires slid. Hannah jumped back out of the way. Ghost bounded to her side with a thunderous bark.

The truck stopped in the middle of the street. The driver's

door opened, and a man clambered out. He wore a police uniform beneath his winter coat, a pistol holstered at his hip and a rifle slung over his shoulder.

He shoved back his coat and rested his hand on the grip of his service weapon. "Can we help you?"

She could hardly get the words out. "You're from Fall Creek. You're the Fall Creek Police Department."

"Yes ma'am. We are."

He looked familiar. A Hispanic man in his forties, he was thick-necked and built like a tank. He looked like he could smash watermelons with his fists. He was tough, but his face wasn't unkind.

Ghost pressed against her outer thigh. He didn't growl, but his stiff, guarded stance was warning enough. *Don't mess with us, or else.*

The officer looked at Ghost. His eyes widened. "Big dog you got there."

"Yep."

"He friendly?"

"Only sometimes."

"Guess that's fair." He smiled a little. "You wanna put away that pistol? I'm happy to talk if you want to talk, but it's a bit difficult to focus with a deadly weapon flailing around."

He sounded nice. Nice could mean anything. Anyone could act nice.

She kept her guard up. She lowered the gun, aiming it at the ground, but kept it in both hands. Finger tickling the trigger guard. If she needed to, she wouldn't hesitate to shoot.

"No offense," she said, "but I'm not putting it away."

"No offense taken." He was watching her, studying her. He frowned in confusion. "Do I know you?"

"I think so. Maybe." She exhaled. Memories from another lifetime flooded her head. "You worked with my husband. He's a Fall Creek police officer. His name is Noah Sheridan."

The officer's face went ashen. His mouth contorted. He opened his mouth, then closed it. He shook his head back and forth. "No. No way."

The passenger door opened. A female officer hopped out, a shotgun in her hands. She circled around the front of the truck and stopped beside the first officer.

She was Hispanic as well, full-figured and broad-shouldered, her black hair cut in a bob at her chin. She looked like she could hold her own in a fist fight, gun fight—any kind of fight.

She tucked the shotgun against her shoulder and aimed it at Hannah. "Is there a problem, Reynoso?"

"I'm hallucinating," the first officer—Reynoso—said. "I've finally lost my marbles. That's what's happening."

The female officer glanced from Reynoso to Hannah. Her eyes narrowed. "You look familiar."

"You recognize her?" Reynoso asked. "I'm not crazy, right? She's really there."

"I'm really here," Hannah said.

Reynoso looked at her like she was a ghost. He crossed himself. "Perez, she says she's Sheridan's wife."

The female officer—Perez—made a face. "Sheridan's wife is dead."

"I'm not dead," Hannah said quietly. "I'm very much alive."

She recognized Reynoso now. He and Officer Perez had both been Noah's coworkers. She didn't remember their first names. She hadn't known them well, not like Noah's good friends. Not like—

Ahead of them, the black truck's door slammed open. A big, burly black man sporting an afro barreled out of the truck and sprinted toward them with surprising speed. He was dressed in jeans and a purple and yellow Hawaiian shirt beneath a worn leather jacket.

Hannah's heart skipped a beat.

The man slowed as he approached her. His mouth dropped open. "Holy mother of—Hannah? Hannah Sheridan?"

Her blood rushed in her ears. Her whole body tingled from her toes to her scalp. She felt like crying, screaming, and laughing, all at the same time. Too many emotions to name washed over her like a tsunami.

He knew her. And she knew him. "Atticus Bishop."

His whole face lit up. Grinning broadly, his arms spread wide, he strode toward her.

Ghost leapt between them with a growl. Bishop stopped short.

"It's okay, Ghost," Hannah said, tears choking her voice. "It's Bishop. He's...he's a friend."

Ghost gave a reluctant chuff but allowed Hannah to push him out of the way. Bishop crossed the space between them in one long stride and enveloped her in his arms.

He squeezed her so hard that she could barely breathe.

She thought she would hate it, that she'd instinctively recoil from a stranger's touch, but he didn't feel like a stranger. He felt like the old friend that he was.

She'd forgotten the overwhelming strength of his bear hugs—but it came rushing back in an instant. A flood of memories that had been locked away for years, locked away so that she could survive, just waiting for this moment to break free.

Reynoso and Perez watched them, gaping. Slowly, Perez lowered her shotgun.

Bishop pulled Hannah back at arms' length and gazed down into her face. "Hannah! It's really you. It's you. I can't believe it. You're alive! This is a miracle. Truly, a miracle! How can this be?"

She didn't wipe away her tears. She let them stream down her face. "It's a long story."

"I bet it is!" He grinned, his white teeth gleaming, his whole face beaming. "But we're not the ones you want to tell, I bet. Not yet."

He let out a loud, exuberant whoop that echoed in the crisp air.

"Look at me!" he shouted. "I'm happy as a kid on Christmas morning. What a gift! Praise God! He brings joy even in the midst of sorrow. And what a joy this is. Noah will be—he'll be ecstatic!"

"And Milo?" Hannah whispered. Her throat went tight. She could barely say his name. So much could have happened in five years. She had no idea if he was even—

Bishop saw the look on her face. "He's fine! Milo is fine. Oh Hannah, wait until you see him. He's a good kid. Just fantastic. You'll be so proud."

She sagged in relief. Only Ghost pressing against her legs kept her upright.

"I hate to break up the reunion," Reynoso said. "But we're on our way back to Fall Creek now. We were only in Watervliet to pick up the father of one of our people and bring him back to town with us. We were on a rescue mission searching for some missing residents. We found a couple of them. It's damn lucky you even saw us."

"It's providence," Bishop said, not an ounce of doubt in his voice. "A miracle. God is watching over us all, even now."

"Whatever it is—luck, aliens, voodoo—we'll take it." Reynoso turned to Hannah. "I've got a police chief who'll kill me if I don't bring you back to him ASAP. Hop in and we'll bring you home."

Her heart surged at the thought of home.

Finally, after five long years, Hannah was going home.

28

HANNAH
DAY TWENTY-SEVEN

Hannah led the group from Fall Creek back to the house. She introduced them to Liam, who greeted them at the front door with a scowl and the barrel of his AR-15.

He didn't warm up to them, but at least Hannah convinced him to allow them inside the house.

Bishop wept with joy when he held Charlotte. "Children are such a gift," he said in a choked voice.

Ghost circled him, whining anxiously like an overprotective mother hen. Ghost clearly didn't trust these people with the baby he'd been tasked to protect from all threats.

Liam looked just as flustered. He didn't like his sanctuary invaded. He didn't like strangers.

They weren't strangers to Hannah. They were her people.

No one asked who the baby's father was, but she saw the inquisitive looks from the officers. They were itching to interview her, to find out where she'd been and what had happened to her.

"There's more," Hannah said, soft but steady. She went to the basement door. "The man who kidnapped me five years ago. His body is down there. You should probably see it."

She opened the door. The fetid stench of a decomposing body assaulted them. Perez stepped back with a gasp.

Hannah remained at the top of the stairs while Reynoso and Perez descended, covering their mouths and coughing from the stench. Ghost stood beside her, a low growl rumbling in his chest.

She wasn't afraid to go down in that basement. She simply didn't need to. Not anymore.

At the base of the stairs. Reynoso crouched over the body. Perez flicked on a flashlight and examined the remains.

She heard their voices as if far away. "Where's his throat? Look at this, he's basically been eviscerated."

"Holy hell," Perez said. "Do you see this?"

Reynoso looked up at Hannah, his face gray. "You know who this is?"

She said nothing, just watched him carefully.

"This is Gavin flipping Pike. Rosamond Sinclair's son."

"I know."

"The superintendent is going to freak the hell out," Reynoso said. "She's gonna go postal over this."

Perez straightened. She stared at Hannah with a grave expression. "Who killed him?"

Before she could open her mouth, Liam spoke from behind her. "I did."

29

NOAH
DAY TWENTY-SEVEN

Before Noah signed off for the day and headed to Quinn and Molly's place to pick up Milo, he'd stopped at the shelter in the high school gym to check on things.

It was just as depressing as he remembered it. A couple of hundred people crammed into far too tight a space, cots and sleeping bags covering the floors, kids running around, babies crying.

He heard the people murmuring, everyone watching him while pretending not to. Some of them looked disgruntled. Others angry or downright miserable.

Their faces were thinner, some gaunt. Even with the militia feeding everyone, no one was eating as much as normal. The stress was taking its toll.

"How are things going?" Noah asked the former principal, Annette King. She'd volunteered to run the shelter along with Shen Lee, their pediatric nurse.

"They're going," Annette said. In her mid-forties, she looked frazzled and tired. She wore no makeup. Her pixie-cut silver hair still looked good, unlike most people's hair these days.

She gestured behind her. "There's a small group of slackers. That sullen group in the corner over there. It's like high school all over again, just with grumpy adults."

"Hey, chief!" Lee said as he strode up to Noah and Annette. A slightly overweight Chinese American in his mid-thirties, Lee was a friendly, gregarious guy and a damn good nurse.

"We've been working hard to get everyone involved and invested," Annette said. "Everyone has a rotating schedule so no one's stuck on latrine duty all the time. We've divided them into teams to deal with cooking, meal clean up, sanitation, trash, childcare, and education. A couple of people remain in charge of a certain area without rotating for continuity and efficiency.

"Norman Clay is a chef, so he's in charge of the kitchen, for example. Rachel is one of my best teachers. She makes sure the kids are getting at least two hours of instruction every day, along with some arts and crafts and outdoor play time. Some of the parents are really struggling. We're trying to keep things as healthy as possible for the children."

Noah took a second look. On closer inspection, he saw the three tables in the corner covered with construction paper, scissors and glue, and scattered textbooks. Three people were sweeping, and in the cafeteria kitchen to his left, several folks were busy doing an enormous load of dishes.

Annette pursed her lips. "I think we need to add some new curriculum to the basics of math, reading, writing, and science. Maybe foraging? Identifying edible plants? How to build a fire? We're going to need to learn those skills again, I fear. All of us."

Lee made a face. "We'll be fine. This may last longer than anyone wants it to, but in the end, it's temporary. Next year at this time, we'll have Netflix and Facebook back, and things will go back to normal."

Annette frowned, but she didn't argue with him. Noah didn't feel like it, either. He was tired of delivering bad news.

"I've asked Sutter to retrieve some books from local libraries, but he doesn't seem too keen on it." Annette glanced at Noah, as if weighing her words. "It's almost like they don't want us doing anything for ourselves."

"They're just incredibly busy," Noah said. "I'm sure we have some residents with knowledge of the old ways. I know Molly knows her stuff. Maybe she'd be willing to come by."

"That would be great," Annette said.

"Any issues lately? Everyone getting along?"

Annette's frown deepened. "Everyone's still talking about what happened at Winter Haven."

"It was an unfortunate situation," Noah said tightly. "One I hope we can avoid in the future."

"Agreed," Lee said. "People just need to do what they're supposed to, that's all."

"Two people are dead," Annette said quietly. "A lot of people are shocked and upset."

"Hey, law and order are important," Lee said. "Folks gotta know they can't just do whatever they want. Not in a crisis. We all have to work together for the good of everyone else. You ask me, the militia are a Godsend. They're keeping us fed and warm, aren't they? I don't have a negative word to say about them. Rosamond's doing a great job. So are you, chief."

Annette made a face like maybe she disagreed. But when she turned to Noah, her smile was genuine. "We appreciate you coming over so often to check up on us, Chief Sheridan. That matters."

"You're welcome. We've got to take care of each other. Anything else I can help you folks with?"

Lee grinned. "Now that we've got the water issue ironed out and people are properly filtering their water, things have been better. We're still dealing with pneumonia and a flu bug going around."

Annette half-turned to look at the people huddled behind her. "People are stressed. It's one thing if you're in your own home, but with everyone squeezed together and no privacy, and no end to this crisis in sight? It's wearing on people."

"I admit, I am getting a little worried about mental health issues cropping up." Lee lowered his voice. "I'm seeing a lot of depressive symptoms, anxiety, PTSD. Anger issues, too. Kids are acting out. Adults, too."

"I'll talk to Sutter about looking for Prozac and anti-anxiety meds."

Lee shook his head. "You can't just dope people up. Not when their whole lives have been upended like this. I don't know. I try to keep everyone's spirits up, but a good pep talk just isn't doing it."

"I wish we had some psychologists on hand," Annette said. "We could really use some help on that angle."

"I'll try to figure something out," Noah said. As if he needed one more thing on his plate.

"Before the collapse, I read about a recent study that suggested Tylenol could be used to block or deal with emotional pain as well as physical pain," Lee said. "It's worth a shot."

Noah nodded. "I'll talk to Sutter."

"There's something else." Annette took a step closer. "Tina Gundy told me that the gas station is no longer open to regular folks. I went over during a break to check for myself, and she's right."

"Did they give you a reason?" Noah asked.

"The militia standing guard said supplies were running low. What was left was needed for those that are keeping the town safe."

Lee gave an easy shrug. "Hey, things aren't easy, but they aren't easy anywhere. It's true that our first responders need the gas more than we do. I don't have a problem with that."

"Can you spread some of that positive attitude around? We desperately need it." Noah sighed and scratched at his stubbled chin. He was three weeks past a good shave, but lately, a smooth face had been the last thing on his mind. "It's only temporary, until the militia finds a fresh supply."

Annette nodded, but she didn't look convinced. "This wasn't voted in by the council, Noah."

"We didn't get a chance to vote." The meeting three days ago hadn't gone well. People too stressed, too divided. Half were on Rosamond's side, the other half loudly against. It had dissolved into a shouting match between a bruised Darryl Wiggins and a furious Mike Duncan. Before it came to blows, Rosamond ended it early and kicked everyone out.

"Still, that's not exactly protocol—"

His radio belched static. Grateful for the distraction, Noah stepped outside and raised it to his mouth. "Sheridan here."

"Noah!" Bishop nearly shouted.

Noah pulled his head back. "Woah there. What's wrong?"

"Nothing! Absolutely nothing's wrong!"

Noah hadn't heard such happiness in Bishop's voice since before his family had been slaughtered. He couldn't imagine what this could possibly be about. If it was good news, he'd gratefully take it. "What is it?"

"My friend, you're going to need to sit down for this."

"Just tell me."

"It's a miracle! I still can't believe it. I'm standing here looking at her and I don't believe it."

"Atticus Bishop, if you don't—"

"It's Hannah."

Noah's heart froze inside his chest. The world stopped. The birds ceased singing. The sun went still in the sky. "They—they found her body?"

"Oh no! It's so much better than that. We found her. We found Hannah. And Noah—she's alive!"

Noah sat down hard. Right on the curb. His legs turned to water and his stomach flipped upside down. Cold, wet snow leaked through the butt of his pants. He didn't feel it.

He couldn't breathe. He couldn't speak. He struggled to form a coherent thought. His mind buzzed like a beehive, everything fuzzy and distant.

He couldn't comprehend Bishop's words. They didn't make sense.

He'd dreamed this scenario a thousand times. Each and every time, he'd awakened drenched in sweat, pulse racing—only to return to a cold silent bedroom and grief punching another hole through his heart.

"Did you hear me okay?" Bishop's booming voice brought him back. "Noah, did you hear?"

"I—I heard you. This...it can't be. Bishop, don't lie to me. Don't do this to me."

"It's real. She's real. This is real, Noah. This is happening."

Bishop would never lie about this. He wouldn't make a mistake, either.

Noah ripped off his gloves with his free hand and let them drop to the snow. He stared at his wedding ring glinting in the sun. His hands trembled. His whole body trembled.

"Chief Sheridan, are you okay?" Annette King asked, bending over him. "Is something wrong?"

He barely heard her, barely registered her voice. He was shaking all over. Hope, however frail, never died. Never. It sprang to life in his chest, stronger and fiercer than ever.

He didn't remember starting to cry. Tears ran down his face into the stubble of his beard. His nerves raw and vibrating. Everything was raw and bright and beautiful.

He swallowed hard. "I—can I hear her voice? Can I talk to her?"

"I'll do you one better!" Bishop bellowed. "Get your son. Get Milo. We'll be at your house in thirty minutes. We're bringing Hannah home."

30

HANNAH
DAY TWENTY-SEVEN

"I shouldn't be here," Liam said.

"No!" Hannah seized his hand. Guilt pricked her. She immediately dropped it. "I mean, I don't know. I want you here. Please. I'm sorry. I don't know what's wrong with me."

They stood on the front porch of her family's new home in Winter Haven, the self-sufficient community in Fall Creek. Large beautiful chalets, cabins, and lake cottages were nestled amongst the trees at the edge of the river.

The house itself was huge and a little imposing: a modern two-story log home with an expansive wraparound porch and huge windows.

A few moments ago, Bishop had dropped Hannah, Charlotte, Liam, and Ghost off at the front drive. He'd radioed ahead so Noah and Milo knew they were coming.

A tsunami of emotions roiled through her. "What if he doesn't recognize me? He was three. He won't know me. I shouldn't expect him to. That's asking too much. What if he doesn't like me? What if it's not—if it doesn't turn out—what if it's all wrong—"

Liam touched her shoulder. "They're your family. That's all you need to remember."

She nodded and patted Charlotte's back. The infant was swaddled against Liam's chest, tied with strips of a sheet beneath his coat. He'd offered to carry her so that Hannah would have her arms free to hold her son, to hug her husband.

She could hardly believe it was real. That this could really be happening.

She turned and glanced behind her. The sun was shining. The sky was a rich cobalt blue. The white snow sparkled like diamonds. It was so bright it was nearly blinding, but she did not look away.

Ghost had been prancing around in the front yard, trying to catch the melting clumps of snow falling from the branches. He seemed to sense that she needed him.

He dashed through the snow, bounded up the steps, and skidded to a halt. He didn't bump into her but halted neatly at her side. He pressed his muzzle into her hand with a comforting chuff.

She breathed deeply. "I needed that, boy. Thank you."

She steeled herself and lifted her chin. A lifetime of memories cascaded through her—washing Milo in the tub, Milo covered in soap bubbles and giggling; dancing with Noah in the kitchen; singing Milo to sleep, snuggled together in his too-small bed.

She rang the doorbell. Her hands shook. Her emotions were too big for this. Anticipation, hope, anxiousness, longing, fear.

She'd waited for this moment for so long. Prayed for it. Yearned for it. Lived through hell to get here.

The door opened.

A boy stood on the other side. Tall, so much taller than she remembered. The chubby baby face of her memories lengthened into an eight-year-old's. His body slim and gangly, all elbows and knees. But that familiar olive skin. The unruly black hair curling around his ears. Those big, solemn eyes.

"Milo," she whispered.

He stared at her, not speaking.

It was all she could do not to grab him and pull him against her, to enfold him in her arms.

She restrained herself. She would be a stranger to him. Of course, she would. She had to remember that. She had to think of his feelings.

Her eyes stung. The lump in her throat too large to swallow.

"Hi, Milo," she tried again. "I'm—" *I'm your mother. I love you more than the whole world. I went through hell and back to get to you.* She didn't say any of those things. Not yet. "I'm Hannah."

Milo glanced back at someone inside the house, then back to Hannah. He scrunched up his face. He looked nervous, confused. Maybe a little frightened.

The door opened wider.

Noah stood there. Her husband. The man she'd married. Danced with. Slept with. Made a home with.

He looked the same, but different. The same build, the same easy, athletic gait and dark brown hair. He looked older. His face was harder, leaner. Still handsome. He'd always been handsome.

Noah's features contorted. He stepped around Milo, strode onto the porch, and opened his arms. His eyes were red, tears glistening on his cheeks. He'd already been crying.

"Hannah," he said. "Is it really you?"

"It's me," she whispered. "It's me."

Noah hugged her. She wrapped her arms around him and hugged him back. Nothing had prepared her for this. She didn't know what it was supposed to feel like.

They had fit together so easily before. Now they didn't know where to put their arms. It was awkward, like they were pieces of a puzzle that didn't quite fit.

With a low growl, Ghost shoved between them.

She stepped back. Noah released her.

He wiped at his eyes. His wedding ring glinted in the sunlight. He still wore it, she realized with a pang.

Five years. He hadn't remarried. He hadn't taken it off. He'd waited for her.

The tears came then. She couldn't hold them back.

"I'm sorry," he said. "I'm so sorry."

"Sorry for what?"

"For losing you. It was my fault. I should have gone after you. I shouldn't have—"

"No. It wasn't your fault. It wasn't my fault. It was the fault of one person, and he's no longer here."

She saw the question in his eyes, but he didn't ask it. This wasn't the time.

She cleared her throat. "Noah, this is Liam Coleman. After I escaped, he found me in the woods. He saved my life. Three or four times, actually. I wouldn't be here without him."

Liam gave an uncomfortable half-grunt, half-cough. "She held her own."

Noah stepped forward. He clasped Liam's hand and shook it vigorously. "Thank you, Liam. Thank you so much. We can never repay you. We can never thank you enough."

Noah seemed to notice the infant swaddled against Liam's chest for the first time. "Oh, you have a baby. How wonderful."

Hannah's stomach clenched. She knew this was coming. There was no good way to say it. "She's not his, Noah. She's mine."

Noah blanched. A complicated array of emotions passed across his face in rapid succession. She saw the moment it hit him.

The words she couldn't say, but they hung in the air like a shroud: *She's mine...and from the monster who kidnapped me. She is a product of the most horrific thing one human can do to another. She's also beautiful and she's mine and I love her. Please, please love her, too.*

Surprise crossed his face, followed by a swift shadow of revulsion, replaced almost immediately by shame. He forced a smile that looked plastered to his face like a sticker. "That's okay. It's okay. Everything will be okay."

He said it more to himself than to her or Milo. She understood his reluctance, that gut-reaction of repugnance. Hadn't she felt the same for nine months?

Still, it hurt. Something dark and hollow opened up inside her chest.

Noah waved his hand, flustered. "Where are my manners? Come inside. Please. We're so excited—Milo and me. We would've been waiting for you outside, but we thought—we wanted everything to be okay for you. We didn't want to overwhelm you with hugs and kisses..." He cleared his throat. "Anyway, I'm rambling. Come in. This is your home."

It didn't feel like her home. She pushed that thought down deep and moved into the foyer.

It was warm and bright, with walnut plank flooring and vaulted ceilings. The house was richly furnished. It looked like a picture out of a magazine. The electric lights hurt her eyes.

She unzipped her coat and removed her hat and gloves. Liam did the same. Noah gathered their things and hung everything in the coat closet.

He turned back toward them. He caught sight of her damaged hand. It wasn't disgust or revulsion that crossed his face, but dismay, pity.

She'd thought pity would be better than the alternative. She was wrong.

Anger mixed with shame flushed through her, followed by defiance. She resisted the desire to hide her hand. She wasn't going to hide anything anymore.

Noah's gaze slid away from her deformity and returned to her face. He smiled then, happy and genuine. "You're here. You're really here. I can't believe it. Milo, it's your mom. She's home."

Milo didn't say anything.

Hannah's heart constricted.

Ghost pushed between Hannah and Liam's legs and entered the house ahead of them.

"A dog!" Milo said. His face brightened. A bit of his reluctance faded. "May I pet him?"

"Of course. His name is Ghost. He's a hero, too. He saved my life."

Ghost circled Milo slowly. He sniffed Milo's socks, his pant legs, his belly, arms, and chest. The Great Pyrenees was so large that he barely had to lift his head to smell Milo's face and hair.

Milo held very still. He didn't look scared, but awed. Cautiously, he reached out and scratched behind Ghost's ears.

Ghost woofed happily, ducked his head, and pressed the top of his skull against Milo's small chest.

"He likes you," Hannah said.

Milo gave a tremulous smile.

Hannah sank to her knees. She couldn't take her eyes off her son. He was so beautiful. He'd grown so much, more than she could have imagined.

He was everything she'd dreamt of, everything she'd held on to so fiercely during those dark, miserable years. The only splinter of hope in a hopeless existence.

The desire to hold him was nearly overwhelming. There was

nothing more in the entire universe that she wanted than to draw him into her arms and never let go. But she couldn't. Not yet.

He was like a deer in the forest, wary and hesitant. One wrong move and he might bolt.

This moment was made of glass. Everything so fragile, so easily crushed.

Sensing her distress, Ghost returned to Hannah and sat at her side. He nuzzled her neck and chuffed softly.

"Milo ... do you remember me?"

Milo dragged his gaze from the dog and looked at her. Slowly, he shook his head.

She had steeled herself for it. Logically, she'd known better than to believe otherwise. It still struck her like a punch to the gut.

There was no going back in time, no recovering the lost hours, days, months, and years. The lost moments of laughter, tears, anger, heartache, joy, love—they were gone forever.

Milo's childhood had been ripped from her. Milo's mother had been stolen from him.

They were not the same people they were that Christmas Eve five years ago. How could they be? Each of them was scarred, damaged, and haunted in their own way.

Hannah wasn't the only one who'd suffered. Her absence had left a gaping hole in their lives. Their shapes had changed into something jagged and broken.

In that moment, with her husband a stranger and her son almost unrecognizable, she feared their broken pieces might never fit back together.

The grief struck her so hard and so swift that her legs went weak. If she wasn't kneeling on the floor, she might have collapsed. Ghost leaned against her side, offering his strength.

"Hannah," Liam said, concern in his gruff voice. He touched her shoulder again. "Are you okay?"

The fear crept in. What if she no longer remembered how to be a wife? Or worse, a mother? The expectations of her reunited family bore down on her with a tremendous weight. She did not bow under it.

"I'm okay." She exhaled, steeling herself, and looked at Milo. "I know it's weird and strange and uncomfortable. I'm...I'm a stranger to you. Whatever you're feeling, it's okay to feel that way. We can get to know each other again. Let's start with being friends. You can call me Hannah. Is that okay with you?"

She didn't breathe until he nodded. He thrust out his hand with that same tremulous grin. "Deal."

Her fingers closed around his, so warm and small and wonderful. She felt her heart shattering and mending itself all at once. "Deal."

31

HANNAH
DAY TWENTY-SEVEN

Later, after Milo had collapsed into sleep and Noah had gotten Liam set up in a guest bedroom down the hall, Hannah and Noah at last found themselves alone with each other. Hannah had fed Charlotte and put her to sleep on the deep sofa surrounded by pillows.

Ghost had settled himself in the kitchen at Hannah's feet. He lay with his head on his paws, his alert gaze alternating between Hannah and Noah. Keeping watch.

He'd taken an instant liking to Milo but kept giving Noah the stink eye. If Noah got too close to Hannah, he gave a low warning growl.

Noah moved nervously around the kitchen, making sure to give the dog a wide berth. "You want some coffee? I can make decaf. Or hot chocolate? We have cookies. The last of our eggs were about to expire, so Milo and I made double chocolate with peanut butter chips."

"I'm fine, thank you." Hannah's stomach was too knotted to eat. She sat at the kitchen island on a wrought-iron stool with a polished wooden top.

Ornate white cabinets gilded with glass doors and crown molding towered on all sides of the huge kitchen. The vaulted ceiling gave her the feeling of vast empty space.

She stroked the large marble island with her fingertips. "This is a beautiful place you have."

"Thank you. After the EMP, Milo needed a house with electricity and heat."

She bit her lower lip but didn't say anything. It felt so strange being here. Sitting in a bright white kitchen with her husband, electric lights shining down on her head, talking about coffee and baking cookies like everything was normal.

Like the world hadn't turned upside down out there; like their lives hadn't imploded in here.

Everything was so far from normal that the sheer normalcy of this pretty house with its heat, lights, and running water almost seemed obscene.

Noah came to stand beside the island, awkward and hesitant. A couple of stools between them. And Ghost.

Ghost's claws clicked over the wood floor as he shifted to his feet and glared at Noah. He didn't growl, but he made his presence known.

Noah looked reluctant, like he wanted to come closer but was holding himself back. Because of Ghost, but also something else. She recognized the torn look in his eyes.

He twisted his wedding ring on his finger. "Do you really like it?"

She thought of their old house—the cozy living room with the red brick fireplace; the mismatched sofa and love seat, the antique coffee table she'd painted herself; the shabby kitchen they'd been meaning to remodel but never had the money for; the nest of blankets in Milo's toddler bed that smelled like apple shampoo and baby powder.

He would've outgrown that toddler bed years ago, she thought with a pang.

"It doesn't feel like home," she said honestly.

Noah glanced at the massive living room, the towering stone fireplace, the heavy dark leather furniture, the hand-scraped wood flooring. Everything pristine and polished, but not theirs. "No, I suppose it doesn't. It could, though. It will."

She waited for him to ask what had happened to her. Where she'd been for the last five years. He didn't. Maybe he was waiting for her to work up the courage to bring it up. Maybe he didn't want to know.

She traced a swirling pattern in the marble with her fingers. "You didn't get remarried."

"No, I didn't. I couldn't."

Her stomach tightened. "No...girlfriend?"

He shook his head. "No one but you, Hannah." He attempted a wry smile. "I never thought of anyone else like that. Not ever. Even though things weren't so good between us. I wanted you back, Hannah. I always wanted you back. It was only ever you."

She stared down at her hands. Her bad hand looked garish next to the perfect, flawless marble. "You aren't beholden to me. I don't...I don't hold you to anything. I want you to know that. I'm broken, Noah. I'm not the girl you knew. The one you married. I'm not her anymore. I'm not sure who I am yet, but what happened to me—"

"I don't care," he said in a rush. "We'll get over it. We'll get through it. It will be okay."

"The things that were done to me...I wouldn't blame you for not being able to get over that. For not being able to unknow it."

"That won't be a problem."

She wanted to share her past with him, the way she'd shared it with Liam. But Liam wasn't her husband. She understood that this was different. That it was an incredible burden to ask another to bear.

"Do you...is there anything you want to know? About what happened to me?"

He looked up at the ceiling, blinking rapidly, not meeting her gaze. "You didn't run away."

"No. I was—taken."

He exhaled like he'd been holding his breath for a long time. "I'm a cop. I know what happens. You don't have to go through that pain again, Hannah. It's okay, now. Everything will be okay."

She nodded, waiting for him to say more.

"I know we had problems before. I know we weren't perfect. But we loved Milo. We loved him with all our hearts, and that has to count for something, doesn't it? We can start again. Start over. I loved you. I love you."

"And Charlotte?"

He hesitated. She saw it in his face—a flash of doubt.

Her stomach dropped to her toes. She looked away.

"I'll—I'll try," he said, faltering. "I'll learn to. I will."

It was too much to ask. She couldn't demand more of him than he could give. It was unfair. Wasn't it?

An image flashed through her mind—big, strong Liam cradling tiny Charlotte in his arms, his hand cupped around her soft skull, a light in his eyes. Pride and affection. A fierce devotion.

She shook the memory away. It did no good to think about that now.

"Do you want to hold her?" her voice was raw, a whisper. She didn't breathe.

He glanced at the baby on the couch. He looked down at his hands, his wedding ring, then back up at Hannah. "She's sleeping now. Maybe later?"

He must have seen the disappointment in her expression. "It'll be okay, Hannah. Everything will be okay. We're together now. You're back. Like Bishop said, it's a miracle. This will work. I know it will."

He didn't want to see the cracks. He didn't want to see the ugliness. He didn't want to acknowledge the difficult terrain that lay before them.

Today was the first step in a tremendous journey. A journey their little family was attempting as the world crumbled around them.

The odds were stacked against them. The odds were stacked against them all.

There would be as much pain and heartache as joy and happiness.

She knew that. She understood it, accepted it.

She wasn't sure if Noah would. If he could.

She tried not to let the hurt show in her face. Maybe he would be ready later. It was a lot to take in—her miraculous return, a wife long dead suddenly very much alive. Alive, but damaged, and different in almost every way.

She needed to tell him who had done this to her, but it could wait for a bit. A few minutes, at least.

She changed the subject to something happier, some shared common ground. "Milo...he's so big. Tell me about him. I want to know everything."

Noah's expression brightened. His love for their son was obvious. That had never been the problem.

"He's so smart. And brave. That kid is fearless. When he was four, he tried to jump off the diving board at the YMCA pool. No arm floaties or anything. I'd already jumped in before he hit the water. But man, I had to watch him like a hawk. He's a little quiet, a little more serious." He flashed her a grin. "He takes after you that way. He loves reading and Legos. The Avengers. The usual kid stuff."

"Does he still love peanut butter?"

"Oh man. He'd eat Jif at every meal if I let him."

She smiled. "Pancakes slathered in creamy peanut butter topped with whipped cream?"

"His absolute favorite."

Hannah's heart squeezed. He was still her son. Still her Milo.

They would find their way back to each other. She had absolute faith in that.

"There's something else you need to know," Noah said quietly. He stared down at his hands. "Milo has a serious illness."

Dread filled her. "What? What is it?"

"Two years after you disappeared, he started to get sick. Real sick. The doctors diagnosed him with Addison's disease. He's fine. He's healthy and happy. He just has to have his medication."

Hannah imagined Milo sick and scared in a hospital room. And she hadn't been there. His mother hadn't been there.

Remorse struck her. How much she would give, how many mountains she would move to erase the last five years, to go back and change everything. Her heart ached with love and sorrow.

"What happens if he doesn't have it?"

Noah didn't answer. His silence was answer enough.

Her chest was too tight. It was hard to breathe. "Without it, he'll die."

Slowly, Noah nodded.

The hammer fell, slow and terrible. Medication meant pharmaceutical companies, production, distribution warehouses, open pharmacies, and a functioning supply chain. Because of the EMP, that was all gone now. For years, at least. "Where is he going to get it?"

"We have plenty, don't worry. The militia, they've been going out and getting food and supplies for the community. They've brought back at least five years' worth of medication. Five years, Hannah! By then, the country will be back up and running. The supply chain reinstated." He smiled at her. "He's fine, Hannah. We're fine."

It was difficult to imagine how Milo would be fine in a world without hospitals, ambulances, and top-notch medical care.

The giant hand squeezing her heart did not let go.

32

HANNAH
DAY TWENTY-SEVEN

"I'll make some hot chocolate," Noah said, though she hadn't asked for it. With a wary glance at Ghost, he circled the island to reach the counter and banged around in the cabinets.

She understood that he was seeking a distraction. Noah had never been great with uncomfortable emotions. He would rather smooth things over and pretend everything was okay, even if it wasn't.

Even amid catastrophic change, some things remained the same.

Ghost nosed her thigh. She reached down and absently scratched his ears.

"It was so good to see Bishop," she said, once again attempting to change the subject to more neutral territory. "We should have him and Daphne over. I can't wait to see Juniper and Chloe."

Noah went very still. He paused, his back to her. His hand hovered over the hot chocolate canister.

A chill raced up her spine. "What?"

He turned to face her, his expression somber. "Daphne. The girls. They're...they're dead."

She stared at him, stricken. "What happened?"

Noah told her about Ray Shultz and his gang of thugs. The massacre at Crossway Church. How many had died. Milo and Quinn's ordeal. How Bishop had been forced to watch his wife and daughters die in front of him.

By the end, she was shaking. Tears stung the backs of her eyelids. Her heart ached with sorrow and compassion and burned with anger. The senseless cruelty and death. The horror Bishop had endured. The loss of his beautiful family.

A month into the collapse, and everything was coming undone. Everyone in this town had already lost so much. So much pain, grief, and hardship.

She shook her head. "What Bishop went through...I had no idea."

"The militia took care of it. They caught the monsters and brought justice to Fall Creek. That will never happen again. Never. We've...sacrificed. We've made sure of it."

"The militia?"

"We invited them to Fall Creek. They get homes in Winter Haven in exchange for protection. Gangs and organized criminals are attacking nearby towns. With the supply chain down, people are already desperate and starving. The governor has made it clear that he doesn't care what happens to his citizens. Not in the rural communities, anyway. FEMA and the National Guard are busy elsewhere. We've been abandoned. For the foreseeable future, we're on our own."

She'd seen the soldiers in camouflage uniforms toting semi-automatic rifles at the checkpoint into Fall Creek. More patrolling Main Street and Winter Haven.

She'd been so focused on getting home to Milo and Noah, her mind had barely registered them. Until now.

"They're keeping us safe." Noah put his elbows on the island

and leaned toward her, his eyes bright, his expression earnest. "This place is safe, Hannah. We can start over. We can build a life here."

"I hope so."

"I know so. We have a house with electricity and heat. We have food, supplies, Milo's medication. Rosamond made sure of it. She took care of us."

Her heart constricted at the mention of Rosamond Sinclair. Gavin Pike's mother. Her mouth went dry and thick, like it was stuffed with paper towels.

It was time to tell him. Even if he wasn't ready for the details, he needed to know this.

Noah narrowed his eyes. "What? What is it?"

"Did—did Bishop tell you about the body in the basement? Did he tell you who it was?"

"No, he didn't. I doubt I would've heard it even if he did. I couldn't focus on a thing after he told me about you."

She swallowed. "It was the man who took me. Who stole me from my life. The man who held me captive and tortured me for five years."

Noah went still. "Who?"

"Rosamond Sinclair's son. Gavin Pike."

Noah stood quickly. He leapt back from the island like she'd burned him. The stool clattered to the floor. He took three swift steps backward, until his back pressed against the wall of cabinets.

His face went slack. He shook his head incredulously. "No. No, no, no..."

She said nothing.

He pressed both hands to his chest and stared at her in shock. Horror, confusion, and disbelief warring in his eyes. "How..."

"He kept me in his hunting cabin up north. In the Manistee National Forest."

Noah flinched. He staggered to the sink on the opposite side of the island. He barely made it. He bent over the sink, gagged, and vomited into the basin.

He remained there, a hand gripping either side of the porcelain, breathing hard, his face sweating and pale. "Every time he went up there…every weekend…all this time, he was…what he was doing to you…"

Noah turned on the faucet. He cupped a handful of water—fresh, clean, running water—and splashed it over his face. He grabbed a washcloth and wiped his mouth.

He closed his eyes. "The baby. She belongs to…She's …"

He couldn't bring himself to say the words aloud. So Hannah did. "Charlotte does not belong to Pike. She is not his. Her conception does not matter. She is innocent."

Noah opened his eyes, blinked, and nodded his head. He looked like he was on the verge of despair. "Okay," he whispered, more to himself than to her. "Okay, okay."

He straightened, still shaking. "I never liked him. Never. There was always something… off about him. Like he despised you even as he smiled at you. But I never thought…we never suspected him. No one did. He was here, this whole time. I spoke to him. I had meals with him at Rosamond's house…"

He grimaced, aghast. "Oh, hell. He would talk to Milo. He would watch him. I never liked it. I never…"

He shoved himself away from the sink. He paced in a tight circle in the expansive kitchen, his hands balled into fists and pressed against his temples. He looked like he was in shock.

The hackles on Ghost's back rose. He growled softly. Maybe he didn't like Noah's erratic movements. Maybe he sensed who it was they were talking about.

Hannah buried her hand in his fur and stroked the top of his head. It steadied them both.

Noah met her gaze with a stricken expression. "How could I have not known? All this time. He was right here, underneath my nose. I should have suspected!"

Empathy welled within her. Her husband had suffered. She could see it etched in every pore and line of his face. "You didn't know. You aren't responsible for what you didn't know."

"I should have done something!" Noah cried, anguished.

"He was good at what he did," Hannah said softly. "I trusted him when he pulled over that night and promised to help me. I got right in his truck. He was a chameleon. A shapeshifter."

"He's a psychopath," Noah spat.

"He *was* a psychopath. He's dead now."

That brought Noah up short. "How?"

"I killed him. Me and Ghost together." She hesitated. "Liam told Reynoso that he did it."

Noah had gone still. The blood drained from his face. His mouth worked soundlessly for a moment. She could see the cogs turning in his mind, the pieces falling into place. One by one.

"Rosamond," he said. "Julian."

"What about them?"

"She'll never believe it. Not of her precious son."

Hannah stiffened. "I don't care what she believes."

He shook his head. "Your soldier friend was smart. I don't want her blaming you for this. Julian has a hot temper. You remember how he is. Rosamond...she's not going to take this news well. It will be better if it wasn't you."

"But it was."

"I know that. You know that. That's all that matters. Just... trust me, okay?"

She stared at him. "What aren't you telling me?"

Noah came around the island toward her.

Against her side, Ghost bristled. He padded between her and Noah.

Noah stopped two feet away. "Don't worry. I'll keep you safe, Hannah. I'll protect you."

Hannah didn't ask why she would need protection from the Sinclairs. A cold chill trickled down the back of her neck. Something—some deep primordial instinct—was warning her.

Killing Gavin Pike might have ended one nightmare—only to begin the genesis of another.

33

JULIAN
DAY TWENTY-EIGHT

Julian was sure he hadn't heard correctly. Noah's living room was suddenly stifling. A low buzzing filled his ears. "What did you just say?"

Noah's long-lost wife sat in a soft white leather armchair in Noah's living room in Winter Haven. Noah stood on one side of her, anxious and hovering. On the other side stood a tall, wary stranger who'd introduced himself as Liam Coleman and a giant white dog. Noah's wife held an infant in her arms.

Julian stood facing them, Perez and Reynoso flanking him, old-fashioned notebooks and pencils in their hands. Milo had been sent to his room when they'd arrived. They were debriefing Hannah Sheridan and the man she'd brought back to Fall Creek with her yesterday.

"Maybe you shouldn't be here," Noah had said when he'd first arrived with Reynoso and Perez. "It's a conflict of interest."

"Like hell," Julian had shot back. "I've got just as much a right to be here as you do! Should I bring the superintendent instead?"

Noah hadn't argued after that.

Hannah's mere presence was shocking. Every word she spoke

shocked him even more. How she'd been kidnapped on the side of the road and locked in a basement up north for five years. What she'd endured. How she'd escaped.

And who it was who'd done this to her.

She looked at him steadily, without flinching or dropping her eyes, without fear or shame. "It was Gavin Pike. He was the one who did this to me."

Julian felt like he'd been punched in the gut by a giant unseen hand. It was suddenly hard to breathe. Gavin Pike, his brother, a demented psychopath?

"No way," he said, because that's what he was supposed to say. "That can't be true."

"It is true," Hannah said calmly.

His mind raced. It was difficult to believe. But was it, really? It wasn't out of the realm of possibility. Not where his brother was concerned.

"That's impossible."

Hannah didn't say anything. Just watched him.

The more he thought about it, the more everything began to fall into place, to finally make sense. Gavin's obsession with those weekend camping trips. That throwaway phone he didn't want anyone to know about, that he would furtively check during council meetings or at family dinners at their mother's house.

Hannah reached up to tuck a stray strand of hair behind her ear with her left hand. Something was wrong with it.

Julian cleared his throat and pointed. "What happened?"

"I was tortured."

He couldn't take his eyes off her grotesquely disfigured hand. "How?"

"He broke my fingers. On purpose. As punishment, if I did something he didn't like. A few times, just for fun. They healed crookedly, and then he broke them again. And again."

Noah flinched. Liam Coleman's expression darkened. Perez scribbled notes, her mouth agape.

Hannah didn't move. She didn't take her eyes off Julian's face.

A shiver raced up his spine. Instinctively, his right hand strayed to the two fingers of his left hand, broken in childhood. An accident, his mother had always insisted.

He saw his brother's face in his mind's eye. That cruel, thin-lipped smile. An approximation of a smile. A facsimile. All the more chilling for how similar it was to the real thing.

Fifteen years later, and he hadn't forgotten. Could never forget.

It was true, then. It was all true.

He met Hannah's gaze and saw recognition in her eyes. She knew that he believed it. Her chin lifted a little.

"So where is he, then?" he asked, keeping his voice and his expression neutral. "What does he have to say for himself?"

"He's dead," Coleman said. "When he hunted us to the house in Watervliet, I confronted him. He tried to kill Hannah and myself. In defense, I shot him three times and stabbed him in the stomach."

Dizziness washed through him. Gavin's death was more shocking to him than what had come before. His half-brother. His mother's precious, favorite son. Dead.

A competing jumble of emotions snarled in his gut. He waited for the sorrow, the gut-punch of grief. It didn't come.

He knew how he should feel. He should be weak-kneed, overcome with horror and loss. He felt none of those things.

Numbness spread through his body. Maybe it was shock. Maybe it was something else.

His older brother had cast a large and ominous shadow. He'd always seemed larger than life. Too evil to die.

A cruel and cunning bully. Brutal enough to torture his own

flesh and blood and enjoy it. And smart enough to get away with it.

No one but Julian had ever seen it. Not until Hannah, anyway. Certainly not his mother, who'd worshiped the ground Gavin walked on.

Now, the truth was finally out. And Gavin was dead.

Julian inhaled a steadying breath. His mother would be devastated, furious, beside herself. He would have to deal with her, figure out the fallout and get ahead of it. But as for Julian himself...

His brother would never taunt or ridicule Julian again. He would never be their mother's golden boy again. Julian was free of him for good.

Maybe even the apocalypse had its perks.

"You killed Gavin," Julian said. "That's what you're telling me?"

"Yes, I did," Coleman said again.

Hannah's eyes flickered. Julian shifted his gaze to Coleman. He looked like a man familiar with killing. A man who killed often and without conscience.

"You're under arrest," Julian said, already pulling out his cuffs.

"No," Noah said. "He isn't."

"It's protocol—"

"You heard them," Reynoso said. "It was self-defense."

"Even so. We need to take him into custody and conduct an investigation."

Noah took a step forward. "We just did."

"Everything we found at the scene is consistent with their statements," Reynoso said. "The dog got ahold of the corpse, making an autopsy more difficult—if we could even get one."

"We could always send someone up to Pike's cabin in Manistee," Perez said. "Examine the basement."

"True," Noah said.

"It'll take you awhile," Coleman said. "It took us over three weeks to make the journey. Plenty of anarchy between here and there. And it's only getting worse."

"We'll get it done, but I don't see how we can make it a priority right now," Noah said. "As chief, I decide. We're not taking anyone into custody or pressing any charges. Michigan is a Stand Your Ground state. By law, Liam Coleman had the right to use lethal force to protect himself—and my wife—from the imminent threat of great bodily harm and death."

Julian wanted to argue further, but he wasn't the one in charge, was he? He'd needed to tell his mother that he'd tried, at least. It wasn't his fault he'd been overruled by *her* choice for police chief.

He felt no personal animosity toward Coleman. He wasn't the one Coleman needed to worry about.

"Fine!" He swallowed the bitterness on the back of his tongue and raised his hands, palms out, in a sign of surrender. "This is on you, *chief*."

"I accept that," Noah said through gritted teeth. "I think we're done here. My wife has been through a lot and needs to rest."

Perez and Reynoso folded their notebooks and tucked them back in their pockets and zipped up their coats.

"Sure thing, chief," Reynoso said.

Julian shrugged carelessly and tucked the handcuffs back into his coat. "You're the one who has to deal with the superintendent. I don't think she'll be as understanding as I've been."

Noah paled.

Julian turned to leave.

"Julian," he said quickly. "Can I talk to you for a minute? Outside?"

Noah followed Julian out to the snow-covered porch. Reynoso

and Perez waited for Julian in the truck. Coleman and Hannah remained inside the house.

It was still mid-morning. The air was chilly, but the sun peeked out from behind a ribbon of gray clouds. There was no wind.

Julian leaned against a post and folded his arms across his chest. "What do you want?"

Noah ran a hand over the growth of his new beard. "What am I going to say to Rosamond? How am I going to tell her?"

Julian hesitated, weighing his options. "I'll take care of it."

Noah stared at him suspiciously.

"I'm serious. Look, man, I know we've been on opposite sides of this thing. It's been a little tense. But I'm happy for you. I really am. You've got your wife back. You need to be with her. Let me do this favor, for old times' sake."

Relieved, Noah's shoulders slumped. "I appreciate it. Still, as chief, it should be me..."

His tone was unconvincing at best. He was just waiting for Julian to talk him out of it, to relieve him of the responsibility.

"She's my mother. It was my brother. I'm the best person to handle her, trust me."

"Look, I don't blame you for any of this. I'm sure you're as shocked as the rest of us. I know you didn't know, I believe that."

Even now, Noah still thought the best of him. Guilt stuck a knife in his gut and twisted.

For a minute, for just a moment, the events of the last weeks slipped away. They were best friends again, years of history between them, just two cops who always had each other's backs.

Julian resisted the urge to slap his old friend on the shoulder, to pull him in for a manly hug like they used to. How easy it would be to slip back into warm and familiar habits. To share in

Noah's joy and celebration. His wife had returned, his family whole again.

Years of good memories flashed through his mind. And the bad, too—all those times he'd nursed Noah through grief and nightmares, never leaving him, never doubting him.

And then he remembered the look on Noah's face when he'd accepted his new role as chief of police. He remembered how his mother idolized Noah for no good reason, just like she had Gavin. The pain of betrayal still stung like it was fresh.

"She didn't know him like she thought she did," Noah continued. "He fooled all of us. Tell her that. I don't blame her, either. This doesn't have to change things."

Noah was living in a dream world if he thought Rosamond Sinclair would ever accept that her precious golden boy was a monster. That ex-soldier in there was in trouble up to his neck, and he didn't even know it. Hannah, too, if she kept spouting that stuff about Gavin.

Didn't matter how true it was. No one wanted to hear it, least of all his mother.

"I'll handle my mother and keep her from doing anything rash, okay? I know what to say to defuse the situation. Don't worry about it."

Noah looked immensely relieved, like Julian had just lifted a massive burden off his shoulders. "Thank you. I owe you."

Julian smiled like it was nothing. "I'm your brother. I have your back."

Julian turned to go, then paused. "You should keep your wife quiet. You don't want her making enemies when she's just gotten back."

Noah nodded. "I'll talk to Hannah. I'll get her to see. It helps no one to keep dwelling on it. If Gavin were here, I'd kill him myself. Honestly, I would. But he's dead. It's over. What's done is done."

"That's the spirit," he forced out, feigning nonchalance.

Noah was as naïve and stupid as he'd always been. Julian couldn't believe he'd felt anything for him, that for half a second, he'd even considered forgiving this moron. "The past stays in the past, is that it?"

"Something like that," Noah said.

Julian had to turn away to hide his sneer. The past never died. That was the painful lesson Noah Sheridan still hadn't learned.

It always came back to haunt you, to nurse grudges, to exact its revenge.

34

JULIAN
DAY TWENTY-EIGHT

There was a knock on the exterior door to the superintendent's office.

Julian leaned against the wall of bookcases, his arms crossed over his chest. Rosamond Sinclair sat behind her pristine mahogany desk in her home office, papers stacked neatly on the dusted surface.

Mattias Sutter and Sebastian Desoto sat on the opposite side of Rosamond's desk in antique wooden chairs. Noah would normally be in the meeting, but he was otherwise engaged at home with his newly returned wife—a fact that Rosamond was not yet privy to.

"Come in," Rosamond said tersely. She did not appreciate interruptions.

The office had a rear entrance off the back deck, which the militia and council members used. Officers Reynoso and Perez entered, a blast of cold air following them, and stood near the door. They were tense and anxious, their faces grim.

Julian had instructed them to wait an hour before reporting to the superintendent. Instead of telling his mother immediately, as he'd promised Noah, he'd decided to let the two officers do it.

Rosamond had a way of hating the messenger, if not killing them. It would be better for Julian if the news didn't come from him.

"What is it?" His mother shuffled several papers, sighed, and steepled her fingers on the desk. She fixed her gaze on them. "Out with it."

"Ma'am, I'm so sorry," Reynoso said. "But we've found a body."

"Whose?"

Julian waited for it, holding his breath.

"Gavin Pike, ma'am," Perez said.

Rosamond went absolutely still. "What?"

"I'm sorry, Superintendent Sinclair," Reynoso said grimly. "Your son is dead."

His mother gripped the lip of her desk with rigid fingers. "No. That's impossible."

Reynoso glanced at Julian. "His body was discovered in Watervliet. Identification collected confirmed his ID. It's him."

Rosamond sank back into her office chair. Her face went bone white. Her hands fluttered around her throat as if she didn't know what to do with them.

"Rosamond?" Sutter said, rising to his feet. "Are you all right?"

Rosamond shook her head, her eyes huge and wild. Her gaze flitted around the room without landing on anything. "No," she whispered. "No. Not my Gavin. No, no, no!"

"Get her some water," Sutter ordered.

Desoto hauled himself from his seat and lumbered for the kitchen.

Julian barely registered his departure. Sutter was speaking to

Rosamond, but his words sounded far away. He stared at his mother, gauging her reaction.

Desoto returned with a glass of water. Sutter seized it from his hands and offered it to Rosamond. "Drink this. You need to drink."

She took it with shaking hands. Her whole body was trembling, quivering with grief. She looked like she'd aged a decade in five minutes. Her eyes were red and wide, but she did not weep.

Julian had never seen her cry, not once.

Julian realized he should've been the one to check on his mother, to get her a drink, to comfort her, but he couldn't bring himself to move.

Rosamond waved Sutter away, and he and Desoto returned to their seats. Reynoso and Perez watched her like she was a bomb about to explode. Probably because she was.

She set the glass back on the desk so hard, the *clink* echoed in the room. She wiped her eyes and smoothed her coiffed blonde hair. She set both hands palms down on top of the desk on either side of the glass and took a steadying breath. "What happened to my son?"

Perez and Reynoso exchanged wary glances.

"Tell me," Rosamond said, her voice like ice. "Right now."

"He was killed," Reynoso said.

"Gavin was murdered?" Rosamond faltered. She was struggling to maintain her serene, unruffled demeanor and failing. "By whom?"

Reynoso and Perez glanced at each other again.

"Who killed my son?" Rosamond whispered.

Reluctantly, Reynoso cleared his throat. "Apparently, ma'am, it was in self-defense."

"Impossible," Rosamond said.

"We also found a woman. Not just any woman. Hannah Sheridan."

Rosamond stiffened. "What?"

"Noah Sheridan's missing wife," Perez said. "She's alive. She's been alive all this time. She was kidnapped and held captive in a cabin up in the Manistee National Forest."

"That's fantastic," Rosamond said, her voice wooden. She didn't sound like it was fantastic news at all. "What does that have to do with my son?"

"Hannah says..." Reynoso shuffled his feet. His gaze flicked around the room like he was desperate to be anywhere but here. "She claims that Gavin Pike is the one who kidnapped her five years ago."

For a moment, there was absolute silence. No one moved. No one breathed.

Mattias Sutter raised his eyebrows in surprise and shifted his gaze to Rosamond. Desoto's mouth dropped open.

Julian watched his mother, watched the shock register on her rigid features.

"Is this true?" Sutter asked.

"Of course not!" Rosamond snapped.

"It's what she says happened," Perez said.

Rosamond leapt to her feet. Rage and grief flashed in her eyes. "Then she's insane! She must be on drugs. Or out for revenge. She always was jealous of Noah's close relationship with us. She was always an ungrateful little slut." She paused, breathing hard. "How do you even know it's Hannah Sheridan?"

"We all recognized her, ma'am," Perez said.

Rosamond's eyes flicked to Julian, her gaze begging him to deny it. But he couldn't. He'd seen it with his own eyes. So had plenty of others. "It's her."

"She's playing you!" Rosamond nearly shouted. "Don't you

see? She ran off five years ago to abandon her family and live the good life, free of responsibility. Then the world goes to pot, and she needs security and shelter. Who better to offer it than her former husband? What better place than Fall Creek, with its self-sustaining community of Winter Haven? You're crazy if you believe that drivel!"

"She has a baby," Perez said. "She alleges that she was raped—repeatedly, over a period of five years. That the child is a product of that rape."

Rosamond reacted like she'd been slapped. "Lies! Complete rubbish! Bitter, manipulative lies intended to smear my family's good name! That's all this is. That child has nothing to do with us. Nothing! You can't prove it! You can't prove any of it!"

Reynoso glanced at Julian. Julian kept his expression neutral. Gone were the days of DNA tests. At least, for now. Maybe forever.

Julian had no doubts, but he wasn't going to say that out loud.

"My son is innocent until proven guilty!" Rosamond snapped. "Don't you forget that!"

"Of course, ma'am," Perez said tightly.

Rosamond went rigid. Her mouth contorted, her eyes flashing with rage. She was losing her cool, her precious control. "This manipulative little whore murdered my son in cold blood? Is that what you're telling me?"

"No, ma'am," Reynoso said. "It wasn't her."

Rosamond fixed the officers with a cold, hostile stare. "Then who? Who killed my son?"

35

JULIAN
DAY TWENTY-EIGHT

Julian watched the scene unfold with a dark fascination, like a car crash he couldn't turn away from.

Watching Reynoso and Perez get a dressing-down wasn't the worst thing in the world. Reynoso had been a jerk lately, not the loyal sidekick that he used to be. Well, screw him. Let them twist a little.

"Who killed him!" Rosamond demanded again.

"She has a man and a dog with her," Perez said. "The man is an ex-soldier. He apparently came across her in the woods after she escaped. He rescued her and agreed to escort her to Fall Creek. They've been trying to get here since the EMP. Pike came after her—"

"Allegedly!" Rosamond snarled.

Perez's face lost some of its color. Reynoso looked appalled. They'd both backed against the door.

"Allegedly," Reynoso admitted grudgingly. "According to the witness statement, her alleged assailant stalked her and attacked both her and the soldier in the house they'd taken shelter in. There was an altercation. The soldier shot and then stabbed the assailant in self-defense. Afterward, the dog took a few bites out of him as well."

"According to them," Rosamond said.

"Yes. According to their statements."

She looked furious enough to rip someone's head off. Julian knew his mother's rages. He would not put it past her to try it.

She glowered at the officers. "And my son is not here to provide a statement of what really happened. Seeing as he's dead."

The two cops said nothing.

"What is the soldier's name?"

"Ma'am—" Reynoso started.

"What. Is. The. Soldier's. Name."

"Tell her," Julian ordered.

Reynoso licked his lips uneasily. "Liam Coleman."

No one reacted. The name meant nothing to Rosamond, Sutter, or Desoto.

"And where is he now?"

"He's staying at Chief Sheridan's house," Julian said.

Rosamond's mouth twisted. "Why was this criminal not apprehended?"

"Chief Sheridan declined to press charges." Julian said the words with relish, waiting to see what she would do, how she would react. Her precious police chief had let her son's killer go free.

"Did he?" Rosamond said, shaking.

Julian gave a flippant shrug. "You know he'll pick his wife over...other loyalties."

Perez shifted nervously. "As we said, we determined it was self-defense—"

"GET OUT!" Rosamond screamed at them.

The officers flinched. Julian resisted the urge to shrink away from her, too. His mother was formidable on a good day. When she was angry, she was terrifying.

Rosamond's features were pinched, the tendons of her neck straining. "This woman's...accusations remain in this room. If I hear a word of this breathed by either of you two, you're off the force. You'll be out of a job and packing your things, because you won't be welcome anywhere in Fall Creek ever again. Neither will your families. Have I made myself understood?"

Perez swallowed. "Understood."

Reynoso looked more openly disgruntled, but he didn't say a word. They both valued their careers—and having a roof over their heads.

Julian knew they'd fall into line. Just like everyone else under his mother's thumb. She could crush them like ants whenever she felt like it—and they knew it.

Hannah Sheridan was still free to say whatever she wanted to whoever she wanted, but that was a problem for another day, one Noah might or might not solve. He was certain his mother would not overlook it.

"Go!" Rosamond spat at them. "Get out of my sight!"

Reynoso and Perez scurried out of the office.

Rosamond waited for the door to shut behind them. Her whole body vibrated with outrage. With quivering hands, she smoothed invisible wrinkles from her beige pantsuit and straightened her shoulders. "This Liam Coleman is an outsider. A criminal and a murderer. Such a man of violence does not belong within the borders of this community."

"I agree," Desoto said.

"We are at your command," Sutter said evenly. His face betrayed no emotion. "Simply tell us what you wish to have done."

"Do you want me to arrest him despite the *chief*'s objections?" Julian asked. "Chief Sheridan let him go. No charges. Nothing."

His mother turned her gaze on him. Her eyes had gone shiny and hard. Red pigment from her lipstick leaked into the creases around her mouth.

Julian cringed at the rancor in her gaze—the pure contempt. As if she wished he were the one dead, not her precious Gavin.

"What do you want me to do?" Julian asked. "Beat him up? Toss him out of town?"

When she spoke, her voice was full of razor blades. "Are you that stupid? Do you really think that is a sufficient consequence for the murder of your brother?"

Gavin hadn't been murdered. He'd deserved every gunshot and stab wound and then some. Julian was certain of it. Whoever this soldier was, he'd done the world a favor.

In doing so, he'd also found himself on the wrong side of Rosamond Sinclair. That was his fatal mistake.

Julian knew better than to speak his thoughts aloud. His mother wouldn't change her mind. He had little inclination to try.

This was happening, with or without him.

This was his chance to get back on her good side. To prove his worth to her. To prove that he was better than his brother.

She didn't need Gavin anymore. And she certainly didn't need the likes of Noah Sheridan. Neither did Julian.

It was more than that, though. His mother gazed at him, her glassy eyes a blaze of grief and rage, beseeching him. Begging him.

A longing filled him, that twisted desire for her approval that had haunted him from childhood, that old desperation for a crumb of her stingy love to be flicked his way.

He hated her for it. He hated himself even more. But he couldn't stop it, even now.

"No," he said. "I don't. I'll make it right."

Her lip curled in derision. "Can you handle it like a man, this time?"

He forced himself not to flinch, forced the humiliation not to show on his face. He groveled, because that was what she wanted. "Please! Let me take charge of this. I'll get it right this time, I promise."

She hesitated, her eyes flashing with contempt, even hate. He waited, not breathing.

A shadow crossed her face. Something deflated in her. Almost imperceptible, but he saw it. She gave him a subtle nod and shifted her gaze to Sutter. "Whatever my son asks of you, do it."

Julian tried not to let the relief show on his face. He clenched his jaw. He would claw his way back on top, back to her side. He'd get things back the way they were supposed to be. Starting with Liam Coleman.

Julian had a few names of his own to add to the list.

Sutter rose from his seat. He was a tank of a man—thick-necked, burly, and imposing. A cunning intelligence shone from his dark eyes.

He nodded at Julian before meeting Rosamond's gaze. "That won't be a problem. I'll give you Desoto and Benner to do as you both see fit."

"Where is my son's body?" Rosamond asked Julian, her voice low and dangerous. "What did those idiots do with him?"

"I really don't think you want to see—"

She leaned forward and planted her fists on the desk, her eyes bulging. "Where!"

"They put him in the last body bag and stored him in the freezer at the school for now," Julian said.

"I'm going to bury my son," Rosamond said stiffly. She gave Julian a hard stare. "I don't want to see your face again until it's done."

She strode around the desk, marched past Julian, and opened the door without a backward glance.

36

NOAH
DAY THIRTY

"Chief Sheridan, we may have a problem." Reynoso's voice sputtered over the radio.

"Come in, Reynoso," Noah said. "What is it?"

"Trouble at Crossway Church."

Noah's heartrate quickened. His gloved hands tightened on the steering wheel. He sat in the black 1970s Ford F150 with "Fall Creek Police Department" spray-painted across the sides. The engine was on, heat chugging from the vents.

He'd parked the truck in the road at the roadblock just past the bridge leaving town. The guards had given him an update. Sutter reported to Rosamond daily, but Noah wanted to keep his finger on the pulse of his town himself. It was part of his job.

In the last twenty-four hours, the militia had turned back four groups seeking food and shelter. They all had tales of woe—empty pantries, freezing homes, break-ins and violence in the streets. One group got hostile and had to be turned away by force.

Another dead body to add to the list—and Noah's already burdened conscience.

Things were getting worse out there. No help was coming. No help but what they did for themselves.

Anxiety twisted his guts to water. The only thing that steadied his nerves was the knowledge that fifty-three armed men patrolled Fall Creek. Fifty-three soldiers ensuring the town was safe. Ensuring his son was safe.

That was what mattered. He would tell himself that until he believed it.

"It's Bishop," Noah said, not a question.

"It's Bishop," Reynoso said reluctantly.

He'd been waiting for the other shoe to drop since the day Bishop brought Hannah back, only to discover the Crossway food pantry had been emptied out in his absence. Noah had meant to talk to him, but he'd been more than a little distracted by the miraculous return of his wife.

"Should I contact Julian? He took the afternoon to go ice fishing—"

"No!" The word exploded from his throat.

Silence on the radio.

"That's not a good idea," he said more calmly, though he felt anything but calm.

Guilt pricked him. He ignored it. He and Julian were still barely speaking, especially after their confrontation a few days ago. He should've just let Julian take Liam into custody like he'd wanted to.

He sighed. What was done was done. He already had too much on his plate; he couldn't handle Julian's volatile moods, too.

"What do you want me to do, boss?" Reynoso asked.

"I'll handle Bishop. I can handle him. I'll be right there."

Noah clipped the radio back on his belt. He shifted the truck into gear, made a U-turn, and headed back into town. He squinted against the glare of sunlight reflecting off snow. The roads were freshly plowed. The day was bright and sunny, the temps somewhere in the low thirties.

Maybe the warmth would stick, and some of this damn snow would melt. It was wishful thinking. January wasn't even over yet. In southwest Michigan, they had two months of winter remaining—if they were lucky.

The truck rumbled across the bridge over the widest section of Fall Creek. The river wound around the town in a serpentine C-shape before feeding into the St. Joe River five miles north. South of town, the dam separated Fall Creek from Lake Chapin.

He headed onto Main Street. His shoulders tensed at the sight of his familiar town. Friendly's Grocery was closed now. Vinson Family Pharmacy, too. The pharmacist, Robert Vinson, was working with the militia to deliver medication to the residents who needed it.

Two of the militia's snowmobiles cruised past on patrol. Other than that, the streets and sidewalks were empty. Someone had finally taken down the Christmas wreaths from the light poles.

He passed shuttered shop after shuttered shop—Pizza Palace, Patsy's Café, Gundy's Auto Repair, Clothesline laundromat.

He drove through the single dark stoplight without stopping. To the west was the high school and combined elementary/middle school that now served as the emergency shelter and community food bank; Tresses hair salon, the Brite Smiles dentist's office, and the post office; to the right, the historic Greek revival courthouse featuring large white columns inspired by ancient temples. Township meetings now took place at the superintendent's home.

After a few more blocks, he reached Crossway Church and parked along the curb. There was still plenty of room for snowmobiles, 4x4s, and the occasional vehicle to pass.

Fuller's Hardware, the bank, and Fireside Tavern stood across the street. Their dark windows stared at him like dead eyes.

Fall Creek was a ghost town.

He was getting used to it. That was the part he hated the most.

Movement out of the corner of his eye snagged his attention. About twenty-five yards ahead of the parked truck, a lone figure strode down the right side of the street.

The figure's head was up; he slowly scanned his surroundings from left to right and back again. Noah recognized his broad shoulders, chestnut hair, and confident, purposeful stride.

Liam Coleman.

Bitter acid rose in the back of his throat. In the three days since Hannah's return, Noah's instinctive dislike toward Liam had only grown.

He knew it was petty and spiteful. He knew it and couldn't help it. Maybe he was a lesser man than he'd always believed himself to be.

Jealousy ate away at him every time he saw Liam and Hannah together. Since Liam was still staying in their downstairs guest room, that was a lot. How she looked at him with trust and respect. How she moved and spoke and laughed with such ease around him.

Noah had been trying. He was trying with all his heart and soul to reach her. Things were getting a little better, but they were still awkward.

He loved her. She was his wife, and he wanted her to remain that way, forever and ever. He wanted to raise Milo with her, grow old beside her.

He knew where he stood. He wasn't so sure about Hannah.

She'd been through things he couldn't even imagine, didn't want to imagine. He had to give her time. He knew that.

Noah watched, jaw clenched, as Liam Coleman's figure grew

smaller and smaller. Was he walking the whole town? It didn't surprise him. Coleman seemed like the restless type.

Maybe he'd walk right out of Fall Creek and never come back. In his opinion, the gruff soldier couldn't leave soon enough.

Noah forced his attention back to the church. He didn't have time for another pity party. He had work to do.

Several snowmobiles huddled in the church's parking lot, along with a couple of old vehicles. Noah got out of the truck and pocketed the keys. He stood for a moment, blinking against the sun.

How Bishop could still enter that church, he had no clue. The memories of the carnage still haunted his nightmares. All those bodies. All those men, women, and children, senselessly slaughtered.

The massacre was a blight on Fall Creek. A stain that might never be lifted.

He steeled himself and strode toward the church. The stained-glass windows were broken. Colored glass glinted in the snowbanks beneath the windows. The church steeple towered above him.

Reynoso greeted him at the side door. Officer Oren Truitt stood with him. "Follow me."

They hurried to the largest room with the pass-through window where Daphne had handed out bags of donated food a month ago. It had once been stuffed floor-to-ceiling with supplies; now it was empty of everything but people.

Officer Hayes stood outside the door, his service weapon holstered, but his palm resting on the grip, just in case.

Noah gave him a tense nod. Hayes returned it.

Truitt and Reynoso followed Noah into the room. At least twenty people were crowded inside. Their faces were haggard, their expressions tense. Everyone looked thinner and scruffier.

Noah scanned the crowd, recognizing the gas station owner, Mike Duncan, and his physics major son, Jamal. Next to them stood Dave Farris, Tina Gundy, the mechanic's daughter, and Annette King, the principal of Fall Creek High School.

Standing near Bishop was Mrs. Blair, Thomas Blair's widow, and her daughter, Whitney. Their eyes were red, their faces gaunt with grief.

As one, everyone turned to Noah.

"Chief Sheridan! You need to do something!"

"Tell us you're going to do something to stop these animals!"

"We're starving! I have nothing to feed my children!"

"You're not going to let this stand, are you?"

"We're happy you got your wife back and all, but things aren't so great for the rest of us!"

"Calm down, folks," Noah said loudly. "What is going on here?"

Their grumbling faded. Their heads swiveled to Bishop.

Bishop stood at the back of the room, surrounded by empty, ransacked shelves. His hands were balled into fists at his sides. "They shut down my church, Noah. They stole from me. From us. From this community."

Noah didn't have to ask who. He already knew.

37

NOAH
DAY THIRTY

"The militia took food that didn't belong to them," Bishop repeated. "They stole it."

Noah raised his hands, palms out. His gut twisted, dreading this moment. "It is true that the town appropriated certain goods to expediently serve the community's needs—"

"We didn't vote on this," Dave said. "The town council didn't approve this."

"The town can't vote on every decision," Noah said with a patience he didn't feel. "The superintendent needs the ability to make decisions in the field that will keep the community safe and healthy."

Bishop looked at him like he'd suddenly grown three heads. "Don't tell me you okayed this. Don't tell me you're on board."

Noah hesitated. If he admitted that Julian and Sutter had done this without bothering to ask his opinion or consent, it would undermine his authority.

Bishop's eyes narrowed. Noah didn't have to say a word; Bishop knew him too well.

The others didn't, though. It was vital that they saw him as their leader, as the leader he was trying so hard to be. The leader that Fall Creek needed.

He cleared his throat. "Consolidating the supplies makes it easier to disseminate and keep an active list of who needs what and who's received what. That's all this is."

Bishop's face darkened. His voice dripped with sarcasm. "Oh, is that all this is?"

"They're out of control," Dave said. "You know it. I know you do."

"They can't just come into this town and make up their own rules," Annette said.

A rumble of displeasure swept through the crowd.

"We need to do something," Jamal Duncan muttered. "This isn't right."

They were angry. Hungry, scared, and angry. Noah remembered how bad things had gotten after the Crossway Massacre, before Ray Shultz and his crew were summarily executed in front of the courthouse. The people had nearly rioted.

It wouldn't take much to rile them into a frenzy, to push them over the edge.

Fear sprouted in Noah's gut. These people weren't fighters. Bishop had military training and experience, but not the rest of them.

They wouldn't stand a chance against fifty armed militia. They were liable to do something stupid and dangerous. The militia would retaliate, and good people would get hurt.

He had to prevent that from happening, even if they hated him for it.

"We know what happened at Winter Haven," Annette said. Her gaze slid toward Mrs. Blair. "Everyone knows. Those militia killed two of our people. Murdered them and left them to rot."

"In the act of an armed home invasion," Noah said quickly. "They were assaulting the homeowner—"

Bishop's eyes bulged. "Homeowner? Are you kidding me? You sound like you've been drinking the Kool-Aid, Noah."

Anger flared through him. "Thomas Blair and Ted Nickleson broke the law. They endangered the entire community when they chose to attack and steal another's home. Things are different, you all know that. The consequences for every decision are swift and severe. If we want to make it when every town and city in our state is on the verge of collapse, we have to be willing to make the hard choices. There is light on the other side, I promise. We just need to make it through winter. We can do it, if we work together."

"And what about my dead husband?" Mrs. Blair asked. She was a diminutive woman, thin and pretty. Now, she looked collapsed somehow, her shoulders hunched inward like broken wings. "What about us?"

He pushed aside the guilt, forcing himself to focus on the big picture. "I am truly sorry for the families. We need to take this as a learning experience, as a warning for us all moving forward. The best we can do is to move forward and focus on working together to make it through this crisis. What's done is done. It's over now."

The townspeople looked at each other with skeptical expressions. Annette shook her head. Tina Gundy glared at him.

He clenched his jaw. He was doing the best he could. Rosamond was better at this sort of stuff.

"But it's not over," Mrs. Blair said. "We went to the middle school this morning to get our daily food allotment. The soldiers checked our names on a clipboard and turned us away. We have been labeled 'dissidents,' and as such, are no longer eligible for rations."

Noah tried to keep his expression fixed to hide his surprise.

He had not been privy to this decision, either. He pressed his lips together, forcing his voice to remain steady and confident. "I'm sure that's an error we will get ironed out shortly."

Tina Gundy crossed her arms over her chest. "Who's next? We do or say something wrong, and we starve? Is that the way things are now?"

"No, of course not—"

"Anyone who speaks out against the superintendent or her guard dogs, they're gonna get put on a list," Mrs. Blair said. "How do you think that will go?"

"Let's not succumb to fear-mongering," Noah said, his voice stern to hide his growing dismay. "What-ifs do no one any good. Just worry about what's right in front of you. Take one day at a time. We'll get through this—"

"It's not fear-mongering if it's true," Dave Farris muttered.

Noah shot him a look. He needed fellow council members on his side, not stirring people up even more. "Things are under control. Fall Creek is under control."

Bishop stepped forward. The crowd parted around him. "You need to take a long, hard look at the people surrounding you, Chief Sheridan. The things you think you're controlling aren't so in control."

"Now, that's uncalled for—"

"It's about control," Bishop said. "The consolidation of power in the guise of public safety. It's an age-old game that's been played a thousand times throughout time on government stages large and small. The erosion of our rights is the slow death of freedom. We're the frogs basking in the warm pan bath while the water boils us to death, and some of us don't even realize it."

Noah gritted his teeth. "Bishop, may I speak to you in private?"

Bishop motioned toward the hallway. "By all means."

They moved into the hallway and paused in front of the last storage room. A ribbon of yellow caution tape stretched across the doorway. The room where Bishop had cradled his dead daughters and his dead wife.

Bishop did not look inside. Neither did Noah.

Regret filled Noah. Frustration and anger. He felt torn in two, backed into a corner.

No matter what he did, he disappointed someone. Either way, he was letting those he cared about down.

At least this way, he was keeping people alive.

"You're the one who's losing control, Bishop," Noah said in a low voice. "What are you doing in there? Are you trying to create civil unrest? Are you trying to incite a riot?"

"This is wrong. Real people are being hurt here. Real people are dying. Don't you see that?"

"What about turning the other cheek? Isn't that what you preach? What about peace and harmony?"

"All of those things are important," Bishop said quietly. "But this is tyranny."

"That's a big word you're throwing around. Be careful. Rosamond is doing the absolute best that she can."

"Is she?"

"Of course!"

Bishop leveled his steady gaze at him. "Some of us strongly disagree on that count."

Noah threw up his hands, searching frantically for anything to strengthen his argument. "Aren't Christians supposed to obey the government? 'Give to Caesar what is Caesar's,' or whatever?"

"We honor civil authority wherever possible, to the point where such authority abuses the people it is set up to protect. Where the government threatens freedom and violates those God-given rights, we have a duty to resist."

Noah thought of Mattias Sutter executing Octavia Riley. Julian shooting Billy Carter in the head. Desoto opening fire on Fall Creek citizens.

He had to get Bishop to understand. He needed him to take this seriously. Keep his head down. Toe the line. It was the only way they would all get through this.

At least until spring. At least until the worst of this crisis was over.

"You don't know who you're messing with." Noah was on the verge of panic. His pulse thudded loud in his ears. His palms were damp beneath his gloves. "Sutter is a dangerous man."

Bishop's eyes flashed. "He isn't the only one."

"All the more reason to let this go! It's just food, Bishop. Food the militia are giving back to the people. Who cares who gives it, as long as it happens?"

"It's much more than that, and we both know it."

Noah said nothing to that. What else could he possibly say? He'd tried his best.

Bishop had always been stubborn. He saw things a certain way, and that was it. He was like a boulder in the middle of a river. No matter how furiously the river raged, he was immoveable.

Bishop shook his head. "I've got to get back to work. We've got families going hungry. We've got to figure out how to help them."

He turned away from Noah and strode down the hall.

"Bishop!" Noah called after him. "You need to let sleeping dogs lie."

Bishop paused. He glanced back at Noah, his hands still balled into fists. Emotion flickered across his face—a smoldering anger. "Who says they're sleeping?"

38

QUINN
DAY THIRTY-ONE

Gran held open the door. A blast of cold air gusted inside, but Gran didn't seem to notice.

"I'm so glad you could come," Gran said. "Come in, come in. You must be freezing. Make yourselves at home."

Quinn clicked off "Bohemian Rhapsody," which had been blaring on her iPod, took off her earbuds, and draped them around her neck.

She stared at Gran like she'd grown three heads. She might as well have. Quinn had never seen her act so nice in her entire life.

Gran smiled nervously and gestured to their guests. "Welcome, welcome."

Milo entered first, slower and quieter than normal. The big white dog followed him. He trotted right to the center of the living room and shook himself. Snow and ice pellets sprayed everywhere.

The three cats who'd been sprawled lazily across various pieces of furniture sprang to life like they'd been electrocuted. Aggrieved growls and hisses filled the air.

Thor's orange fluff stood on end. He leapt from the back of the sofa and skittered down the hall toward the bedrooms.

Odin was so startled that he promptly fell off the back of Gran's favorite armchair. He barely landed on his feet. He scooted as far as he could beneath the armchair.

With a screech of terror, Loki shot beneath the couch and disappeared.

The dog merely watched their antics with his head cocked and his ears pricked, looking slightly amused. He didn't chase them, which was a good thing. The cats would probably have jumped into the rafters and never come down.

Milo giggled. Quinn winked at him.

Hannah Sheridan entered Gran's house next, cradling her newborn baby. Hannah freaking Sheridan. Standing in front of them, right here in Gran's living room.

The girl who'd vanished. The girl who'd come back.

The big, muscled soldier Quinn kept hearing about came last. He ducked to enter the low doorway. He was as handsome as she'd imagined. His features rough and craggy, strong and fierce. He looked like he could break a few necks with his bare hands.

He scanned the room, taking in everything with a single glance. His expression wasn't exactly hostile, but wary. Just like a soldier.

Quinn dragged her gaze from Liam Coleman and looked past him out onto the porch. The sky was darkening to twilight. Shadows stretched across the snow. No one else was outside.

"Where's Noah?" she asked.

Hannah's mouth tightened. "He was going to come, then he got called away for work. A couple of neighbors fighting over a stolen snowmobile. It turned into a fistfight. He'll stop by later if he can."

Quinn scowled in frustration. She'd always had a hard time

hiding her feelings. She vacillated between being so irritated with Noah that she could spit and desperately missing their camaraderie.

Noah was changing, becoming someone she didn't recognize. Whether it was the overbearing militia or the pressure of keeping things together after the collapse, she didn't know.

Maybe Hannah being back would fix things. If not everything, at least Noah.

"Welcome, welcome." Gran gave a brisk clap of her hands. "It's not much, but it's our home."

Gran didn't light the fireplace often, preferring the woodstove in the kitchen, but tonight, the fire crackled and popped.

Two Aladdin lamps glowed from the fireplace mantel. They were brighter than normal oil lamps, and gave off both light and heat. Gran had put a mirror behind the lamps to reflect even more light.

"It's lovely," Hannah said quietly.

Gran blushed, her wrinkled cheeks turning red, her blue eyes bright. She turned and shuffled for the kitchen, leaning heavily on her cane. "I'll just be in the kitchen," she said over her shoulder.

Gran was like a whole different person. Suddenly sweet and polite and gracious.

Well, who knew how to act around a woman who'd returned from the dead? Quinn sure didn't.

Should she ignore Hannah's five-year disappearance altogether? Just pretend she'd been on an extended spa vacation or something? Pepper her with questions about her trauma? Stick to small talk and ask her about the weather?

It was weird for everybody. Probably weirder still for Hannah herself.

Quinn touched her lip piercing a little self-consciously. She glanced down at Milo. He stood a few feet from Hannah, looking uncomfortable. Honestly, the kid looked miserable.

Poor Small Fry. His whole world had already been turned upside down. And now this.

Everyone else probably assumed he'd be happy. Thrilled. Elated.

Not Quinn. She more than most people knew the darker side of life.

How things rarely turned out how you'd expected. How the moments that were supposed to be the happiest were often tinged with shadows. How reality could never quite match the fantasies in your head.

Imagining a mother was different than having one appear right in front of you—especially one you didn't remember.

She swallowed the lump in her throat. "Hey, Small Fry. Long time no see. Have you grown five inches since I last saw you? Or do you just really need a haircut?"

Milo gave her a tremulous smile. There he was. The smart, fearless kid she knew was still in there. He just needed a little encouragement.

"I see you got a new horse as a pet. You want to introduce us?"

"He's a dog, silly. A Great Pyrenees." He shot a furtive glance at Hannah. "He's—he's not mine."

"Of course, he is," Hannah said.

Milo stood a little taller. "This is Ghost. He's our protector. He's the best dog ever."

As if sensing that he was the center of attention, Ghost raised his head and pricked his ears. He'd been busy examining every corner of the house.

He trotted over to Milo. He was huge—practically as tall as Milo, with a massive head and a barrel chest and super fluffy. Milo wrapped his arm around the dog's furry ribs.

Ghost nuzzled his cheek and gave a pleased little chuff.

He turned his head toward Quinn, gazing at her with those big brown eyes. It felt like he was examining her, deciding whether she was worthy or not.

Quinn stood still. She held out one hand, palm up. She hadn't realized how much she wanted this magnificent creature to like her—to approve of her—until this moment.

Ghost left Milo and padded across the living room. He halted in front of her and sniffed her hand. The room fell pin-drop quiet. Quinn didn't move.

His hot breath warmed her palm, his whiskers tickling her skin. His black nose was warm and dry.

He was different than most dogs. All the dogs she knew were jumpy, energetic, friendly, and eager to please.

Ghost was regal. A solemn, serious dog. His eyes shone with a keen intelligence. He pressed his muzzle against her hand. His plumed tail swept slowly back and forth.

"That means he likes you," Hannah said with a pleased smile.

Quinn couldn't help herself; she beamed.

Milo snorted. "You should see him with Dad. It's like he thinks Dad's an alien or something. He gets all growly and mad."

Quinn grinned. "I can totally see that."

Hannah shot Liam a wry look. "It does take him a while to warm up to certain individuals."

"I have no idea what you're talking about," Liam deadpanned.

Milo looked around. "Where are the cats?"

"Hiding in terror," Quinn said. "They might not come out for a week."

A loud hissing sound came from the kitchen.

"That'll be Hel," Quinn said. "Ruler of the Underworld. He's just letting us know how displeased he is. Dogs don't belong in his domain. He's got a bit of a temper, but he's protective, too."

As if on cue, a small dark creature streaked from beneath the couch and launched itself at the dog's butt.

With a savage hiss, Loki sank his claws into Ghost's long, plumed tail.

Ghost didn't snap or snarl like Quinn expected. He calmly flicked his tail, and Loki lost his hold. He plopped to the floor.

Before he could make his escape, Ghost turned around and nosed him.

Loki froze, shaking, hackles raised, while Ghost sniffed him all over.

Ghost let out a bemused sigh and plopped down in the middle of the floor, Loki between his front paws.

Surprisingly, Loki didn't flee. He stayed put, and even ventured to sniff Ghost back.

Odin crept out from beneath Gran's armchair. The dog's tail thumped the floor gently. The animals sniffed each other. Satisfied that Ghost wasn't a furry monster attempting to murder him, Odin climbed back into the armchair.

A minute later, even Thor came downstairs to investigate. Valkyrie, who'd been stalking mice outside, strolled in from the kitchen. She was fearless and didn't seem fazed by the new arrival.

The big white fluffy thing was calm and quiet. And soft. The cats decided maybe they liked him, after all. Maybe he'd even make a great warm blanket to sleep on. Maybe.

"Great Pyrenees aren't herding dogs like some people think," Hannah explained. "They're livestock guardian dogs. Their job is to protect the flock. Usually that's sheep and goats, sometimes chickens. Or their human family. I suppose it's not outside the realm of possibility for a Pyr to consider cats his flock."

"Good luck with that, Ghost," Quinn quipped.

Everyone chuckled, even Liam.

39

QUINN
DAY THIRTY-ONE

"Dinner will be ready in fifteen minutes!" Gran called from the kitchen.

"Can I help you with anything?" Hannah asked.

"Oh, heavens no!" Gran said loudly as if she'd been personally insulted. "Absolutely not. Have a seat, chit chat, try not to let Loki attack your toes."

"No one is allowed to even sniff Gran's honey cornbread and pineapple chili before it's ready," Quinn said. "It's her secret recipe she refuses to share."

Liam raised his eyebrows. "Pineapple chili? That's something I need to try."

"You'll never be the same, I promise. It's amazing."

Hannah took a seat on the sofa, the baby asleep in her arms. Liam sat beside her. He helped her out of her coat, laid it across the sofa arm, then settled next to her.

Quinn couldn't help noticing how close they sat, how comfortable they seemed with each other. She also noticed the bulge of a pistol at Liam's hip beneath his sweatshirt. How his eyes never rested on any one thing, but continued to roam, checking the windows, the door, the hallway. Like he was always on the lookout for danger.

Bishop had said he wasn't a man to mess with. Quinn believed it.

"Milo and Noah have told me all about you, Quinn," Hannah said. "You're very important to both of them."

Despite her best intentions, Quinn blushed. She cleared her throat, resisting the urge to say something sarcastic. "Yeah. Well. The feeling's mutual."

"I remember you," Hannah said. "You used to sit right at that window and wave to me when I went running with baby Milo in his jogging stroller. You were smaller, then. And your hair was a different color."

Milo shot Quinn a look, his eyes widening. She'd never told him that story. "Really?"

"Really," Quinn said. "See? We were destined to be friends."

Milo smiled at that. A real, genuine smile. "I knew it," he whispered under his breath.

"What's all this?" Liam pointed at the leaves arrayed across the coffee table and stacked neatly in a cardboard box on the floor next to the table.

"Those are Gran's toilet paper leaves."

"Say what now?"

"These plants are called Lamb's ear," Quinn explained. "They have soft, absorbent leaves that are big and broad. They're edible and medicinal. They can be used as bandages and have anti-bacterial properties. They're best known as a good toilet paper alternative. Mullein works great, too, with its larger leaves."

"Oh, cool," Hannah said. "That's going to come in handy real soon."

"The leaves are dried flat to preserve them for year-round use.

The leaves will remain absorbent even after being dried. They take up a lot less space to store than packages of toilet paper."

"How does she grow them in the middle of winter?" Liam asked.

Quinn explained the winter garden boxes Gran tended in the backyard. "Lamb's ear can be grown indoors in small pots in winter, too. Once you dry them flat, you put them in a jar or Ziploc baggie to use whenever you need it."

"That's a genius idea," Hannah said. "What about homemade diapers?"

"Those too. And menstrual pads."

"Oh gross," Milo muttered.

"If Molly has a few seeds to spare, I'd love to grow some of our own," Hannah said.

Milo made a face.

"It won't be that bad," Hannah said. "Trust me."

"For what it's worth, Gran says it feels like a cloud. Personally, I have yet to try it out."

Hannah grinned at Milo. "A cloud, huh? You sure you don't wanna try?"

Milo let out a shy giggle. He blushed and looked away. "Maybe later."

"Toilet paper was only invented a hundred years ago," Quinn said, proud and thankful for all the knowledge that Gran and Gramps had taught her. "People have used plants for centuries. It works fine—as long as it's not poison ivy."

"We'll need to learn to make things from scratch," Hannah said quietly. "With manufacturing plants down and the supply chain disrupted, there is a finite supply of everything we're used to. A lot of things will be going back to the old ways."

"Not everything, I hope," Quinn said. "I'd like to keep at least a few technological advances."

"Speaking of technology." Liam gestured to the cords draped around her neck. "What do you have there?"

Quinn grinned broadly. "Music."

Hannah was rocking the baby in her arms. She went still. "Music?"

"My grandpa put an old iPod in a Faraday cage to protect it. The EMP didn't hurt it. I have a solar charger, too. And even a nifty little speaker to play it loud."

"Me and Quinn sing and dance sometimes," Milo said shyly.

Hannah swallowed. Her face had gone pale. Liam was watching her intently, a concerned look on his face. "Can you—do you think—can we listen to something?"

Quinn fished the iPod out of her pocket.

The baby gave a little cry. Liam reached for her. "I'll take her."

Without a word, Hannah handed Charlotte to him. The baby almost disappeared beneath the soldier's big, calloused hands.

Surprisingly gentle, he cradled the infant to his chest and patted her back.

She squirmed, then relaxed, settling into the crook of his neck. Almost instantly, she was asleep again.

"Will the noise bother her?" Quinn asked.

"She sleeps through just about everything," Hannah said. She hadn't taken her eyes off Quinn's iPod since it had appeared.

Quinn plugged the iPod into the speaker on the mantel. She clicked through the various artists, searching for something good. She skipped over "Eye of the Tiger," "Dancing Queen," and "I'm a Believer."

She stopped on a Beatles song, remembering how Milo had told her they were his mother's favorite band. She hesitated, then pressed play.

The soft strums of "Blackbird" filled the room. Paul McCartney's haunting voice and acoustic guitar blended in perfect harmony.

Hannah expelled a sharp breath and closed her eyes. Her features softened.

Quinn couldn't take her eyes off her. She looked so beautiful, so serene.

Everyone listened intently until the last notes faded. No one moved.

A strange look crossed Milo's face. He glanced at Hannah, his eyes wide and bright. "You sang this song. You sang it to me at bedtime. You changed the tune a little, though."

"I did. It was our favorite." Hannah scooted forward off the couch and sank to her knees, her expression so full of hope that it hurt Quinn's heart. Her hands knotted in her lap. "You remember?"

Milo nodded. "I remember."

Hannah's chin quivered. In a shaky voice, she began to sing acapella. Her voice grew stronger, more confident as she sang the words about broken wings learning to fly. "Blackbird fly, blackbird fly..."

Quinn stopped breathing. Milo and Noah hadn't exaggerated. Hannah Sheridan had the most beautiful voice she'd ever heard—pure and rich and powerful.

The song hit her straight in the heart, in her very soul.

Milo joined in. They sang together, their voices sweet and harmonious, echoing beautifully in the small room.

Tears streamed down Hannah's face. She sang the last line about waiting for this moment to arise.

Milo went to her. Not hesitantly, not awkward or uncomfortable or nervous, but full tilt. Arms opened wide, he flung himself at his mother.

Hannah wrapped her arms around him and drew him close,

burying her face in his dark curls. They held each other tightly, like they never wanted to let go.

Quinn's chest filled with warmth. Her eyes were wet. She felt like crying and laughing at the same time.

She knew how much this meant to Milo. She knew how much Hannah must need this.

She couldn't imagine what Hannah had gone through to get here, the battles she had fought and won to make it back to her family.

What a gift this was: to have lost something precious, and after all hope was gone, to find it again.

Quinn knew about pain. She knew about loss. She had her own grief and nightmares to contend with, her own missing mother who was never coming back.

She would never begrudge them their happiness. Their happiness was her own.

She loved Milo. She liked Hannah, had always liked Hannah. It was good that she was here. More than good—it felt right.

Quinn glanced at Liam. His gaze was locked on Hannah, his eyes dark, his face shadowed with emotion. Whoever this man was, it was clear to anyone in the room that Hannah meant something to him.

In the doorway between the kitchen and living room, Gran leaned on her cane, watching them. Quinn couldn't be certain, but it looked like Gran had tears glittering in her eyes, too.

"Come, friends," she said, her voice thick with emotion. "Dinner is served."

40

NOAH
DAY THIRTY-ONE

Noah hesitated in the doorway of Molly and Quinn's house. He'd let himself in the front door but found himself strangely reluctant to enter.

"You're letting all the heat escape!" Molly called from the kitchen. "Either crap or get off the pot!"

Laughter echoed from the kitchen. Milo's voice, high and bright. And Hannah's, pure and sweet as chiming church bells.

Noah smiled. He shook the snow from his coat. He shut the door behind him, removed his boots, stuffed his gloves in his pockets, and strode through the small living room into the kitchen.

The fire flickered merrily in the wood stove. A blast of warmth greeted him. The delicious scent of cinnamon and baking dough filled his nostrils.

The kitchen exuded peace and joy. Everyone was together, happy.

Molly's old ranch was much smaller than his new house in Winter Haven. Cramped, a bit shabby, and plain. Somehow, it didn't feel like it.

Noah's chest tightened, a twinge of envy pricking him. In

here, it was warm and inviting. Easy to forget the chaos and anarchy that raged just outside these walls.

The last few days had been rough. His mind was burdened with so many worries—the greedy overreach of the militia, the devolving state of the town, the rising tensions between Julian and Bishop. Gavin Pike's death, and how Rosamond Sinclair might or might not be unraveling. He had avoided her until now, a part of him afraid that she would see the truth written all over his face.

Then there were the disconcerting news reports regarding the violent attacks on towns in the region. It was only a matter of time until Fall Creek became a target, too.

How would they stand against an attack from outsiders if they were too busy turning on each other?

Fall Creek was a powder keg waiting to explode. Another outburst like the assault on Winter Haven, and the militia might kill even more citizens. The militia were edgy and uptight. The townspeople were rebellious, resentful, and angry.

The residents might hate him for it, but Noah was doing his best to placate everyone, to keep things stable. He'd made the hard choices so the people he cared about could have this. Food and warmth. Shelter. Fellowship and community.

Too bad most of them didn't appreciate it.

He tried to push it all out of his mind. For tonight, at least, he could be present with his friends and his family.

His son. His *wife*.

"You hungry?" Molly stood at the counter, flour everywhere as she kneaded dough. "I'm making my famous cinnamon bread."

She glanced back at him. Flour smudged her round, wrinkled cheeks. Her blue eyes danced. "Your son put peanut butter on it, which is a sacrilege in this house. He's lucky he's cute, so I forgave him." She winked at Milo. "This time."

"He didn't get the peanut butter thing from me," Noah said, forcing brightness into his voice.

"It's from my side of the family," Hannah said. "My brother, Oliver. He slathered that stuff on everything he could."

The sofa was still in the kitchen, shoved against the window with the round table beside it. Liam sat at the table across from Milo, a chess board between them. Quinn squeezed next to Hannah on the couch. She was rocking the baby in her arms while Hannah watched.

Quinn gave him a wry grin, her piercings glinting in the firelight. "Hey, Noah the Cop. I put Charlotte right to sleep. Turns out I'm not half bad at this kid stuff."

"You're better than I am," he said with a pang. He'd meant it as a joke; it didn't come out that way.

Hannah's huge dog, Ghost, lay sprawled on the small rug before the woodstove, his paws sticking straight out, his long, plumed tail thumping rhythmically.

Odin was curled up between Ghost's paws beneath his muzzle. Thor, the fluffy orange one always begging for affection, sat on the dog's haunches, licking his paws. Loki crouched behind him, his yellow eyes locked on Ghost's tail, the cat's butt wriggling in the air as he prepared to pounce.

Ghost ignored the cats' antics completely. He didn't growl, but he turned his head, ears pricked, his gaze alert. He didn't take his eyes off Noah.

Noah paused in the archway between the living room and the kitchen, hesitant again. The dog made him nervous.

"He's a friend," Hannah said to Ghost. "Don't bite him."

Ghost's ears tilted toward her. He let out a low petulant whine, like he was voicing his disagreement.

"I don't think he likes me." He waited for Hannah to assure him otherwise, but she didn't.

He glanced at Milo. His son's ankles were wrapped around the chair legs less than a foot from the dog's powerful jaws. Noah imagined those teeth could bite clean through a leg or an arm.

He cleared his throat. "Is he safe?"

"Not at all," Hannah said.

"Don't make him *want* to bite you," Liam said gruffly. "That's the trick."

Hannah flashed Liam a smile. "Is that the trick? Are you sure? I recall him nearly taking a chunk out of you a time or two."

Liam's rugged face creased. His lips twitched. "I don't remember that at all. You must have been delirious."

Hannah laughed again. High and sweet and musical.

Noah stiffened. The sound filled him with joy and pain in equal measure. How he'd loved her laugh. How he'd missed it, once it was gone.

He'd thought he'd never hear it again. Now, here it was. A miracle.

But it wasn't Noah she was laughing with.

Hannah turned her gaze on Noah. Those emerald green eyes shining with mirth. That delicate, beautiful face seared into his memories—right here, alive, not ten feet away from him.

It might as well have been an ocean between them.

"You'll be fine, Noah," she said, laughing. "It's okay. I promise."

Milo patted the empty chair beside him. "Sit with us, Dad. Liam is teaching me how to play chess. It's really fun! I took out his rook with my knight. That's the cool horse-shaped one."

Noah wanted to sit next to his wife, but that seat was already taken.

Liam sat at the far side of the table, his chair next to the edge of the couch, half-turned so his back was against the wall, facing the room. An AR-15 leaned against the table within his reach.

Less than a foot from him, Hannah was curled up on one end of the sofa, her legs tucked beneath her, a handknit afghan blanket pulled over her lap.

She looked content and at ease, not tense and nervous the way she'd been at the Winter Haven house. The way she was around him.

"Your turn!" Milo said.

Liam made a move. Milo leaned forward, seized his queen, and knocked one of Liam's black pawns off the board.

"Another one bites the dust!" he crowed.

"Nice move," Liam said.

Milo beamed at him.

Something dark and ugly sprouted in Noah's chest. With shaking hands, he unzipped his coat, took it off, and draped it across the back of the chair. He sat down stiffly and folded his hands on the table to still them. He pasted a smile on his face.

He was supposed to be happy. He was supposed to be the luckiest guy on the planet.

How many thousands of times had he dreamed of this? His wife alive, as beautiful as ever, right here in front of him.

And yet, he felt numb. Discouraged. More than a little disillusioned.

It wasn't how he'd imagined it—how they'd fall into each other's arms. How they'd cling to each other like each was the other's life raft, their salvation. The past forgotten, erased. A new start. A new future.

Even in the midst of all this, they could make it work as long as they were together. He believed that.

Hannah was back from the dead— that was all he'd wanted for the last five years. He'd begged God, bartered his soul. He'd never even looked at another woman. He'd never removed his wedding ring.

She was here. He was here. They didn't feel together.

She wasn't even sleeping in the same bedroom. He'd offered her the master, but she and the baby had taken the guestroom instead.

An invisible wall stood between them. He'd tried to hug her, to hold her. When he'd reached out to touch her, the big dog had gotten in the way.

It wasn't just the dog. Or the baby she was always holding. She'd shied away from him like he was a stranger.

He wasn't a stranger. He was her *husband*.

Liam Coleman was the stranger. The tall, muscular soldier, the loner with haunted eyes. This man who had a connection with his wife.

Hannah and Liam had barely touched each other since Hannah's return, but they didn't have to. It was more than just gratitude he saw flashing in his wife's eyes whenever she looked at him.

Noah couldn't pin down exactly what it was, but he couldn't dismiss his suspicions, either.

He was a cop. He trusted his instincts. And his instincts were screaming a truth he wasn't sure he could face.

Every time Hannah smiled at Liam, every time Noah caught the soldier watching her with that look in his eyes, that look every man recognized in another—desire, longing—the claws of jealousy dug deeper.

Resentment pierced his heart. He didn't want to feel this way. It made him feel small and spiteful. He hated himself for it.

This wasn't him. It wasn't who he was, who he wanted to be. And yet.

These were *Noah's* friends. This was *Noah's* family.

Then why did Noah feel like the intruder?

41

QUINN
DAY THIRTY-THREE

Quinn wasn't alone.

The back of her neck prickled. She whipped around, staring behind her. The shadows were thick and dark. The storage shed in Noah's backyard smelled of wood and grease.

The flashlight wavered in her hand. Dust motes swirled in the narrow cone of light.

The shed was huge, more like a pole barn, maybe twenty by twenty. The shelves along the back wall were lined with lawn care equipment: sprinklers, coils of hose, hedge trimmers, cans of wasp spray. Hooks hung on the wall for rakes of various sizes, brooms, and a big shiny snow shovel.

A hulking John Deere riding lawn mower was parked on the right side. The huge stack of seasoned firewood that the militia kept replenishing lay beneath a tarp on the left.

The flashlight beam revealed nothing out of the ordinary. Nothing out of place. Everything quiet and still.

It just was a feeling she couldn't shake.

Images of the ravaged, bloody church flashed through her

head. Billy Carter leering over her. Ray Shultz's hands around her throat.

She expelled a white puff of breath. "Don't be stupid. You're fine. There's nothing to be afraid of."

But that was just as stupid. There was plenty to be afraid of.

It was the terrors of the past refusing to let her go that she hated.

She turned back to the firewood, her heart still thumping against her ribs, already regretting her offer to grab more firewood from the shed.

It was after nine p.m., almost pitch-black, and freaking cold. She just wanted to get back inside Noah's house with the warm fireplace, real lights and running water, and the frozen pizzas that Bishop had tossed into the oven.

Bishop had stopped by to visit Noah—"To make peace," he'd said—but Noah had driven Hannah to their old house to gather toiletries and some of her old clothes. Apparently, Noah had never had the heart to get rid of her stuff. They'd taken Ghost with them.

Quinn was reluctant to see Hannah and her dog go, even for a short while.

The more time she spent around Hannah, the more she liked her. Hannah was both different and the same. Still genuinely kind and thoughtful, but also strong and brave. The bravest woman that Quinn had ever met.

She liked Liam Coleman, too. He looked dangerous. It wasn't just the weapons strapped everywhere, but the rugged jaw and the intensity in his dark eyes, his lean body radiating strength, competence, and power.

She felt safer every time she was in a room with him. She imagined him as an assassin or terrorist-hunter. He probably knew sixty exotic ways to kill a person.

Maybe one day he could teach her some, if she could ever work up the guts to ask him.

And Ghost. If she ever had a dog anything like Ghost, she'd think she'd died and gone to heaven.

Milo had just gone to bed. Quinn had been teaching him to draw superheroes and monsters while Bishop chatted with Liam Coleman.

Liam didn't seem like the chatty type, but he and Bishop had hit it off. They talked about their time in Iraq, exchanging war stories and other soldier stuff. They'd discussed the state of affairs in Fall Creek, too.

It was easier to talk about stuff without Noah around. He got all irritated and snippy whenever Quinn tried to point out how bad things were getting.

He didn't want to see it. He refused to see what was right in front of him.

He wanted to believe that as long as everyone kept their heads down and followed Mattias Sutter's orders, everything would be okay.

She liked Noah. They'd been through a lot together. But in this, he was as dumb as a box of rocks. And she couldn't understand why.

She didn't get why every citizen in Fall Creek wasn't gearing up to fight back.

The militia didn't own this town. They were the outsiders. They'd been invited in—they could be disinvited.

By force, if necessary.

She sucked on her teeth in frustration. She could feel the crackling tension. They all could. Fall Creek was like a rubber band stretching tighter and tighter. Eventually, it would snap.

But how? And when? And who would be the ones who snapped?

Quinn shivered. It was cold and getting colder. Time to get herself inside. She tucked the flashlight between her upper arm and her ribs, the beam aimed at the firewood, and pulled up the tarp.

A soft skittering sounded from somewhere nearby.

Adrenaline kicked her heart. Quinn went still. She strained her ears, every sense on alert.

Silence from outside. Inside the shed, there was nothing but her own juddering pulse.

The skittering sound came again.

She craned her neck, searching for the source of the noise.

A rat darted from a hole between several logs at the bottom of the wood pile. It scampered across her boot, scurried toward the rear of the shed, and vanished into the darkness.

She swallowed a squeal. Gross. So, gross.

Quinn Riley wasn't squeamish. She'd hunted squirrels, raccoons, pheasants, and deer. Gran and Gramps had made sure she knew how to gut and skin an animal and cook it for food.

She'd survived the Crossway massacre by spreading the still-warm entrails and blood of another human being over herself and Milo. She wasn't squeamish, not by a long shot.

Rats, though. They were a different story. Ever since she was six and a big black rat had scuttled across her pillow in her mother's junky trailer, she'd hated—

A soft rustling came from the back of the shed.

She grabbed a log from the top of the pile, intending to chuck it at the revolting rodent, and spun toward the sound. "Listen, you little—"

Movement in the darkness.

A large shadow lurched toward her.

Panic spiked through her veins. Before she could react, the log was bashed from her fingers. The flashlight fell and went skittering across the concrete floor.

Something struck her in the belly, knocked her breath from her lungs. Pain exploded beneath her ribs. She staggered back and nearly fell.

A strong hand seized her arm. A second hand clamped over her mouth.

She was shoved back against the wood pile. The spiky ends of the logs poked her spine.

A body pressed against hers—large, muscular, and strong. She glimpsed white eyes in a thick slab of a face.

A chill raced up her spine. Even in the shadows, she knew him. Sebastian Desoto.

Desoto's teeth flashed. "What a pleasant surprise."

A second shadow emerged behind him. This one was tall and lanky with a gaunt face. He was dressed completely in black with black grease smearing his face. So was Desoto. They wore heavy gear like soldiers, with body armor and big menacing weapons hanging from slings.

The gaunt-faced one flicked on a flashlight and shone it in her face. She squinted against the harsh glare. "Is this the girl that shot you with the BB gun?"

"It was a slingshot." Desoto's voice was still raspy. The welt on his throat had turned a nasty shade of purplish green. "This is her. Hard to miss that blue hair."

She tried to scream but the sound was muffled against Desoto's thick ham of a hand. She attempted to bite him, but his fingers were clamped down so tight across her jaw that she couldn't move her mouth at all.

She writhed and squirmed. Desoto's body might as well have been a brick wall for all the good it did her.

"Stop fighting," Desoto said. "It's pointless."

She didn't stop. She thrashed against him, struggling to free her arms so she could punch him or claw at his eyes. She kicked frantically, desperate to connect with whatever part of him she could.

Her foot connected with his shin. Desoto cursed. She kicked him again. He grunted but didn't falter. Grimacing, he punched her hard in the side of the head.

Lights flared behind her eyes. Her ears rang. Against her will, her body wilted like a rag doll.

"Don't let her scream," the gaunt one said.

"I don't plan to." Desoto shifted and glanced around the shed. "Toss me the rag hanging from that hook."

Gaunt brought Desoto the rag. She fought him, kicking and flailing as hard as she could, but it didn't matter. He outweighed her by a hundred and fifty pounds at least.

Gaunt pointed a pistol at her head with one hand and held the flashlight in the other while Desoto stuffed the filthy rag into her mouth and knotted it tightly against the back of her skull.

The harsh chemical taste of oil and cleaning agents stung her tongue and choked the back of her throat until she nearly gagged.

"I've got some paracord," Gaunt said. "We can tie her to the riding lawn mower. She won't be going anywhere before the job's done."

"She won't be going anywhere ever," Desoto said. "Not when I'm through with her."

She screamed through the rag. The sound was pitiful. Pathetic. It wouldn't even carry outside the shed itself, let alone all the way to the house.

Dizziness from the fumes swept through her. The pain skewering through her skull made it hard to focus. She jerked and flailed anyway, desperate for an opening, a way to slip free.

She managed to shove her hand in her coat pocket, searching

for the slingshot, but it wasn't there. Her fingers closed over empty air.

She had taken it out at Noah's house to show Liam and Bishop. They'd both been impressed with her skills. She'd been so proud.

Pride was worthless to her now. She'd neglected to put it back in her pocket. And the .22 she'd brought with her was left back inside the house, too.

Stupid, stupid, stupid. Who was the idiot now? A mistake like that could be fatal. She pushed down the panic and fought to calm down, to freaking *think*.

Gaunt frowned. "She's not the job."

Desoto grunted as he wrestled her against the woodpile. "She is now."

"But he said to just take out—"

"I am aware of what was said, Benner. Things change in the field. You have to be ready to adapt. Liam Coleman is in the house. Atticus Bishop, too. You know what he said about Bishop."

"Two for the price of one," the guy called Benner said.

Desoto's eyes gleamed with loathing—and malice. "Now it's *three* for the price of one."

42

QUINN
DAY THIRTY-THREE

Desoto was going to kill her.

Quinn saw it in his flat, hard face, in his cruel eyes. Desoto wasn't going to let her go. He was going to murder her for what she'd done to him.

Her breath came in shallow, desperate gasps. Her heart jackhammered so hard that it felt like it was going to break out of her chest cavity.

"I don't know, man," Benner said, his voice hesitant. "She's a kid."

"No, she isn't. She just looks young. She's old enough to attack a soldier, so she's old enough to pay the price for it."

Fake soldier wannabe! she thought but couldn't say. She screamed helplessly against her gag. *Screw you!*

"Just look away if you have to. It'll be over in a minute. Which is faster than this little slut deserves. Then we'll get Coleman and Bishop."

Benner gave a reluctant sigh. "Fine. Make it quick, before the targets start getting anxious and come looking for her. We need the element of surprise against those two."

Desoto grunted dismissively. "The pastor and that ex-army flunky? Nah. He's no badass. We'll get the drop on both of them. Shut up and let me get this done."

If Quinn didn't do something right freaking now, she was dead meat.

She wouldn't be able to warn Bishop and Liam. She wouldn't be able to help Milo. She'd be no good to anyone if she died.

She didn't want to die. Every cell in her being thrummed with her will to survive.

Another breath. Another day. No matter how hard. No matter how much it sucked. She wanted to live.

She forced herself to focus, to take everything in, to be smart. Her back was to the wood pile. Her flashlight was somewhere on the floor.

Desoto in front of her, Benner a few feet behind him and to the left, between Quinn and the shed door. It was ten feet from the wood pile to the exit. At least a hundred feet from the shed to the house.

She wouldn't make it. They had size and speed on her. And weapons. All Benner had to do was grab her, and she was done before she'd started.

Desoto held her in place with one hand. With his other, he fumbled at his belt and withdrew an object. A wicked-looking curved blade glinted in the dim light.

Quinn didn't give him a chance to use it. She used the slight distraction to act. With everything she had in her, she surged forward and rocketed her leg up, punching hard into his groin, kneeing Desoto in the crotch.

With a groan, Desoto hunched in on himself. She didn't stick around to notice anything else. She wrenched from his grasp and catapulted herself sideways.

Pulse roaring, legs pistoning, she plunged into the shadows toward the back of the shed.

"Get her!" Desoto rasped.

She banged into the back shelves and grabbed at whatever was closest. A bunch of dark shapes and glinting objects. Her fingers closed over sharpened steel.

With a scream no one could hear, she grabbed the hedge trimmers and spun around.

Benner was lunging for her, arms outstretched, flashlight in one hand, rifle still attached to the sling.

Handles held tight against her ribs for leverage, pointy ends out, Quinn turned and thrust herself at him. She shoved with everything she had in her.

He wasn't expecting that. He'd expected her to keep fleeing, not turn and fight. He shifted to the right at the last second. The sharp ends of the hedge trimmers sank into his lower left side beneath his body armor.

He let out a shriek of agony and jerked back.

Instinctively, she let go of the shears.

Damn it! Another mistake. She should've held on. Should've yanked them out and used them to defend herself.

She had no time to react. Desoto was already coming at her, gripping that curved knife.

She half turned, fumbling along the shelf for something else, for another improvised weapon. She seized a clay gardening pot, whirled, and hurled it at him.

It struck his right shoulder and crashed to the concrete. He kept coming.

Nails. A box of three-inch nails on the shelf at her eye level. She scrambled for them, fingers stiff and unwieldy in her fear.

She could poke one between her fingers and make a fist. Stab him right in the throat or maybe through his eyeball, finish him off the right way this time—

Desoto reached her just as she closed her hand over the box. Something hard struck her in the back of the head.

Pain exploded inside her skull. More stars filled her vision. Her legs sagged.

He took hold of the back of her coat and hauled her around to face him. He slammed her back against the shelves, his left forearm pressed hard against her throat.

Her larynx felt crushed. She couldn't breathe. Couldn't even swallow.

"Benner, you okay?" he growled.

Benner leaned against the far wall next to the hooks holding the shovels, rakes, and weed trimmer. He'd pulled out the hedge trimmers, dropped them, and now held his hand to his stomach. "She nailed me good. I got a decent gash here. You think that thing was rusted? How do we get a tetanus shot these days?"

"No idea," Desoto said.

Quinn struggled weakly. She scratched and beat at his hands and tried to pry his forearm from her throat. She cursed helplessly against the gag.

"I'm sorry, I couldn't hear you." Desoto grinned. He leaned in closer. "Too bad we don't have more time. You're a mouthy little slut, but you've still got some worthwhile parts."

She wanted to claw his eyes out. To bite and scratch and kick until she was free, and he was dead. Deader than dead.

It was no use. Her vision was fading, her brain deprived of precious oxygen. Her body was doing its best. This time, it wasn't good enough.

Desoto jabbed at her coat. He hooked it with something and lifted the bottom. Something sharp scraped against her belly through her sweatshirt. "This is a karambit knife blade. Have you ever heard of it?"

She refused to shake her head. She refused to give him anything. She clung to consciousness, clung to her outrage.

She couldn't believe this was actually happening, that this pathetic thug was really going to be the last face she ever saw.

Desoto smiled at her. It looked garish on his flat face. "I'm gonna gut you and spill your insides all over the floor for what you did to me, you little—"

"Desoto," Benner said, his voice tense. "Hurry up. We need to go. I'm really bleeding, man. We need to get out of here."

"Not before we finish the job!"

"But I'm hurt, man—wait, did you hear that?"

Desoto stilled. "What?"

Quinn didn't hear anything. She didn't hear anything but the rush of blood in her ears as unconsciousness took hold of her.

43

LIAM
DAY THIRTY-THREE

Something was wrong.

Liam stood beside the wall next to the window and peered cautiously outside.

Clouds covered most of the moon. In the dim moonlight, he could just make out the tracks. Quinn's footprints went into the shed. They didn't come out. The shed door was closed.

She wouldn't have closed it behind her. She wouldn't have had a reason to.

Go in, grab a bundle of logs, come back out. Thirty seconds, tops. A minute or two maybe if you were a sixteen-year-old kid. Maybe you didn't like the dark. Maybe you dropped the flashlight or stubbed your toe.

It took moments for him to make the assessment, determine a course of action.

He shrugged on his coat, which had been slung over one of the kitchen chairs. His Glock 19 was holstered at his hip, his tactical knife tucked snugly in its sheath on his belt.

Atticus Bishop stood in the kitchen. He'd just checked the oven. He glanced at Liam and tensed. "What is it?"

"She should've been back by now. I'm going to check it out."

"I'll go with you."

Liam shook his head. "Stay here and watch Hannah's kid. Any hostiles out there, I don't want to leave the house unprotected." He inclined his head at the AR-15 leaning against the island. "Keep that close."

Bishop gave a curt nod. He was already moving toward the weapon. "Got it."

Liam exited the house by way of a side basement window so that any potential hostiles watching the rear or front of the house wouldn't see him.

He unholstered his pistol and held it in the low ready position. Seventeen rounds in the upgraded magazine, with an eighteenth in the chamber.

He let his eyes adjust to the moonlit night. He missed his night vision goggles. Every sense on high alert, he took in his surroundings.

Moonlight reflected off the wide expanse of unbroken snow. It was quiet. The trees were still. There was no breeze. An owl hooted to the east. The air smelled clean and cold.

He sensed no movement. The shadows did not stir. No telltale gleam of a muzzle in the moonlight or crack of a twig betrayed the enemy's presence.

Thin straggly trees and underbrush ringed the property. The frozen river lay just behind a thin line of pine trees. Noah's house was on the eastern side of Winter Haven, at the end of one of the cul-de-sacs.

Eight more houses lined the road on this side, nine across the street. The houses on either side were visible through the trees, maybe twenty yards away.

With its emphasis on self-sufficiency, Winter Haven was a luxury retreat for the wealthy and eco-minded. As such, the community removed as few trees as possible, preserving much of the natural wildness of the area.

Liam appreciated the concealment and cover it provided him.

It also meant that intruders could enter the community from numerous points, not just along the main, militia-guarded entrance.

The militia regularly patrolled the community on their snowmobiles. He saw no militia now. Not a single soul.

Liam crept through the trees, using the thickest trunks for cover. He moved cautiously, conscious of every movement, careful not to make a single unnecessary sound.

He reached the edge of the tree line and again stopped and listened for any sign of movement. He breathed slow and steady, controlling his heart rate.

Tension thrummed through him. The importance of stealth warred with the need for expediency. Every moment of delay could cost the girl her life. Going in rashly could mean the death of them both.

He tightened his grip and picked up the pace. He circled around the house to the backyard, stepping lightly, searching for the most concealed approach.

The day had been sunny, but with nightfall, the chill had returned with a vengeance. It tunneled through his clothing and froze his breath.

He shut it out. He shut out the dull throbbing pain in his back. That niggling concern that his body would fail again. That he'd lost a step.

He focused solely on his senses, on the mission at hand.

He drew parallel to the shed. The building was constructed of wood on a concrete slab, maybe twenty by twenty, no windows, no other doors but the one in the front, facing the back of the house.

Behind the shed, he located a second and third set of footprints. In and of itself, multiple tracks in the backyard weren't alarming. Except that these prints trekked from a cluster of pine trees forty feet behind the shed.

No reason to hoof it through woods in deep snow when the road was right there. Not unless you were up to no good.

The prints were long and smeared. Like they'd been heading surreptitiously toward the house, were startled by Quinn exiting the back door, and had quickly sought concealment inside the shed.

Adrenaline spiked through him, icing his veins. If they were hurting that girl, they'd pay with their lives.

His senses heightened. He was in the zone. Crouching low, Liam darted across the ten open yards between the trees and the shed. He pressed himself against the left side of the shed.

This close, he could hear voices. Low murmurs. A female voice, muffled, making low cries of terror. An aggressive, threatening male voice. A second male voice joined the first, this one higher-pitched, anxious and apprehensive.

Liam's heart rate accelerated. He had two targets to take out and a hostage to save. He couldn't fire indiscriminately. He needed to be precise and exact.

He didn't know Quinn Riley well, but she was feisty and tough. She wasn't Hannah, but he still felt a responsibility to keep her alive.

No one was hurting women and children on his watch. No way in hell.

He crept along the wall, edged around the corner, and quickly approached the front—all the while keeping a close eye on his surroundings.

Keeping most of his body concealed behind the wall for cover, he reached over and tried the shed's handle. The door was unlocked.

If the shed had windows, he might have attempted a silent entry or even sniped the scumbags through the window with two swift headshots. He scanned quickly for a distraction but didn't see anything. He did not have flash bangs or frag grenades—none of his usual arsenal.

If he had the luxury of time, he could wait for one of them to exit to relieve themselves and eliminate the threats one by one. He could start a fire and flush them out.

He discarded each option in a fraction of a second. He did not have time on his side.

The decision was made in a heartbeat. Go in hard and fast, using the element of surprise to his advantage.

No matter how trained or skilled the combatant, there was always a fraction of a second of reaction time. Inside that delayed reaction, he'd have to make his move.

Time to go.

44

LIAM
DAY THIRTY-THREE

With propulsive force, Liam kicked the shed door inward.

Immediately, he dropped into a prone position. The hostiles inside would instinctively aim for a chest or a head shot. Return fire would go over his head. Glock up and ready, he scanned from left to right.

Time slowed. He took in the scene in an instant.

Moonlight spilled through the doorway. A couple of flashlights on the floor threw garish shadows.

Two hostiles were turning toward him. Men dressed in black with black grease on their faces. They were both armed.

To his right, the first hostile pulled a bound and gagged Quinn toward him like a shield. Liam spotted the glint of a weapon: a karambit knife. The hostile jerked the rounded outer edge under her chin.

Fifteen feet to the left, toward the rear of the shed, the second man was raising what looked like an AK-47.

Liam ducked low as the hostile dumped half his mag in a thunderous burst. Staccato rounds screamed over his head, faster than a semi-automatic. *Boom! Boom! Boom!*

A wild volley of gunfire blew holes in the wall and shredded the door behind him. Splinters of wood sprayed his back.

Ears ringing, Liam squeezed off three shots.

All three rounds hit their mark, punching the hostile's chest. He staggered but didn't drop. Plate armor in that chest rig. *Damn!*

Rounds peppered the wall behind him. A burst of slugs smashed into the ceiling, splinters raining down. Spent cartridges clattered against concrete.

Liam fired at the hostile's head. Two quick shots drilled right between the eyes.

The gunman's head snapped back. He collapsed against the wall of lawn care supplies in a heap. A metal shovel fell from its hook and clattered to the cement floor.

Liam sprang to his feet, spine on fire as he crouched and spun to the right, the Glock trained on the man holding Quinn.

Liam recognized the squat slab of meat Bishop had pointed out earlier: *Desoto.* The cretin huddled behind the girl, keeping her between himself and Liam—the curved blade pressed to her throat.

Gun up, finger itching the trigger, Liam advanced toward Desoto. Heart thudding, not for himself, but for the girl. He couldn't fire on Desoto without posing considerable risk to Quinn.

Desoto stepped back, his heel striking one of the flashlights. It spun, throwing wavering shadows. "You shoot me, she's dead! I even twitch, her neck splits wide open!"

"You sure about that?" Liam said, still moving, slowly, cautiously, seeking an opening.

Liam was a big man—six-foot-one, two hundred pounds—but this guy outweighed him by at least thirty pounds. Solid muscle, by the heft and breadth of him.

"Stay back!" Desoto cried.

"If she gets even a nick from that blade," Liam hissed, "I'll gut you slowly. I promise you that."

Quinn's eyes flashed wide and white, laser-focused on Liam. Fear in her face. Dark blood staining her forehead. She yelled something, but the gag stifled her cries.

Anger surged through him. He was going to kill this man for hurting a defenseless girl. Right here, right now.

"You're dead for killing Pike!" Desoto spat. "Now you'll pay for Benner, too!"

Liam came within ten feet of them. He didn't take his eyes off Quinn; she didn't take her eyes off him.

"I think you have it the other way around." He gave Quinn a slight nod of his chin.

Quinn understood him. She kicked Desoto in the shin with the heel of her boot.

Desoto let out a ferocious growl and threw Quinn aside. She went to the ground hard but rolled out of the way, her arms over her head.

Desoto dropped a shoulder, zig-zagged hard, and rushed Liam like a bull seeing red.

Liam fired.

The round caught Desoto wide. His big body jerked, but he kept coming, knife flashing.

Instinctively Liam shifted, his knees slightly bent, weight centered over his hips, left hand in a blocking position, right hand close to his body.

He dropped his pistol to free his hands. He wanted to kill this scumbag with his own shiny toy.

Desoto lunged. The karambit blade slashed through the darkness. Liam dodged. It nicked him in the ear. He barely felt it, barely felt his back.

His entire focus narrowed to a single point. He was in the zone, a killing machine.

Lightning fast, Liam sidestepped. He used the edge of his hand to deliver a powerful strike to Desoto's throat, crushing his windpipe. Desoto gagged.

Liam seized the top of the man's knife hand, bent his wrist inward while simultaneously pulling him off-balance and twisting the knife. Liam forced his hand backward and drove the karambit through the top of Desoto's throat and up into his brain.

Desoto dropped to the floor, choking and flailing. Liam followed him down.

Grunting from the effort, Liam shoved the curved blade forward through meat and sinew, puncturing the larynx, trachea, and esophagus, nearly through to the concrete on the other side.

Desoto writhed violently, but he was pinned like a butterfly to a spreading board. Blood bubbled up his throat and spilled from his lips. Warm, wet blood gushed over Liam's hands.

A moment later, Desoto was dead.

45

LIAM
DAY THIRTY-THREE

His heart thudding, Liam wiped his hands on the man's pant legs. He climbed to his feet, breathing through the pain. A flashlight was within reach; he grabbed it with a wince.

He hadn't yet recovered fully from his back injury or his bout with hypothermia. His muscles ached. His lower spine felt like molten lava.

Slowly, it subsided. Too slowly, and not enough.

He felt his ear. It was bloody and mushy. A quarter-inch chunk was missing. Nothing important. He could still hear fine.

The wound would heal with some antibiotic ointment and bandages. Once he got inside, he'd administer first aid with his IFAK—individual first aid kit—in his go-bag.

He turned to the girl.

She crouched in the corner next to the wall of hanging lawn equipment. She was shaking. She gripped a snow shovel in both hands, ready to strike.

"Hey," he said, steady and calm, like he might soothe a frightened horse. "Hey. It's over. It's finished. They're dead."

He expected her to be terrified, panic-stricken. Stunned, even catatonic. He'd seen plenty of civilians traumatized by war and violence. Soldiers, too.

Fear shone in her eyes, but so did anger, bright and sharp. She was alert. She was present.

She was breathing heavily, her chest heaving, but she appeared okay. Blood leaked down her forehead from a cut to her scalp, and the red line across her throat would leave an ugly bruise.

She dropped the shovel, and it clattered to the concrete floor. She pointed at the rag gagging her mouth.

Liam unsheathed his knife and handed her the flashlight. "Hold still."

She didn't move as he sliced the gag free at the back of her head. It had been knotted so tightly that a red line indented her face on either side of her mouth across each cheek, like a twisted Joker's smile.

"Disgusting." She spat several times and rubbed her face. She touched her bloody temple. "I blacked out for a second. I wanted to nail that sucker in the head with the shovel."

"You did fine." He examined her pupils, checking for a concussion. "You feel okay? Dizziness or blurry vision?"

"I'm...I'm okay." Her voice came out raspy. She sucked in several ragged breaths and spat again. "That dirtbag choked me. He was going to gut me with that knife."

"He got what was coming to him."

"Hell yes he did! You have no idea." Rage thrummed through her voice.

"I just wish I did it myself!"

"No, you don't."

She shot him a sharp look. Her piercings glinted in the moonlight. "Hannah said you go around saving people. She said that's what you do."

Liam snorted. "That might be stretching the truth a bit."

"Looks plenty true from where I'm standing. You were like Wolverine!"

Liam grimaced. *Not quite.* Nothing ever came so easy as in the movies, especially killing. He glanced at the bodies. "You did your share."

"Yeah, and I got that one with the hedge trimmers. I wanted to live. Anyone would've done the same."

"You'd be surprised how many men freeze in fear. More than you'd think."

"And women?" She crossed her arms over her chest and glared at him. "Not as many as you think."

He eyed her. A smile twitched at the corners of his lips. She reminded him of Hannah. That same steel flashing in those eyes. "Touché."

Liam bent to pick up his pistol. It was wedged beneath the tire of a hulking shape—a riding lawn mower.

His back spasmed. The electric shot of pain reminded him that he was far from one hundred percent. Not even close.

He didn't want to admit to himself how much his back was affecting him. All the training and skills in the world didn't matter when your own body betrayed you. He'd need to ice his lower back tonight.

Quinn didn't take her eyes off him. "You're hurt."

"It's a war wound. I'm just getting old."

"I doubt that."

The adrenaline dump hit him, and his legs went to Jell-O. He leaned against the rear shelves with a weary sigh.

Fighting took so much out of him. Killing, even more.

He was tired. He was hurting. But he could manage it, put it in a box. He still had work to do.

He did a quick systems check. Twelve rounds in the magazine. He exchanged the half-spent magazine for the full one in his back pocket. He'd reload it tonight.

He was running dangerously low on ammo. He needed to fix that problem, and soon.

Especially if more assassins were coming.

Quinn stared at Desoto, the dark puddle spreading rapidly beneath his body. Her hand went to her throat. "They were hiding in the shed. I should've seen the footprints. I should have paid attention."

He nodded. "Do better next time. Always pay attention to your surroundings. It's called situational awareness."

"I will," she said.

Liam kept the Glock in one hand as he squatted painfully and examined the bodies.

Both men wore black camo. Grease paint smeared their faces. In addition to their plate carriers, one carried an M4 carbine, and the other, an AK-47 retrofitted with a bumper stock.

He patted down the corpses. Each plate carrier held three thirty-round magazines. He helped himself to the magazines, the rifles, and Desoto's karambit blade. He discovered two frag grenades in Desoto's rig, pocketed them, and relieved Desoto of his plate armor.

Apprehension lurked in the back of his mind. The bumper stock concerned him, as the modification enabled the semiautomatic rifle to fire almost as quickly as an automatic.

And where did they get the M4 and the grenades? Some police departments had them, and the National Guard.

How many weapons like this did the militia have? Where was their weapons depot?

Wherever the militia had gotten these, there would be more.

He slung the M4 and modified AK-47 over his shoulder and

handed the magazines and plate carrier to Quinn. "Can you carry these?"

She nodded gravely.

"That one you practically beheaded is Sebastian Desoto," Quinn said. "Mattias Sutter's righthand man."

"He's the one you nailed with your slingshot last week?"

"That's the one." She shot him a grim smile before pursing her lips. "Are you going to fight them?"

"Unless these two reanimate, they're already dead."

"I mean the militia. They're bad. All of them. They're just like this."

He shook his head. "That's not my battle."

"They're dangerous! They're destroying our town!"

"This isn't my town," Liam said as gently as he could.

She frowned. "You saved Hannah."

"That's different."

"You saved me, too."

"They were here for me," he said darkly. "I had to put them down."

He never wanted another soul put in harm's way because of him. The idea sickened him. It was anathema to everything he stood for.

"Exactly!" Her expression clouded. "They took control of the food. They stole it right out of our pantries! They made all these rules and regulations and curfews. Now they're killing people. They have no right!"

He felt her righteous anger seething off her. She had a reason to be angry. Hell, he was angry himself. Those scumbags had made it personal when they'd come after him and hurt Quinn instead.

But that didn't change the facts. Fifty against one weren't odds anyone could defeat, especially armed with bump stocks, military-grade weapons, and gear. Not even a special operator.

"They're a small army," he said wearily. "I'm one man. A man with a broken back."

"You're more than that," she said, not a shred of doubt in her voice. "I know it."

An engine splintered the night air. The sound came from the road in front of the house.

"Hannah and Noah are back," Quinn said.

Liam heaved himself to his feet. "Go back to the house. I'll do a check of the property and meet you there. Lock the doors, keep the lights off, don't let anyone in until I come back. I'll whistle 'Happy Birthday' so you'll know it's me."

Quinn wrinkled her nose. "Lame choice."

He narrowed his eyes at her.

She grinned back, the red line on her face giving her that garish Joker's smile again. "Whatever, Wolverine. I'm going, I'm going."

46

LIAM
DAY THIRTY-THREE

After he watched Quinn safely enter the house, Liam checked the property.

He holstered the Glock and used the M4. It had been a long time since he'd used one. Too long. It fit in his hands like a glove.

He hadn't gone a dozen yards when Ghost came hurtling toward him, a big fluffy cannonball. Growling fiercely, he tore past Liam and headed into the shed.

Once he was sufficiently satisfied that the bad guys he'd smelled were indeed dead, he bounded back to Liam's side. He loped beside him, tail sticking straight out, hackles still raised.

"Stay alert," Liam said in a low voice. "I think they were the only ones, but we need to make sure."

As if instinctively understanding this was a clandestine operation, Ghost chuffed softly. He remained at Liam's side as they cleared the woods surrounding the house.

Liam had grown used to the dog's steady presence. Expected it, even enjoyed it.

Ghost had accompanied him on most of the jaunts he'd taken nearly every day for the last week. He was edgy and restless, needing out of that oversized box of a house that still seemed claustrophobic.

That, and he wanted to know the layout of Fall Creek like the back of his hand. He'd studied the map, but he needed to walk it himself—and so he did, putting the topography to memory, every road and river bend, the bridge, the businesses, and the neighborhoods.

He'd analyzed the town for weaknesses, mentally designed exit strategies and pre-planned exit routes, choosing spots where he might hide a cache of weapons and supplies concealed in hollowed-out tree trunks or an abandoned shed. He'd scanned for choke points, potential sniper hides, and improvised weapons.

He'd had no specific threat in mind, only the certainty that it would come, and he would be ready.

The first threat had come sooner than he'd expected. It wouldn't be the last.

He found the two snowmobiles a quarter mile from the house along the edge of the river, hidden beneath hastily chopped pine boughs. As he'd suspected, they'd parked close by and hoofed it through the woods to sneak in undetected.

Twenty minutes later, he was back in the house after he whistled and Quinn let him in. The lights were off except for a camping lantern placed on the coffee table. Everyone's faces were drawn, tense, and bathed in shadows.

Bishop stood guard by the back door, AR-15 in hand. Hannah and Noah stood several feet apart in front of the sofa in the living room, Hannah holding Charlotte, Noah with his hand on his holstered service weapon.

Quinn went and sat cross-legged on the ottoman on the other side of the fireplace, holding an ice pack to her head. Milo was still sleeping.

Ghost shook off his coat and tracked snow across the shiny wood floor all the way to Hannah. He leaned heavily against Hannah's leg, still alert, as if he sensed the tension vibrating through the room.

"Liam!" Hannah's gaze locked on Liam. Her face paled. "You're hurt!"

He looked down at himself. Desoto's blood stained his hands and much of his coat. "Only a little bit is mine. I'm fine."

"Like hell." Hannah was already moving toward him. "Look at your ear."

Quinn reached out and offered to take the baby. Hannah laid Charlotte in her arms and strode across the living room. Ghost followed her.

Liam glanced at Noah. The lantern threw shadows across the room. He didn't miss Noah's narrowed eyes, the naked jealousy flashing across his face.

Hannah halted in front of Liam, put her hands on either side of his face, and examined him, her mouth pursed. "There's alcohol in the bathroom and bandages below the sink. I need a bowl of warm water and some towels."

Noah went for the medical supplies and quickly returned. Noah watched Hannah clean, disinfect, and bandage the gash in Liam's ear—with Bishop's help—in stony silence.

Charlotte cooed contentedly as Quinn rocked her and patted her back. She was good with the baby.

"Thank you," Liam said when Hannah and Bishop had finished.

Hannah flashed him a grim smile. "You're welcome."

"Did you tell them what happened?" he asked Quinn.

"Mostly." Quinn nodded. "I startled them. That's why they had to hide in the shed. If it was someone else, maybe they would've just waited until whoever it was left and then went about their original plan to sneak in and attack you two. But

Desoto saw it was me. He hates—hated—me because I humiliated him. He saw his chance and decided to take it."

She was a perceptive girl. Liam had suspected as much.

"The militia is out of control." Quinn shot Liam a pointed look. "We need to stop them."

"Why would they attack us?" Hannah asked tightly. "I don't understand."

"Not you or Noah," Quinn said. "They wanted Liam. They said 'he' ordered them to take out Liam. Bishop was a bonus if they could get to him. Two for the price of one. That's what Desoto said."

"Who's 'he?'" Noah asked. "Did they say the name of the person who gave them the orders?"

Liam shrugged. "Sutter's the commander of the militia."

"Why would Sutter want you dead?" Hannah asked.

"He wouldn't," Bishop said in a low voice. "But I can think of a few people who would."

"You haven't even done anything," Hannah said, but there was doubt in her voice. A growing trepidation.

She was putting the pieces together. He could see it in her face—what he already suspected.

Quinn twisted around on the ottoman. Holding Charlotte tightly, she pinned her gaze on Liam. "It's because Wolverine here—Liam—was the one who killed Gavin Pike."

The room went silent. They stared at each other, the dread a palpable thing.

"It was Julian Sinclair," Quinn said.

"No," Noah said firmly. "Absolutely not."

Her eyes narrowed. "Everyone knows there's animosity between the Sinclairs and Bishop. Especially Julian. That's why Bishop was named, too. And the Sinclairs have every reason to loathe Liam. Julian sent Desoto to kill you because of Pike. This was revenge."

The back of Liam's neck prickled. He hadn't officially met the town superintendent, but he had no desire to have any further contact with the likes of Julian Sinclair.

Rosamond Sinclair was Pike's mother. That was all Liam needed to know. The apple never fell that far from the tree.

Noah raked his hands through his hair. "You don't know that. All this is speculation and rumor. There isn't a shred of evidence connecting Julian to any of this. Julian wouldn't do this."

"Julian had to know about this," Quinn said. "It's the only piece that fits."

Noah shook his head. "He was trying to help. He told me he would calm Rosamond down, that he would defuse the situation."

"He lied," Bishop said.

"No. You're wrong."

"Possibly, but I don't think I am." Bishop shifted his stance and tightened his grip on the rifle. His mouth was set in a grim line. "Nothing in this town happens without the approval of the Sinclairs. I've said it before, and I'll say it again."

Quinn raised her pierced eyebrows. "You think Rosamond Sinclair herself ordered this?"

"No!" Noah gestured wildly. "This was the work of a few rogue militia soldiers. That's all! Rosamond Sinclair would never sanction anything like this. Never. Listen to yourselves. This is crazy. It's ridiculous."

"It's not that ridiculous," Quinn said. "Not anymore. Not after what's happened."

"It wasn't even Liam who did it," Hannah said.

Liam shot her a warning look. So did Noah.

She ignored them. Her hand tightened in Ghost's fur. "It was me. I'm the one who killed Pike."

Edge of Anarchy

Quinn's mouth dropped open. Bishop didn't look surprised at all.

Hannah turned toward Noah, her expression stricken. "That's why you didn't want me to say anything. This is why you told me to keep it a secret. You knew Julian would come after whoever killed his brother. You knew."

Noah flinched. He opened his mouth, closed it, saying nothing. Guilt was written all over his face.

Anger flashed through Liam at the hurt look in Hannah's eyes. He tamped it down. Noah was a lucky man that so many witnesses were present. He could've wrung his neck then and there.

Liam gritted his teeth. He'd attempted to like Noah for Hannah's sake. It hadn't worked. He was failing completely.

His initial assessment that the man was weak-willed, indecisive, and willfully blind had just confirmed itself.

"Enough." Bishop did not speak loudly. He didn't have to. His larger-than-life presence could command a room without speaking at all. "I've long suspected Julian played a role in the Crossway Massacre. And now this? Enough is enough. It's time to find the truth. It's time to find out exactly just how much he knows. And what he's done."

"No!" Noah nearly shouted. "He's Rosamond's son. He's protected. You can't hurt him."

Bishop's expression darkened. Shadows ringed his eyes. He was a man haunted by a past he couldn't change, by a wrong not yet rectified. "I'll do what I need to do."

"I'll go with you," Liam offered.

In contrast to his initial impressions of Noah Sheridan, Liam had taken an instant liking to Bishop—a rarity for him. Bishop had lost the people he'd loved most in the world, just like Liam. They were both military vets, both bereft, unmoored in a cold and merciless world.

"Thank you, brother, but no. The Lord is with me. This is my task, and mine alone. It's been a long time coming, believe me."

"At least take the weapon."

Bishop set the rifle down and moved for the door. "I have an HK 45 pistol."

Noah strode forward and halted a few feet from Bishop, blocking his path. His hand moved to the holster at his waist, something like panic etched across his face. Real fear. "This is a mistake. Don't do this."

Liam shifted slightly. He didn't raise the carbine or do anything to draw attention to himself. He was ready to act if needed.

"This is a terrible idea, Bishop," Noah said. "You don't know what you're getting into."

"You won't stop me this time, my friend," Bishop said, steel in his voice. "Not unless you're willing to shoot me."

Reluctantly, Noah lowered his hand.

Bishop moved past him. His face a storm cloud, his eyes burning. "Julian Sinclair's reckoning comes now."

47

HANNAH
DAY THIRTY-THREE

"Maybe I should leave."

Hannah stared at Liam, stunned. "No."

"This isn't my home," Liam said grimly. "My home is north. I have a cabin, supplies, land. Everything I need. That's where I belong. Not here."

The cold night air was crisp and sharp. Moonlight reflected off the snow. The trees stood, watching over everything like sentinels.

They were sitting in the swing on the porch. Several inches between them. Hannah was wrapped in a blanket. Liam stiff and straight, the M4 resting on his other side, his gaze constantly scanning the yard.

Charlotte was sleeping inside. Bishop had left a few minutes ago. Noah had driven Quinn home. She had her bright orange truck, but no one had wanted to let her drive home alone, not after what she'd just been through.

Hannah faced Liam and expelled a puff of crystalized air. Her hands had turned clammy inside her gloves, her pulse rushing in her ears. "You do belong here."

"I'm an outsider in your home."

It still felt like Noah's home, not hers. "It's fine."

It wasn't. She knew it wasn't. Liam knew it wasn't. Noah certainly did.

Every time Noah and Liam were around each other—which was often in the same house—it was incredibly awkward. Tension humming in the air.

She knew Liam felt uncomfortable. She knew Noah was jealous.

She could feel it, could feel them both circling each other warily, like wolves jockeying over territory, vying for supremacy.

"I don't want to leave you here." Even in the dim light, she could see his expression contorting, the scowl on his face. "Noah can't protect you like I can. But if I leave, you'll be safer."

Everyone was shaken after the attack on Quinn, and Desoto and Benner's failed attempt to assassinate Liam and Bishop.

Liam had been hurt. And a teenage girl had almost been killed in the crossfire.

Liam now had a target on his back. Because of her. Because he'd taken the burden of her actions upon his shoulders. Still trying to save her, even now.

"It's me they want," Liam said. "Not you."

"Because of me. I'm the one—"

He shook his head sharply. "You can't say that. Not anymore. Not ever. Now Bishop and Quinn know. The more people who know the truth, the more danger you're in."

She stared at his bandaged ear. She hated the thought that she was the reason Liam and Quinn could have died tonight.

As if reading her mind, Liam said, "Whoever is behind this—the militia, Julian Sinclair—their actions are theirs and theirs alone. Not yours."

She bit her lip and nodded slowly.

This last week had been a rollercoaster of emotions. One revelation after another threatening to topple everything like a house of cards.

She felt like she still hadn't regained her footing. They were all standing on thin ice, just waiting for the next crack to show itself.

She watched as Ghost loped across the snowy yard, a flash of white against white. In the moonlight, he'd never looked more like his namesake.

He glanced at them, tongue lolling, before resuming his patrol of the property. He slept during the day and remained alert and watchful at night.

Just like Liam. Both of them protectors to their core.

Her mouth felt dry. She shifted on the swing, the slats digging into her back. "You can protect us."

He turned to her in the darkness. His gaze intense, those gray-blue eyes haunted in a way that she understood now. "It's not safe for you here, either. This place isn't safe."

"It's not safe anywhere."

He gave a noncommittal grunt.

"Fall Creek is my home. Even with everything happening, everything going wrong. This is it."

Despite everything going on with the EMP, the militia, with Pike's death, life still happened. Quinn came over often. So did Bishop and Noah's cop friends, Reynoso and Samantha Perez. Annette King and Dave Farris stopped by, too.

In her old life, her Fall Creek friends had mostly been Noah's. Daphne and her little girls had come over often for playdates. Daphne had been her closest friend here—but now Daphne was dead.

Hannah's best friend from college, Carly, lived in Grand Rapids. Was she okay? Or had something terrible happened to her, too? She thought often of her parents and brother in the Upper Peninsula. They were probably better off than most people, but she longed to call them, hear their voices again. Connect with the people she'd loved most.

The EMP had made the world a much smaller place. No more road trips. No more jumping on an airplane and zipping across the country in a few hours. No more phone calls, FaceTime, or Zoom meetings. No stores to visit or restaurants to enjoy.

The world had shrunk to the borders of Fall Creek. And for Hannah, it was even smaller.

Noah and Liam both felt like it was a good idea for her to stay close—the only thing they'd agreed on. She'd only left the house to visit Molly and Quinn, which she and Milo had done almost daily.

Molly had already taught her how to wash clothes by hand, bake homemade bread on the woodstove, and showed her how to construct her own winter garden boxes.

Milo knew which plants were which, and when the fresh greens were ready to be harvested. He'd proudly pointed out the potatoes, turnips, carrots, cabbage, cauliflower, onions, garlic, and Swiss chard.

She'd watched Quinn and Milo make a few dozen homemade handwarmers. Milo had shown her each step. He'd gestured at the Ziplock sandwich and snack-sized bags strewn across Molly's kitchen table. "You just add a cup of ice melt salt, like what they use on roads and sidewalks. But make sure it has the calcium chloride stuff in it."

He poured the salt into the sandwich bag, then picked up the smaller baggie. "Add half a cup of water to this one and push out all the air bubbles, then seal it." Milo had put the water bag inside the larger ice salt bag and sealed it.

He'd handed it to Hannah, his face beaming. "Keep them in

your coat pocket. When you go outside, squeeze it to puncture the water bag, then shake it to activate. Boom!"

When she'd tried it, the heat had activated immediately and kept her hands warm for about thirty minutes. It was a genius idea, and she loved seeing Milo so engaged in creating something useful.

"We're using them for trade, Hannah," Milo had said proudly.

They were making items to barter with other people in the community for canned goods, split firewood, toiletries, gasoline for generators, and other supplies.

A bit of an underground trading post had sprung up, with tough, practical Molly at the heart of it. She didn't give anything away, but she traded her expertise, teaching neighbors and friends how to build bucket toilets, solar ovens, and Amish buckets to retrieve water from their wells.

Day by day, she felt herself drawn to the warmth and kindness of these people. It surprised her how quickly she'd come to care about each of them, how in such adversity, community meant everything.

When they weren't learning new skills with Molly, Hannah spent time with Milo at the Winter Haven house. They read books, drew superheroes, played with Legos, and cooked and cleaned together.

At bedtime, Milo still asked for Noah. He hadn't asked for Hannah yet. He still called her Hannah. He didn't seem too interested in his infant half-sister, either. It pained her heart, but she didn't press it.

He was just a child. He was overwhelmed and needed time to figure things out.

They were working toward each other, slowly and cautiously, but it was happening. That was all that Hannah could ask for.

She would accept whatever Milo was ready to give her, when he was ready.

Cliché as it sounded, she took each moment as it came.

In the life she'd lived before, she had taken happiness for granted. Now, she took nothing for granted. Just sitting here next to Liam, this small moment of peace and comfort—it was enough.

This type of happiness, this simple contentment, was no longer ordinary. It was precious and fragile. If she moved too quickly, it might slip from her hands and shatter.

"Fall Creek is my home," she said again.

Liam leaned forward and gazed at her intently. "Are you sure?"

She knew what he was thinking. What he wanted to say but wouldn't. He was too honorable.

He would take her with him, if she asked. He would take Charlotte and Milo, too. No hesitation. He would protect her little family with his very life.

She shook her head, her throat thickening. Unable to verbalize how tempted she was, how much part of her wanted to take her children and flee Fall Creek.

Though there was much good here, and good people, there was also a wrongness about this place. A darkness festering at the heart of it.

She couldn't take Milo from Noah. Milo worshipped his father. He would never forgive her. She knew that. Her relationship with her son was budding but still so, so fragile.

She was trying to make things work with her husband. Trying as hard as she could. Every time she thought they were making headway, Noah would do or say something that made her feel unmoored all over again.

The way he couldn't hold Charlotte. How he couldn't bear

the sight of her crippled hand. How he tiptoed around the past, choosing not to bring it up rather than face it head-on.

It was like they were both adrift on a wild and raging sea and couldn't find their way back. Like it was impossible.

But she wasn't going to quit. Hannah Sheridan did not give up easily. It wasn't in her.

She said it more for herself than for Liam. "I have to try, Liam. I owe it to everyone to try."

He nodded once, accepting it.

It remained unspoken, the thing between them. Glimmering like a thread of gossamer. Barely visible, and yet stronger than she thought possible. She felt it, pulling her, tugging on her heart.

She swallowed. "I don't want you to go."

"If you want me to stay, I'll stay," he said.

She didn't hesitate. "I do."

"Not in this house." His jaw clenched. "It's not safe for you. And it isn't...it's not working."

"Our old house is empty," she said quickly. "You can stay there. You can stay as long as you want. Please, I—"

She couldn't say the rest. How the thought of him leaving stole the breath from her lungs and filled her chest with an aching dread.

She bit her lower lip. "Please say yes."

His eyes flashed with something she couldn't read in the dark. He cleared his throat. "Hannah, I'll stay for as long as you need me."

"Thank you." She longed to take his hand and hold tight. To steady herself the way she held onto Ghost. She didn't, but she wanted to.

48

JULIAN
DAY THIRTY-FOUR

Cold, thin puffs of air drifted from Julian's mouth with every breath. Dawn tinged the early morning sky a weak, watery gray.

The Sinclairs owned a little fishing shack on the edge of Fall Creek along the far border of Winter Haven's property line. Gavin had had no use for fishing—preferring to hunt larger prey, including humans, apparently—so it was Julian who used it almost exclusively.

The small ten-by-ten shack smelled musty and dank. Dust motes danced in the gray light trickling through the smudged, dirty window. The wood plank floor was rotting in some places and scuffed with dirt and grime.

He'd packed his gear on a sled—jigging ice fishing rod; tackle box with line clippers, pliers, hooks, and sinkers; a bucket to overturn for seating; a manual ice auger with an ice saw and chisel; a skimmer; and a retractable ice pick, just in case.

He didn't have his usual bait of meal worms, grubs, or minnows that he could just grab at a bait and tackle shop like before the collapse. He'd tried a few hacks he'd heard of from other anglers, which had worked surprisingly well. A few kernels of canned corn threaded onto the hook could lure trout, perch, carp, and bluegill into biting. Gummy worms and marshmallows also worked for bluegill.

He hesitated in the doorway, glancing back a final time. The chest freezer in the corner drew his gaze like a terrible magnet.

There was no electricity to keep it running, but the freezing temperature had served its purpose. The body inside should still be cold enough to keep it from decomposing too much.

He would need to move it soon. The ground was still frozen, but he could weigh the corpse with rocks and chains, roll it over a deep and secluded section of the river, cut a hole in the ice, and dump it in.

Maybe someday the authorities would dredge the river in search of people who'd disappeared during the collapse, but it wouldn't be for a long, long time. Julian wasn't worried.

Chief Briggs had been easier to kill than he'd thought. He'd killed in rage before—Nickel and Billy Carter came to mind—but Briggs was premeditated, calculated. He'd had to work himself up to it.

When the moment came, he hadn't hesitated. He'd needed to do it. It got done.

A bullet to the back of the head when the old man had his back turned. Julian had made sure it was quick and painless. Merciful.

Chief Briggs had been a miserable old bulldog. Now he was at peace. Or, as at peace as a corpse crammed inside an ice chest could be.

He needed to get rid of the damn body. That was all. Then this sour sick feeling in his gut would go away. Then the nightmares would end.

He forced his feet to move, his body to pivot. He marched out of the tiny shack and slammed the rickety door shut behind him.

Cold blasted his exposed cheeks and slithered down the back of his neck. He was dressed for a day of exposure to the elements.

He wore a moisture-wicking base layer with long underwear and a flannel shirt beneath snowsuit bib overalls, followed by a waterproof winter coat, waterproof boots with good traction, and the usual hat, gloves, and thick wool socks.

The frozen river stretched out before him, oily and black beneath the thick gray ice. Thin straggly trees clawed at the sky with their barren branches. A low hill rose behind him, obstructing the view of the houses along the bluff. He had complete privacy.

This little corner of the river was tucked into an inlet. Water moving into the river provided a good source of food for game fish. Lots of deadfall beneath the surface also made it a good spot for fish to congregate.

Julian stepped out onto the ice, lugging the sled behind him. It creaked a little but easily held his weight.

The recommended thickness to walk on ice safely was four inches. Julian sometimes went out on only two or three and had never had a problem. He'd never been one to adhere to rules and guidelines anyway.

He moved out further, searching for one of his favorite spots. Fish liked to run edges. Julian usually targeted drop-offs or changes in underwater terrain to look for gamefish. Today, he was planning to fish the deeper side.

His boots squeaked. Five yards. Ten. Fifteen.

He planned to spend all day ice fishing. It was Sunday, as if anyone remembered what day it was in the apocalypse. He'd been working his butt off for a month and had only been able to escape out here a few times.

He needed a break. And he was sick to death of dinner out of a can. He craved fresh meat—even if it was just fish.

He also needed to get his damn head on straight. There was too much going on, too much to process.

He'd waited all night for the radio confirmation that Desoto and Benner had achieved their mission objectives: Liam Coleman dead. And Atticus Bishop, too.

Two birds with one stone. And why not? Liam was for his mother; Bishop was for himself.

He deserved it, didn't he? Bishop had been a thorn in the side of Fall Creek for years. The collapse had just brought out the conflict in sharp relief. Bishop never had any intention of falling in line. He incited discontent and rebellion with every breath he took.

It wasn't enough to take the church or the community pantry from him. It wasn't enough to take his family.

As long as he was alive, he was a threat to everything that the Sinclairs had worked so hard to build.

Fall Creek was a small town. Nothing but a blip on the map. But it was theirs, and no one was taking it from them.

No one. Not Chief Briggs. Not Bishop or Liam Coleman. And certainly not Noah.

He shifted the sled rope from his right hand to his left and checked his radio once again. It was on. He was in range. What the hell was the problem?

They'd probably gone on a bender and slept it off afterward and just hadn't bothered to check in. Or they'd gone straight to Sutter and cut him out of the loop entirely.

Frustration slashed through him. He cursed.

How much longer could he wait? Should he wait? If something had gone wrong, he needed to be back with the superintendent. He needed to be there to take care of it, not Sutter. And certainly not Noah Sheridan.

This was a mistake. He needed to go back.

He started to turn.

"Julian Sinclair!"

The shout was loud and clear as a gunshot. He recognized the distinctive, deep booming voice. The voice of someone he'd hoped was already dead.

Julian completed his turn and faced his nemesis. "Bishop."

Atticus Bishop was very much alive. He stood at the shoreline, dressed in jeans, black boots, and a lemon-yellow Hawaiian shirt beneath his usual leather jacket, a Lions scarf tied around his neck.

He carried a handgun, held low and pointed at the ground. He didn't need to point it directly at Julian. The threat was clear enough.

Bitter disappointment coiled in his gut. Julian tried to hide his anger, but he'd never been any good at controlling his feelings. He scowled. "What the hell are you doing here?"

"I came for you."

Julian feigned ignorance. "What do you mean?"

He had his knife sheathed inside his right boot, but he'd left the shotgun and his service weapon in the patrol truck. He cursed silently.

What the hell had happened to Desoto and Benner? Benner was a little green, but Desoto was strong, tough, and relentless. Maybe they hadn't tried for Bishop. Maybe they'd just killed Coleman and planned to go after Bishop another night—and hadn't bothered to inform him.

As if reading his thoughts, Bishop said, "Benner and Desoto are dead."

Stunned, he inhaled a sharp breath. That part, he didn't have to fake. "What?"

They were dead? Both of them? Clearly, they hadn't been up to the task. He should've done the job himself.

A needle of fear pricked him. He knew exactly why he'd handed it off. He was a decent cop. Serviceable with weaponry and physical prowess, but he was certainly no super soldier.

He'd never put in more time at the range or gym than he had to. There were always better things to do. Downhill skiing, snowmobiling, fishing, and women.

He'd let the militia do the dirty work. That was what they were there for. That's what powerful leaders did. They never got their own hands dirty.

Bishop took a step forward. "They infiltrated Noah Sheridan's property with the intent to break into the house and murder myself and Liam Coleman."

"That's a pretty wild accusation," Julian said evasively. "Why would they do that?"

"That's what I came to ask you."

"I don't know what the hell you're talking about."

Bishop's expression hardened. "Oh, I think you do."

49

JULIAN
DAY THIRTY-FOUR

Julian took a step back. The ice gave the smallest creak.

He felt a sudden rush of seething contempt. That familiar bite of bitter jealousy as he stared at Bishop. How he'd felt his whole life. Bishop and his family had had that aura, that appealing contentment that certain families exude—the kind that makes you wish you'd been born into some other family rather than your own.

He tilted his chin at Bishop's gun. "Just what do you plan to do with that?"

"It's time to talk."

His lip curled. "I have nothing to say to you."

Bishop shifted the weapon, the muzzle lifting slightly. "Yes, you do."

Anxiety shot through Julian. Bishop couldn't know. How could he know? He was just fishing for information. Working a hunch.

Julian just needed to get rid of him. The faster, the better. The question was, how?

"I'm an officer of the law!" He shouted across the ice. "Threatening an officer is a crime. So is assaulting an officer. To be quite frank with you, Bishop, I'm getting pretty threatening vibes from you right now."

Bishop's expression didn't change. "Do I have a good reason to threaten you, Julian? Is that why you're acting so antsy?"

"Don't play mind games with me! You can't manipulate me. I'm not gullible like your little flock."

Bishop took a tentative step from the bank onto the ice. The ice held. He took another step. "You sent the militia to assassinate Liam Coleman in retaliation for the death of Gavin Pike. You sent them to kill me for personal reasons."

"That's—that's crazy! You can't do this. You can't just come out here making insane accusations without consequences."

"What consequences, Julian? What else could you possibly do to me? You've taken my church, my ministry. You stole the supplies my wife and I had saved for years to share with our community, on our own terms. My wife and children are dead." Bishop's features went rigid. "Did you have something to do with that as well?"

Julian's chest seized. Guilt speared him. "Of course not. Are you listening to yourself right now, Bishop? You aren't even making sense. You've been in the cold too long. You're crazed with grief. Go home. Go spill your guts to Noah. He's good at that sort of thing."

Bishop advanced a few more steps. Only twenty feet separated them. He fixed Julian with a cold, hostile stare. "You've been lying for so long, you've forgotten what the truth sounds like. That stops now, Julian. That stops today."

Trepidation rolled through him. Julian glanced around wildly. The far bank was another twenty-five yards behind him. The ice in the middle was thinner—the river there flowed deep and fast.

The wind-scoured ice was slick. Running wouldn't get him far.

He had zero desire to face Bishop one-on-one in a hand-to-hand altercation. Bishop was a big guy. Six-two and solid bulk underneath that stupid Hawaiian shirt.

Beneath that placid religious façade, he was capable of violence, just like everyone else. With his former military experience, he knew how to wield that violence better than most. Probably better than Julian himself.

"Shut up, Bishop! You never shut up!"

Bishop kept moving toward him. He took deliberate plodding steps, his jaw set, steely determination flashing in his eyes.

The man was relentless. He wouldn't be put off. He wouldn't be misled or deluded, not like Noah.

His heart jackhammering against his ribs, Julian looked downriver. Just before the bend that rounded the peninsula of woods loomed the bridge that crossed Fall Creek and led into town.

The bridge where he'd stood that day. The blizzard raging around him. The brick in his hands tied to the rusty antique key.

The key that had unlocked the cage that held Ray Shultz and the Carter brothers. The maniacs who had unleashed a rain of carnage, death, and destruction upon Crossway Church.

The shockwaves from that single devastating act reverberated through Fall Creek even now. Julian felt the tremors rocking him to his very core, vibrating beneath his feet.

Not my fault! his mind shrieked. It wasn't his fault. None of it. He didn't deserve the guilt and recrimination. He didn't deserve any of it.

"Someone made you feel weak once," Bishop said. "And now the only way you can make that feeling go away is by hurting someone weaker than you. Only it never really goes away, does it?

That soulless void in the center of your chest. So you have to keep hurting people, over and over and over."

"You don't know me!" Julian raged.

He tore his gaze from the bridge. He searched the banks, the wide flat plane of ice with increasing desperation.

Bishop wouldn't stop until he'd killed Julian. That fact was becoming clear with each passing second. Julian needed to figure out a way to defend himself, and fast.

Several ten-inch diameter iced-over holes pockmarked the frozen river here and there that he'd marked with a pine bough or small stack of rocks. They wouldn't be enough to fall through. Not like he needed.

He surreptitiously scanned the ice, searching for the telltale discoloration, holes, and pressure ridges that indicated poor ice quality. He thought of the old adage that had guided ice fisherman for ages: *Thick and blue, tried and true. Thin and crispy, way too risky.*

There. His gaze snagged on the section of rotten ice he'd bypassed the last time he'd come out.

The ice was thin and ridged, a sickly yellow. He could see the water rushing beneath it. It wouldn't hold the weight of a man. Not a man like Bishop.

Julian just needed to lead Bishop to the rotten ice. When Bishop stepped onto it, he'd fall in.

It wouldn't be enough to drown him. Bishop would crawl out eventually, but it would weaken him, render him helpless as he struggled to clamber out. The brutal ice-cold water would drain his strength.

At his most vulnerable, Julian would come in to save him. He was a cop, after all. To serve and protect was his duty.

When Julian was close, he'd seize the knife from his boot, dart in, and stab Bishop in the chest or the throat.

Bishop would sink below the ice, the current dragging him away and carrying his body to Watervliet or St. Joe or even all the way to Lake Michigan.

He'd vanish completely, never to trouble Fall Creek or the Sinclairs again.

Anticipation quickened his pulse. Yes, that would work.

Julian moved further out onto the ice. He felt carefully with each backward step, testing the thickness before settling his weight. A breeze kicked up, sending clouds of ice crystals skittering across the river.

Bishop took three strides, then hesitated. He narrowed his eyes, as if sensing a trap. "What are you doing, Sinclair?"

He was still ten to twelve feet from the weak spot. Julian needed to distract him. Blind him with anger so he didn't notice he was being led to the slaughter.

Bishop was a dead man walking. It didn't matter what Julian said, what he admitted to. Bishop wasn't leaving this river. Not ever.

The thought was almost freeing. Julian smiled. "If I tell you what you want to hear, do you promise to leave? You don't use that gun. You turn around and go back the way you came."

"I don't make any promises other than that I will act justly."

Julian made a face. "That a Bible quote?"

"Not exactly, but close. 'What has the Lord required of you but to act justly and to love mercy and to walk humbly with your God.'"

"Whatever. Sorry I asked. Ask your questions and then leave me alone."

Bishop watched him, his gaze cold and shrewd. Gone was the warm, gregarious pastor. This man more closely resembled a shark. "Did you send Despot and Benner to Noah Sheridan's home with the intent to kill Liam Coleman and myself?"

Julian sucked in air through his teeth. His lungs felt seared. One step back, one step to the east, eyes flicking to the rotten ice and then quickly away.

The air hummed with a sizzling, crackling energy.

Bishop was already dead, he reminded himself. Anything Julian said now was like shouting into the wind. His words tore from his mouth and sailed out into the great wide nowhere.

"Yeah, I did," he said finally. "And I stand behind it. Liam Coleman is a murderer and deserves the death penalty. And so do you!" Anger boiled through him. He practically spat the words. "You're a dissenter and troublemaker. We're trying to keep the peace and protect the town and all you do is rile people up. You exaggerate and spread rumors. You're a fearmonger. You deserved everything you had coming to you."

Bishop's mouth tightened. His neck constricted, tendons straining. He matched Julian's steps. One forward, one to the east. "And the night of the massacre? What happened?"

"I'll tell you," Julian said. "I'll tell you everything."

50

JULIAN
DAY THIRTY-FOUR

Julian swallowed. He flexed his stiffening fingers, imagined the knife in his hand. Pictured himself stabbing it straight through Bishop's heart. "They were there for *you*."

Bishop's face contorted in a rictus of pain, an agony like Julian had never experienced. Or ever wanted to. "For me."

"You were the perfect target." The words were easier to speak than he'd thought. Actually, it felt damn good to get it out. "You wouldn't shut down that stupid food pantry. Why it was so precious to you, I have no idea. It wasn't even a big deal until you made it into one. You always have to go against the grain. You always have to make yourself important somehow, don't you?"

"What happened, Julian?"

"The council wouldn't vote the militia in. We needed them. Anyone with half a brain could see that. Chief Briggs was too bullheaded to see anything but his own agenda. Noah was too weak to go against the town."

Julian shrugged. "It fit together like pieces to a puzzle. Ray Shultz had it in for you. Let him out, and he and his goons would take care of you. That was the deal."

"The gold," Bishop said, his voice raw.

"Shultz was happy to do it. He'd have done it for free. The gold story was a bit of insurance. To make sure his goons were on board, too. To make sure it happened. It was stupid, in hindsight, but those meth heads weren't exactly geniuses. It kept them from looking at their benefactor with suspicion or too many questions. Money talks, you know. It always talks. It was a currency they understood."

Bishop made a sound in the back of his throat like a wounded animal. "You unlocked the door. You let them out of the cell in exchange for the death of myself and my family."

Julian stifled a wince. "Not your family. Just you. I didn't know what they would do. I had no idea they'd go and shoot up the church and hurt all those people. How would I know that?"

Bishop's booming voice went ragged with grief and rising fury. "You unleash a tiger and then cry ignorance when he does what he was born to do, what is in his nature? Ray Shultz, Tommy and Billy Carter—they were killers!"

"Now, wait just a minute—"

Bishop raised the pistol with both hands and pointed it at Julian's face. He flicked off the safety. "You are as guilty for every single one of those forty-seven deaths as they are. You are culpable for the deaths of my wife and daughters!"

Julian averted his gaze. He couldn't bear the righteous fury radiating from every fiber of Bishop's being. He was a father wronged. A widower bent on avenging the death of his family.

His shoulders quaked, his jaw bulging, the cords standing out in his neck. Even from five feet away, he loomed over Julian. "Because of you, I am a husband without a wife! A father without children!"

Julian cowered before his wrath. Trepidation filled him. In

that moment, Julian feared Bishop really would shoot him. "You don't want to do this, Bishop!"

Bishop's features twisted with rage and grief. His expression broke, full of loss. A man unmoored, untethered from everything he'd ever believed in.

"Please!" Julian cried.

Bishop surged forward. "I should do it! I should kill you!"

The ice popped and creaked.

Bishop halted. The muzzle of the gun aimed at Julian's head. The gun trembled in his hands. "You deserve to die!"

Dark energy thrummed through Julian's veins—fear and dread and a terrible excitement. They were five feet from each other. Bishop one step from the rotten ice.

Julian raised his hands, palms out, in a gesture of supplication, of surrender. "You win, Bishop! Arrest me. You take me in. Throw me in that jail cell and feed me through the bars. Whatever you need to do, man. You don't want to kill me. I'm unarmed. Won't the guilt eat you up inside? Don't you preach about mercy?"

"Sometimes death is the mercy," Bishop growled. A shadow moved behind his eyes. A flicker of doubt, of hesitation.

"Here! Take my handcuffs. There's a pair in my pocket. You can slap 'em on me right now." Julian moved his hand slowly to his coat pocket. He pulled out the cuffs and held them out. "Here. Come get them. Put them on me yourself."

A long, tense silence stretched between them. Bishop wrestling with his conscience, Julian breathless, humming with that dark, nervous energy, sensing the thin ice between them, silently begging Bishop to take one more step. Just one.

The river made no sound—not the ice, not the dark water beneath it. Julian could feel it flowing like his own blood, rushing dark and cold and silent.

Only a shelf of frozen water between Bishop and a watery grave.

Something shifted in Bishop's demeanor. His shoulders slumped. His face cleared.

He lowered the pistol. "You deserve to die, but not by my hand."

Julian stared at him in disbelief.

"I'm not going to kill you. But you *will* face justice. Your fate will be up to the council—and to God."

Bishop gestured with the pistol. "Put the cuffs on yourself. But you come to me, Sinclair. You don't think I see what you're doing? Make sure you skirt that weak spot right in front of me." He gritted his teeth like it pained him to say it. "You wouldn't want to fall in."

Despair filled him. Bishop hadn't fallen for it, after all. Julian was out of plays. He had no plan, no way to get out of this.

Julian wanted to believe his mother would save him, but he didn't believe in anything anymore. Not even her. If only—

Crack.

The sound stopped them both cold. A sound they felt as much as heard—a great popping in the floor of the world.

Julian's heart stuttered. He strained his ears, listening hard for any creak or pop or crack.

He could hear his breaths, Bishop's shallow gasps. The wind whistling through the boughs of the pines and scouring the wide flat surface of the river.

And then—the shifting, crackling ice soft as a whisper, as a lover's sigh.

That same popping sound. The ground beneath his feet shuddered.

"We're out too far," Bishop said. "We need to go back. Nice and slow—"

A terrible groan shattered the air. The ice splintered, exploding in blasts like gunshots. The ice beneath their feet shifted, rising on its axis, slanting dangerously.

Julian's boots slid sideways as Bishop skittered backward, leaping back as the ice split between them, a great crack opening up, a fissure like a mouth grinning wider and wider.

The ice sighed like it was taking a breath. Julian squatted, arms wide to balance himself, terrified to move in either direction lest the ice crumble beneath him.

They were fifty feet out. The water was deep, the current strong.

Terror gripped him. If the ice collapsed, he could get pulled under the ice. He wouldn't be able to break through from beneath. He would drown and freeze simultaneously.

The chunk of ice he stood on pitched beneath him. A sharp edge rose up like a huge fin. He felt his boots slipping down the incline, the traction failing, the grade too steep.

Dropping the handcuffs, he fell to his chest and clung like a barnacle to the upended slab. It was maybe the size of a car, not much more.

The angle tilted to ninety degrees; he slid into the water legs-first. He plunged downward, struggling frantically to cling to the ice, to keep as much of his body above the surface as he could.

He sank past his waist, his ribs, then his chest.

The brutal shock of the cold stunned him, squeezed the breath from his lungs.

He released the smaller slab and beat at the water with arms that already felt like blocks of ice, splashing and kicking, sputtering and flailing for the closest ledge of solid ice.

The broken slabs scraped and knocked against each other. The current shoved him against the ledge and yanked at his legs. His coat, snow pants, and layers of clothing filled with water.

Everything suddenly felt fifty pounds heavier, his boots like anchors.

He clutched feebly, desperately at the ice. Up close, the ice was thick and bubbled and fissured with dozens of hairline cracks. Ugly and yellowish and harsh.

Rotten ice. Nothing beautiful about it at all.

He blinked water from his eyes, the droplets already freezing his eyelashes together. Shivering violently, he gazed up at Bishop, who stood six or seven feet from the hole in the ice.

Bishop stared at Julian with shock and something like awe on his face. His pistol hung limply at his side.

"Help me!" Julian screamed. "I'm drowning!"

Bishop said nothing.

"Give me your hand! Save me!"

Very carefully, Bishop took a step back. Then another.

Panic constricted Julian's chest. He was so cold. Colder than he'd ever been in his life. He could feel his cells freezing, the cold scalding his nerve endings.

"You can't do this! You can't leave me to die!"

Bishop just watched him, his expression impassive, unreadable.

He wasn't going to help. He was going to stand there and watch Julian die.

"Where's your faith, Bishop?" he cried. "Where's your God now?"

"God is love. Love is just," Bishop said like a chant, a prayer. "God is justice. This is justice."

"No!" Julian screamed. "NO!"

"Daphne Bishop," Bishop said, his baritone voice clear and deep and booming. The sound echoed across the ice. It filled Julian's ears and ricocheted inside his skull. "Chloe Bishop. Juniper Bishop."

Julian scrabbled at the ice with numb fingers, but it was useless. He was dying. He was going to die.

"May God have mercy on your soul," Bishop said. "For I have none left to give."

The blood roaring in Julian's ears turned slow and sluggish. He couldn't wrap his foggy brain around it. It made no sense. This was all wrong.

It should be Bishop dying on the ice, not Julian. It shouldn't be him.

He stared at Bishop in shock, in growing despair, but Bishop offered him nothing. Nothing at all. He simply stood and waited—a silent witness.

Like the cold and brutal landscape, the vicious winter, the greedy river sucking at him, pulling, pulling, eager to drag him under.

The seconds ticked away like a bomb counting down to zero. The cold was a vise squeezing the strength and vitality from him, draining the very life from his veins.

He'd stopped shaking, he realized dimly. His teeth had stopped chattering. He was no longer cold. He felt nothing below the ice, not even the current pulling at his legs.

He couldn't feel his limbs. They were dead. His legs, dead. His arms, dead. His heart, dead.

"It wasn't...just me," he forced through numb lips.

Maybe it was the guilt talking. Or a deep-seated rage. A hatred he hadn't been able to acknowledge, even to himself.

He was going down. He didn't have to go down alone.

"Tell me," Bishop said.

"S-she knows...everything. She's always known. S-she acts like she d-doesn't to make her f-feel better about h-herself. She's the o-one who approved it, approved everything. W-who sent me to the prison cell that night."

Bishop went absolutely still. His iron gaze drilled into Julian's soul. "Say her name."

The cold was taking him. His brain thick, stuffed with cotton. Everything growing distant and fuzzy.

The current was pulling harder and harder at his concrete legs. His numb aching fingers barely able to grip the ice.

He thought of the key, still tied to a brick somewhere in this same river. He thought of his hated brother, who was dead, too. He thought of Noah, the best friend who'd betrayed him.

His mind clouded around a single bright splinter, one last thing.

He said, "M-my mother. Rosamond Sinclair."

Julian let go. The cold dark water drew him down, down, down into its shadowy depths. Down and away.

51

ROSAMOND SINCLAIR
DAY THIRTY-FIVE

Rosamond Sinclair's sons were dead.

Both of them. First Gavin, maliciously murdered. And now Julian, lost to the ice.

His death was no accident. She was sure of it. One of her still loyal police officers had spotted Atticus Bishop at the river with him two days ago.

Julian had been murdered as surely as Gavin had.

Shattering grief ripped through her. Grief, loss, and a terrible black rage. She shook with it. Trembled with it. Her whole body thrummed with feverish fury, with hatred, with a relentless desire to destroy everything she could get her hands on.

With a growl of outrage, she spun and seized an antique china plate from the stack piled on the counter, waiting to be put away.

She hurled it as hard as she could. It struck the wall on the opposite side of the kitchen and crashed to the floor in several pieces. She grabbed the next plate and threw it.

The china shattered. The crash reverberated in her ears.

She flung every plate, bowl, and saucer she had, until hundreds of ceramic shards glinted across the wood floor. Her manicured hands curled into shaking fists, her whole body quivering with black rage.

"Are you done?" Mattias Sutter asked.

She'd nearly forgotten him.

She turned to face him, chest heaving, heat flushing her face and neck. The adrenaline drained from her veins.

Darkness tugged at her. A great howling emptiness.

Her carefully calibrated control was cracking, fissures appearing in the façade she'd worked so hard to maintain. All she could see was red. Grief and rage mingling into a toxic, radioactive soup eating away at her insides. She was losing it.

Mattias sat quietly on the other side of the island, his back straight, a glass of cabernet sauvignon wine in one hand. "What do you want to do?"

"I want to burn this whole town to the ground," Rosamond spat.

Mattias cocked his brows. "That may be a bit...premature."

"I've given these people everything! Everything I have! And still, they've betrayed me."

She had dedicated her life to Fall Creek. All the stress, sleepless nights, the politics and games—she'd taken it all on. She wasn't being paid for this. Hell, who knew if she'd ever get paid again.

Still, she was willing to shoulder the burden. She was willing to make the necessary sacrifices to protect the town.

Fall Creek had been spared the ravages of disaster because of her. Because of her, this town was safe and whole.

Every citizen had food on the table to satisfy their needs and firewood to keep their children warm—every obedient citizen, anyway. She knew what they needed even before they did. She knew what was required and had the guts and fortitude to ensure it happened.

What other town or city could say that? Certainly none in Michigan. Maybe none in the entire country.

She had accomplished that. No one else.

How had the town repaid her for her unfailing generosity? With ingratitude, whining, and disrespect. With backbiting and betrayal. With the death of her sons.

She'd never expected to lose her precious Gavin. Or Julian. Her sons had been everything to her.

What did she have without them?

Only the town. Only Winter Haven. Only her legacy.

Fury slashed through her, severing her grief like a knife. A righteous outrage. "My sons have been taken from me. They've been murdered by...by dissidents. By *terrorists*. I will not rest until we weed them out. Until we destroy this threat to Fall Creek once and for all!"

Mattias nodded. "Don't let your emotions get in the way. They'll only hamper your ability to see clearly, to get the job done."

He was right. She took a deep, steadying breath. Willed her fractured emotions under control.

She was Rosamond Sinclair. She did not bend under pressure, no matter how immense, no matter how formidable the enemies arrayed against her.

She would not crack. She would not break.

She would maintain the strength and power she'd so meticulously amassed. She would not be defeated.

Rosamond flicked a ceramic shard from her charcoal pencil skirt. She straightened her shoulders and smoothed her blonde hair behind her ears. She did not speak until she had regained control of herself and buried her grief somewhere down deep.

"You're right, Mattias," she said evenly. "Thank you for the reminder."

"What do you want to do?"

"I want them dead." She counted them off on her manicured fingers. "Liam Coleman. Atticus Bishop. And anyone else who aided and abetted them. Anyone who has anything to do with them—they're dead."

"We will need to be more careful this time. They are trained operators. I'm unwilling to lose more men unnecessarily."

"Just don't take too long. I will not sleep until my sons are avenged."

"It'll be done." Mattias took a sip of wine. He set the crystal wine glass on the marble island. "And what about Chief Sheridan?"

She stiffened. She cared for Noah. And for Milo.

Hadn't she taken Noah and Milo under her wing after the wife's disappearance? She'd treated them like family. Better than family.

She had groomed Noah for years to serve as one of her most loyal and dutiful confidants. Julian had been too much of a hothead to deal with certain politically delicate matters.

Gavin had been absolutely dependable in dealing with the undesirables she'd needed taken care of. However, he'd been too... extreme...in his proclivities.

Noah was steady, levelheaded, the peacemaker. Easy to direct, to manipulate. Not to mention morally weak, though he liked to consider himself otherwise.

But Noah continually chose to surround himself with malcontents, instigators, and troublemakers. His friendship with that rabble-rousing pastor, Atticus Bishop. With that churlish old woman, Molly Dũng, and her mouthy granddaughter, who always seemed to pop up in the wrong places at the wrong times.

Everyone had their flaws, even Noah. Rosamond could almost overlook it. She *had* overlooked it, until now.

Until Hannah. Hannah Sheridan and her loose cannon of a soldier.

Just the thought of the man who had killed Gavin filled Rosamond with a seething hatred. A black rage that threatened her careful control.

And Hannah. The weak, vile woman spreading vicious lies about her precious son, when he was dead in the ground with no way to defend himself. Who the hell did she think she was?

Rosamond took a deep breath and reigned in her emotions. Mattias was correct; she could not afford to act rashly.

She prided herself on her practicality. Handicaps like morality and ethics didn't cripple her ability to lead. She was willing to do what was necessary.

Rosamond had no qualms about ordering Hannah's death. She longed to turn to Mattias right now and say the words. She'd enjoy watching them all die, truth be told. The soldier. The pastor. The girl.

Yet Hannah meant something to Noah. And Noah was an integral piece of Rosamond's strategy. With Gavin and Julian gone, she needed him more than ever.

If Hannah died now, even by some grotesque, unfortunate accident, Noah's response would be unpredictable at best. Hannah's demise would have to wait. For now.

Rosamond wasn't stupid. She knew her allies were shrinking. Noah's support was not optional. He was necessary.

As long as she still had Noah as her police chief and Mattias with his militia behind her, she would be fine.

"I know how to handle Noah," she said. "I know exactly what strings to pull. He's under our complete control and will remain that way."

Mattias nodded. "I see the wisdom in that. He'll keep the

other cops in line. And the police chief's approval provides that shiny veneer of respectability you seem to care so much about."

She shot him a sharp look. "Don't underestimate it. Most people are just looking for a reason to capitulate. They're as meek as sheep. Authority is the oldest and most useful tool in the book."

"Noted." Mattias swirled the wine in his glass. Beneath the pendant lighting, the dark liquid looked red as blood. "And the rest of the town?"

Rosamond stepped carefully across the floor, avoiding the shattered china. She reached for her own wine glass. It was nearly empty. No matter. She had plenty more in the basement.

She had everything she needed. This place was a fortress, stuffed with supplies to last her years. And with her own personal army, she could defend it.

She had lost much in the last few weeks, but she had not lost everything. She still had this town. She still had her legacy. And she would fight for that with her last breath.

"We need to send a message. Loud and clear. Noncompliance will not be tolerated. Anyone who dissents doesn't get fed. No more freeloaders."

"Consider it already done." Mattias swirled his wine without drinking. "And maybe it's time to be done with that council of yours. All they do is complain and hold back progress."

"I'll consider it."

Rosamond studied Mattias. Though they had been separated by distance for several years, she and her cousin had always been close. They'd been raised together; their fathers were brothers who maintained absolute control over their families and ruled with iron fists.

They understood each other in ways that others never would.

Mattias wasn't invested in the town like Rosamond. He wasn't driven by anger and resentment like Julian had been. He did not desire to rule or lead or usurp her role.

He was cunning, and he was brutal. Like Rosamond, morals played no part in his decision-making. If he had any flaw, it was greed. He liked nice things.

He was family, but it was still wise to keep him well-satisfied. And close.

Rosamond raised her glass to Mattias. "Your loyalty does not go unnoticed, cousin. Nor unrewarded."

"To loyalty." Mattias smiled broadly. "And to Winter Haven."

She took a long, deep swig, careful not to smear her ruby-red lipstick. She did not smile back. "To Winter Haven."

"I have another idea," Mattias said. "To send a message. To punish the guilty."

"As long as they pay for what they've done."

His dark eyes glinted. "Oh, they will."

Rosamond tightened her grip on the stem of her empty glass. She would still succeed. She would rule. And she would utterly destroy anyone who got in her way.

52

NOAH
DAY THIRTY-SIX

"I made some coffee," Hannah said.

Noah looked up with a strained smile.

Hannah stood on the front porch without a coat on, a blue mug in her hands. She wore a thick gray sweater and black leggings. Her shiny dark brown hair brushed against her shoulders.

Noah's chest tightened. He wiped his hands on a dirty rag and closed the F150's hood. The truck had stalled a few times, and he was trying to fix it on his own without asking for help.

After banging around for a couple of hours, he was just about to give up. Molly had given him a spray bottle filled with three parts vinegar to one-part water to spray on his windshield the night before snow to de-ice it—at least the truck windows were nice and clear.

It was Sunday, and he was taking a rare afternoon off. He desperately needed the mental and physical break after the wreck of the last few days.

Liam Coleman had finally moved out. Noah didn't even care

that it was to move into their old house. He'd rather have him gone for good, but at least he was out of their hair.

It was a relief for Noah, and it was safer for Hannah. That man brought trouble wherever he went.

Liam still couldn't seem to stay away from Hannah. He'd stopped by earlier on the pretense of taking Ghost for one of his long walks. Hannah had been happy to see him. It had made Noah sick.

At least he was out of the house. At least there was that.

Noah, Hannah, and Milo had used the precious family time to play a few games of Monopoly Deal. After lunch, Hannah had gone into the guestroom to feed the baby, and Noah took Milo outside to get a little work done.

Milo was busy building a snowman in the front yard. He trotted around the house and ventured into the woods a bit to gather pine boughs for his Christmas tree forest.

For a couple of hours, life had seemed almost normal.

Noah strode across the yard to the porch steps. He took the hot coffee mug from Hannah, his fingers barely brushing hers. It was her healthy, good hand. A jolt went through him.

With an apologetic look, Hannah pulled away.

Disappointment roiled in his gut. He tried not to show it. "Thank you. Isn't it a blessing that we still have coffee?"

Hannah's brow wrinkled. "Something like that."

"Where's yours?"

She flushed. "Oh, I already had mine. It's difficult to carry both mugs at once."

She meant her crippled hand. He looked away, embarrassed. He hadn't meant to bring attention to it. When he looked at her injury, it filled him with a helpless anger—like he was personally responsible.

Whenever he thought of Gavin Pike hurting Hannah, what monstrous things he'd done to her, his mind swerved away. It felt like he was skating along the edges of a bottomless pit; it would be the end of him if he fell in.

"I'm sorry," he mumbled.

"It's okay. It takes a bit of getting used to."

For a long moment, they didn't speak. Mentally, he scrambled for something to say, something to bring them together instead of pushing them further apart.

They'd barely had a moment to speak in private since that first night. There were always other people around—namely Liam—or things to do. He had a million things on his to-do list, both at home and at work, to keep things running without the power grid.

At home, there was always Milo, the dog, or the baby between them. The baby that was Hannah's, but not his. The baby that Gavin Pike had created, that represented every awful thing that had been done to his wife.

He swallowed bile. It was just a child, innocent in all of this, but he could barely look at her. He hated himself for it, but it was true.

He told himself it would just take time, like everything else. He told himself everything would be okay.

As long as he had Hannah and Milo, that was all that mattered.

"Do you remember that last day we had together?" he asked. "How we went skiing with Milo? How happy we were for him?"

"I remember." Her expression softened. "How could I forget? We got those giant peanut butter cookies for Milo. They were as big as his head."

"I thought about that day all the time, you know. Every year on Christmas Eve, Milo and I went back to Bittersweet. To remember you. To make more happy memories. The day of the EMP, we were there."

She glanced at him. Her eyes were so deep and green in the wintry light. "I didn't know that."

"Milo talked me into riding their biggest ski lift to the top."

She raised her brows. "You? Willingly riding ski lifts?"

"I know, right? I was nervous the whole time. Then the EMP took out the power right before the top. It took out the generators, too."

"What happened?"

"In the chaos, we were overlooked. We got stuck up there in the middle of a snowstorm. I had to climb the cable to the nearest tower to get down. Quinn Riley was there, too. Her grandfather died of a heart attack when his pacemaker went out. I had to climb the cable. It was the only way."

He recalled that day. He'd taken charge and saved them. Everything had been so black and white—do what was necessary, or people died. Things weren't so black and white anymore.

Every decision came with costs. Every choice had repercussions, not all of which he could anticipate or mitigate. The immense burden was overwhelming.

Hannah paled. "I had no idea. What an ordeal. Milo has been through so much. You both have."

"We have," Noah said. His throat tightened. "Everyone has. I'm just so glad you're here. I'm so glad we got you back."

She gave him a soft smile. It lit up her whole face. "Me, too."

He wanted to hold her. To kiss her. After that first night when she'd pulled away from him, he'd been reluctant to try again.

She needed time. He knew that.

He hoped that was all it was. He hoped with all his heart that Liam Coleman had nothing to do with it.

He was too afraid to ask. The answer might break him.

He wanted things to go back to the way they were before. When they were first married, young and happy and blissfully unaware of how incredibly difficult life would become.

"We're going to be okay," he said. "We're going to be fine."

"Are we?"

"Of course."

She half-turned toward him and leaned against the porch railing. She wrapped her arms around her ribs and hugged herself. "Noah, we need to talk about what happened."

Noah's chest constricted. "What do you mean?"

She flashed him a look. "About Julian."

Sorrow thickened his throat. He'd been trying his best not to think about it at all. His grief over his friend's sudden death. His shock at the accusations Bishop had made when he'd returned from the river—alone.

What had happened on the ice. How Julian had died. His confessions before the black water took him. And lastly, the body that Bishop had found stored in the ice chest in Julian's fishing shack.

Noah, Reynoso, and Hayes had gone to the cabin to investigate and confirm Bishop's testimony. It was true. Briggs' had been shot in the back of the head.

Now Chief Briggs' frozen body was wrapped in industrial garbage bags and stored with all the other victims of the collapse in Paul Eastley's large metal pole barn outside of town.

As much as he wanted to, Noah could not justify his friend's actions in this. Julian had done this horrible thing. He'd murdered Chief Briggs for getting in the way. There was no other explanation.

He took a sip of coffee to steady his nerves. "It's hard to

believe he could've had a hand in that—in what happened." He couldn't bring himself to say the words.

"I'm sorry. I know he was your friend."

He'd barely slept the last few nights, tossing and turning alone in his bed, his mind a jumbled blur. He didn't want to believe that Julian was capable of such things, even with the evidence of Chief Briggs' corpse staring him in the face.

You know it's true, a voice whispered inside his head. Julian had shot Billy Carter in cold blood. He had killed Nickel Carter at Crossway Church before the man could out him. Julian had claimed self-defense, but Nickel had recognized Julian—Noah realized that, now.

The truth was, he didn't want to talk about it. He didn't want to think about it. It was too terrible. Too awful.

The friend Noah had trusted and loved was a murderer. He had been a part of the massacre that had killed forty-seven people and nearly killed Milo.

Noah had believed Julian when he'd promised that he would defuse the situation—instead, Julian had betrayed him and ordered the deaths of Liam Coleman and Bishop.

And not only that, a dark voice whispered in his mind. Julian was also Gavin Pike's brother. Had he known what his brother had done? Could he have known about Pike? About Hannah?

His mind recoiled. Everything in him revolted. He felt the past dragging him down and struggled to resist it.

He buried Julian down deep with all the other ugly things he couldn't bear to think about. He had to move forward, to bury the past and leave it there. It was the only way to survive.

He had to survive—for himself, for Milo and Hannah, for the town.

"Julian has paid for what he did," Noah said in a choked voice.

"He's dead now. Bishop's family is avenged. It's over. We can all move on. It's best for everyone if we move on."

"It's not over." Hannah frowned, a line appearing between her brows. "Julian told Bishop that Rosamond knew. That she approved of Julian releasing those monsters to create mayhem. She played a part in the massacre."

Hannah's words hung in the air between them like a threat.

This was the fear he couldn't bear to face. The unspoken whisper that haunted his waking hours, that tormented his dreams.

Noah shook his head. "Bishop was mistaken. Julian was delirious, out of his mind. He just wanted someone to blame. He acted alone. I know Rosamond. She's a good person. I know her."

"Like you knew Julian?"

He balked. "That's not fair."

"Rosamond is Gavin Pike's mother."

"What does that have to do with anything?"

Her eyes narrowed. "A mother has two angry, violent sons. Where do you think that violence comes from?"

"I don't believe that."

"A mother knows," Hannah said quietly. "How can she not?"

Noah shook his head wildly. She was wrong. Hannah was wrong. Rosamond was like a mother to him—a good mother. She cared about him, about this town. She loved Milo like her own grandson.

She'd welcomed him into her home, her family when his own parents couldn't have been bothered. To let those ugly doubts even enter his head was a betrayal. He didn't want to betray her. He couldn't. "I can't believe that."

"You can't or you won't?"

"I need you to trust me, Hannah—"

"Wait." Hannah pushed off from the porch railing. She

shielded her eyes with her hand and scanned the yard. "Where is Milo?"

"He was right here. He must be in the back." Noah turned and looked. "Milo!"

No answer.

Noah turned in a slow circle. Took in the trees, the houses, the empty road. The front yard was a mess of crisscrossing footprints. Broken-off pine boughs stuck up everywhere like little Christmas trees.

The snowman was finished. Milo had stuck in twigs for the arms, stones for the eyes, nose, and mouth, and wrapped his own scarf around the snowman's neck. It flapped forlornly in the breeze.

"Milo!" His voice echoed across the frozen lake behind the house. "Milo!"

There was no answer.

A frisson of fear lanced through him. "Check inside!"

Hannah was already heading toward the front door.

Noah jogged around the house, his boots sinking in the melting snow, his heart jackhammering as he called his son's name again and again.

By the time he'd circled around to the front, Hannah was back on the porch. She carried the baby wrapped in a thick blanket. She bit her bottom lip. "He's not inside. Noah, where is he?"

"I'll check the neighboring houses."

"I'll call Liam on the radio," Hannah said. "He and Ghost can help search. Ghost will find him."

Resentment flashed through him at the thought of asking Liam Coleman for help, but he said nothing. Noah started toward the driveway, then hesitated. He glanced back at his wife. "Be careful."

She nodded. She didn't ask why.

The fear threatened to strangle him. Adrenaline and panic surged through his veins. If someone had hurt Milo. If someone had done anything to his son...

Milo wasn't here. He felt it.

His son was gone.

53

NOAH
DAY THIRTY-SIX

Noah ran down the driveway. He shouted Milo's name. The cold air stung his throat and nostrils. Crystalized clouds puffed from his lips with each ragged breath.

He knocked on every door. None of the neighbors had seen Milo. No one had heard or seen a thing.

His panic grew. Noah finished one cul-de-sac and moved to the next. Time slowed. Every minute felt like an hour.

He didn't hesitate when he reached the superintendent's house. Maybe he should have, but he didn't. He couldn't think about anything but Milo's safety.

He jogged up the expansive stone steps and banged on the glass-plated front door. He glimpsed movement through the glass. Two figures sat at the huge island in the kitchen.

Noah seized the door handle, twisted, and pushed it open. The door opened easily. It was unlocked. He stepped inside.

He took in the familiar lavish furnishings, the Brazilian wood floors, ornate vaulted ceilings, and crystal chandeliers.

"Hello, Chief Sheridan," Rosamond Sinclair said from across the great room.

Relief lurched through him. "Milo."

Milo waved. "Hey, Dad. Look what we're doing!"

Milo sat next to Rosamond in the kitchen, who stood behind the island. A mixing bowl sat on the marble surface, a large gleaming kitchen knife beside it.

The island was cluttered with glass jars of flour and sugar, measuring spoons, and a baking tray lined with small mounds of dough. Flour was scattered over the counter and smudged Milo's flushed cheeks.

"What are you doing here?" Noah struggled to keep his voice even. His heart still thumped against the cage of his ribs like an animal frantic to escape. "You know you aren't supposed to leave the yard."

Milo lowered his eyes and nibbled his bottom lip, just like Hannah. "Sorry, Dad. I was looking for more 'trees' and walked too far. Nana Rosamond found me. She said she had a surprise."

He raised a gooey ball of cookie dough and squished it between his fingers. "And look! Cookies with peanut butter chips!"

"That's great, buddy. It's time to go home now."

"That would be such a shame," Rosamond said brightly. "We're just getting started."

Her voice was artificially cheery. A red-lipped smile plastered across her face. It was disconcerting. Shouldn't she be grieving? Shouldn't she be a sobbing mess?

Noah had been, after Hannah.

"Yeah, Dad. We've gotta finish first. We just got the first batch in the oven."

Noah's mouth was dry. It was hard to swallow. "Your mother wants you home."

Rosamond's smile remained fixed. "I'm sure Hannah understands how much children need their nanas, right Milo?"

"Right," Milo chirped.

"Children need their parents, too. Don't they, Noah? It is so horrible when a child loses a parent. Truly, simply heartbreaking."

"Yes," Noah said.

Rosamond's eyes never left his face. She plucked a spoonful of cookie dough onto the baking tray and molded it into a perfectly round ball. "But when a parent loses a child. Oh, that is a pain that cannot be measured. It is an unfathomable loss."

"I loved Julian, too, Rosamond," Noah said, his throat thick. "I—"

"I have never felt a pain like it," Rosamond continued as if she hadn't heard him. "To lose two children...your only progeny...your hope, your future."

Milo glanced from Rosamond to Noah, a small frown creasing his face. The adults were talking about things he didn't understand.

He didn't know Julian was dead. Noah hadn't been able to bring himself to say the words aloud. Milo didn't know about Gavin Pike or any of the rest of it.

Rosamond steepled her fingers on the counter. "I don't think a mother would ever get over that, do you? Or a father?"

"I—I'm sure they wouldn't."

"I'm glad we agree. I don't think so, either."

Noah swallowed. He'd expected tears. He'd even expected rage. But this—this rigidity, this dangerous calm—it discomfited him more than anything else.

"I'm sorry, Rosamond. If there's anything we can do for you—"

"I'm sure Hannah wouldn't. I know you wouldn't, either. I hope you never see that day, Noah. I truly don't."

For a moment, Noah couldn't speak. His legs felt weak. He looked at Rosamond and tried desperately not to see Gavin Pike. He tried not to hear Bishop's accusations ringing in his ears.

He couldn't explain the fear sinking claws into his mind. He couldn't shake the dread infiltrating every fiber of his being.

"Accidents happen, Rosamond," he said. "Unfortunate events. It's no one's fault—"

"There's no such thing as an accident," Rosamond said. Her voice was ice. It sent shivers running up and down Noah's spine. "For every action, there is an equal and opposite reaction. That's physics, isn't it, Milo?"

Milo completed a row of dough balls. He swiped his finger over the spoon and stuck it in his mouth. "Newton's law."

"His third law, to be exact."

Normally, Noah didn't allow Milo to eat raw cookie dough. Right now, salmonella was the least of his worries. It was suddenly too hot in the house. He was sweating bullets beneath his coat. "Milo, it's time to go."

"Oh, not quite yet." Rosamond put her arm around Milo's shoulder and squeezed him to her side. Her other hand rested next to the butcher knife. Her red manicured fingernails glistened. "Your dad and I aren't quite finished yet."

"Dad?" Milo glanced at Noah, confused.

The vise around Noah's chest tightened. "It's okay, buddy. Have another bite of cookie dough if you want."

"When certain things happen, leaders are forced to act," Rosamond said, each word slow and precise. "Mothers are forced to act. It is not something we would wish or even want. But there are consequences."

Was she referring to Liam Coleman killing Gavin? Or Julian's death? Could she possibly suspect Hannah? Or was it something worse, something he couldn't begin to contemplate?

Milo tried to pull away, but her hand tightened around his shoulder. "It is the natural order of things. There must be control. There must be order. Otherwise, the world is chaos."

Noah cared for this woman. Loved her, even. He'd been loyal to her since the beginning.

He'd never once been afraid of her. Until now.

"I would have done anything for my children." Her voice remained serene but with an edge, the soft sound of distant thunder before the storm, a portend of terrible things to come. "Anything. The question is, will you?"

"Yes," he croaked. "Yes."

Finally, she released Milo.

Relief flared through him. Noah sank to his knees. Milo slid off the stool and scurried to Noah.

He wrapped his arms around his son, felt his little heart beating against his chest, the warmth of him, the soft tickle of his hair beneath his chin.

Noah took in his first full breath since he'd entered Rosamond's house. He felt like he'd just received a reprieve that he didn't completely understand. He already knew that he would not tell Hannah about this. He wouldn't tell anyone.

"What would you do for your child, Noah?" Rosamond asked.

He knew the answer to that question. So did she. He didn't need to speak the words aloud. "Tell me what you need me to do."

Rosamond stood facing him. Her blonde hair glossy beneath the bright kitchen lights. Her cashmere sweater and tan slacks impeccable. Not a speck of flour anywhere on her person.

"It's very simple, Noah," she said. "It couldn't be more simple. All you have to do is nothing."

54

HANNAH
DAY THIRTY-EIGHT

A scream woke Hannah in the middle of the night.

Hannah jolted awake. She jerked to a sitting position, the blankets snarled across her legs, her good hand already reaching beneath her pillow for her loaded .45. She flicked the safety to off.

It was dark. Moonlight streamed through the guest bedroom windows.

Another scream. The distant sound of something breaking. It was coming from outside.

From the living room, Ghost started up his great booming bark.

Her heart pumping, she slipped her feet into her boots sitting beside the bed but didn't bother to lace them. She was already dressed since she slept in her clothes.

She hadn't been able to shake the need to always be ready, no matter what.

Quickly, she checked on Charlotte, who was tucked into a rectangle of pillows in the center of the bed beside her. She still slept soundly, one little arm flung across her face, her tiny rosebud mouth open.

Her next thought was for Milo. She needed to make sure he was safe.

Hannah stood, pistol in both hands, the butt nestled against her bad hand, and moved toward the bedroom door.

The door burst open before she reached it.

Adrenaline spiked through her veins. Instinctively, she raised the muzzle to chest height, finger twitching just shy of the trigger guard.

In the opened doorway, Noah skidded to a halt. With a startled curse, he threw his hands up. "Hannah! Put the gun down! It's me!"

She lowered the gun, didn't apologize. He was the one who'd barged in without announcing himself.

She was starting to think like Liam, she realized grimly. It wasn't a bad thing.

"Where's Milo?" she asked over Ghost's barking.

Noah was dressed in gray sweatpants and a Detroit Tigers sweatshirt. He was still in his socks. His hair was rumpled. He held his service weapon in his right hand. "He's fine. I told him to stay in his bed, that we'd check things out, and I'd come back and tuck him in as soon as it was safe."

She nodded tersely and headed for the doorway. Noah moved out of the way and followed her down the hall.

"You should stay inside," Noah said. "I'll check it out."

"I'm fine. I can handle myself."

"I'm sure you can, but—"

Hannah moved across the shadowed living room. No lights were on, but the moonlight was bright, casting everything in a pale white glow.

Ghost paced before the front door, his hackles raised, barking a thunderous warning to anyone who would dare to infiltrate his domain. He went to her, paused his barking just long enough to press his muzzle against her thigh in greeting, then returned to his guard duty.

She pushed the curtain aside and peered out the front window. Across the street, it was clear. She turned her head to look to the east.

A dozen snowmobiles, Jeeps, and trucks blockaded the road. At least three dozen men in black boots and gray camo milled about the street and the yards of several houses. They held wicked-looking rifles, mostly pointed down but not all of them.

Fear closed her throat. "Noah. What's happening? Are we being attacked?"

Noah looked out the window. He stiffened. "No. It's not that. Those are the militia. Our guys. We need to stay inside. That's all. We'll be safe in here."

She shot him a confused look. She let the curtain drop and went for the front door.

"Hannah—"

"The militia are the good guys. That's what you keep saying. So what's the problem? Are you telling me that I should be afraid of them?"

Noah swallowed. "No. Not you. You're safe."

She hated that she didn't trust him completely. She hated that she wished Liam were here instead. It made her feel guilty. It was still the truth.

The house felt emptier without Liam here.

She felt his absence like a hole in her heart. How quickly he had become a critical part of her life, as precious to her as family.

She pushed those thoughts away and opened the front door. The cold blasted her. She wasn't wearing her coat. She stepped outside onto the front porch, where she could get a better vantage point. She held the .45 low at her side.

Ghost surged onto the porch with a fierce growl.

"Ghost, stay here," she said.

His body strained, every muscle quivering, but he didn't leave her side. His job was to guard his flock—Hannah, Milo, Charlotte—and his flock was here in the house.

She wanted to bury her hand in his fur for comfort, to steady herself, but she needed both hands on her gun. He leaned against her side. She leaned back.

"Can you stop barking, boy? We don't want to draw undue attention."

Ghost woofed his adamant disagreement, but he obeyed. His booming barks lowered to growls that vibrated through his whole body.

A hundred yards to her right, shadows moved in the moonlight. Hannah watched in growing dread as two militia dragged a man and a woman out of the house. Two children huddled on the lawn, crying.

People were sitting in the beds of the trucks. Hunched and huddled against each other. Bundles of suitcases, duffle bags, and laundry baskets were stacked next to them. Several militia members loosely ringed the trucks, weapons in hand, ensuring the people remained inside.

Further down the street on the other side, another family was dragged from their beds and hauled outside. Three men pointed rifles at them.

Hannah's heart stopped. "What are they doing?"

Noah didn't answer. He remained in the doorway. His face was pale, his expression taut.

Her blood rushed in her ears. Anger sprouted in her chest.

"Those are the Millers. And that's Mike Duncan and his son, Jamal."

Across the street from the Millers, Darryl Wiggins stood on his front porch, his shoulders wrapped in a blanket. She couldn't see his bruised face from here.

The militia moved on to the next house, leaving him be.

"The militia are kicking people out of Winter Haven," she said, answering her own question. "Is that it?"

Noah gave a heavy sigh. "Yes."

"But not everyone."

"Yes."

"Where are those families going to go? What are they going to do?"

"Come back inside, Hannah—"

Hannah turned and shot him a scathing look. "Tell me what's happening right now, or I'll march over there and ask Mattias Sutter myself."

Noah rubbed his face. Deep shadows rimmed his eyes. "Rosamond gave these people their places here. She has the right to take them away."

Hannah stared at him, so taken aback for a moment that she didn't know what to say. "Are you serious?"

Noah didn't answer.

"That doesn't even make sense. The Stanleys were here when I first moved to Fall Creek. This is their home. Not borrowed, not taken over temporarily. Theirs."

"The militia has decided that Winter Haven is too difficult to protect with potential dissidents in their midst. They're redistributing housing to fit security needs—"

"Are you listening to yourself? Are those your words or someone else's?"

Noah swallowed. "This is out of my control, Hannah. This is happening, whether we like it or not."

She narrowed her eyes. "I thought you were the chief of police."

"I am, but—"

"How is this not under your purview? How can you allow this to happen under your watch? These are people we know! This is Fall Creek. Your town. Your citizens. Your friends!"

Noah's mouth thinned into a bloodless line. "The militia has been granted certain authority during this crisis—"

"The militia?" Hannah asked. "Or Rosamond Sinclair? Or are they the same thing, now?"

55

HANNAH
DAY THIRTY-EIGHT

Hannah's chest tightened. It was suddenly difficult to breathe. "They're ridding Winter Haven of anyone not aligned with their goals. Rosamond Sinclair is on the warpath. She's cleaning house. Like a tyrant."

A muscle in Noah's cheek twitched. "I understand why you hate Rosamond Sinclair. She's Pike's mother, the man who hurt you. It's easy to lump them both together. But what you said before—you're wrong. Rosamond is not her sons. She cares about this town. She's been trying to do her best for Fall Creek since the beginning of this mess.

"Has she made mistakes? Yes. Has she been forced to make compromises to ensure our safety? Yes. You've seen what it's like out there. Vulnerable towns and villages are being attacked. Lawlessness and anarchy reign. That hasn't happened here, and the only reason is because of Rosamond's quick thinking and strong leadership."

Hannah shook her head, incredulous. "Do you even hear yourself? Look around you. Just who is she keeping safe tonight?"

Noah's gaze darted to the militia and back to Hannah. Tension lined his face—and worry. "Keep your voice down."

"Or what? Or they'll label me a dissident and drag me away, too? Or just attempt to murder me like they did Liam and Bishop?"

Noah's cheeks reddened. "No! I won't let them."

"Oh? You'll stop them just like you're stopping this?"

"That's different."

"How?"

"Do you think I want to do this? Do you think I *like* this? That I agree with it?"

"That's what I don't understand. Help me understand."

His face clouded. "I have to do this, Hannah. I don't have a choice. *We* don't have a choice."

Finally, he was being honest. Finally, he was admitting it.

He took a step toward her, his left hand rising as if to touch her cheek the way he used to, once upon a time, a whole lifetime ago.

Ghost whipped around and pushed between them with a warning growl. He sensed the tension between them, sensed Hannah's growing anxiety. He had no intention of allowing anyone near Hannah—not even her husband.

Hannah didn't rebuke him.

"We always have a choice, Noah," she said. "Always."

Noah's hand dropped to his side. He balled his hand into a fist. His shoulders slumped, his expression defeated. "I'm doing this for Milo."

"What does Milo have to do with it?"

"His medication. The pharmacy is out. So is every other pharmacy in the county, probably the entire state, if they're even still operating. The militia brings his meds. It's at the top of their needs list. Because of Rosamond."

"We could get it somewhere else. There has to be another option."

"There isn't," he said flatly.

She shook her head. "No. I don't believe that. You said you have five years of medication."

"I do, but it's not enough. We may need more. We need more, to be safe."

She saw it in his eyes—he owed them, now. More like, they owned him.

His expression darkened. "I would do anything to protect Milo, Hannah. Anything."

She reared back as if he'd slapped her. "So would I. But there has to be a line, Noah."

His eyes turned fierce. "There's no line except the one that keeps Milo alive. Milo and you. Don't you see? That's what matters. We'll get through this. The three of us."

"Four of us."

He had the decency to look ashamed. "I'm sorry, Hannah. Yes, the four of us. You, me, Milo, and the baby. I'll do the best I can for the town, but you are my priority. That's it. I won't apologize for that. I'll do what I have to do to keep you safe."

She looked out at the street again. The cold stung her face and hands. Her eyes burned.

One of the townspeople was fighting back. He took a swing at a soldier. The soldier struck him with the butt stock of his rifle. The man crumpled to the snow. A woman and a teenage girl screamed and ran to his side.

The soldier gestured to two other militia, who grabbed the man beneath his arms, dragged him to one of the remaining trucks, and slung him into the back like a sack of flour.

Hannah's stomach turned. Sour acid stung the back of her

throat. It was all she could do not to run into the street and try and stop them.

She knew she was outnumbered. She was one person. They had all the guns and the manpower. For now.

"This—" she pointed down the street, "—is not *safe*."

"It is for us."

Anger surged through her. "How can you say that?"

Noah worked his jaw. "I'll make sure each of these families gets situated in the best homes left in Fall Creek. We've had so many deaths that we have a few dozen empty houses with fireplaces or woodstoves, septic systems, and wells. I'll make sure they have enough food and firewood. I'll see to it personally."

"Is that how you live with yourself? Doing a few good deeds to pretend you aren't a part of this?"

He looked wounded. "That's not fair."

"Isn't it? And when Rosamond and the militia decide not to feed them, too? What then? They control the food, Noah. Look how they're controlling you with Milo's meds."

Noah glanced down, unable to meet her gaze. He looked like a man already beaten, a man resigned to a terrible fate. "There's nothing else I can do."

"What if she goes after Bishop again?"

"She won't. Bishop was Julian's enemy, not hers."

"You don't know that, either. And Liam?"

He stiffened. "Liam Coleman can take care of himself."

She lifted her chin. "And what if I tell her that I killed her son? How safe do you think I'll be then?"

He looked up sharply, panic flaring in his eyes. "You can't do that."

"You know she's dangerous. You say one thing, but I can see the truth. You're running around trying to put out fires, but you aren't going to the source. It's all going to blow up in your face, Noah."

He looked bewildered, haunted. A man torn apart.

She recalled a phrase from her college days, in a Psych 101 course she'd taken: cognitive dissonance.

Noah's mind couldn't allow both truths to coexist: the very people he depended upon for his son's life were the people destroying his town and endangering his loved ones.

To admit that his mentor Rosamond and his best friend Julian were corrupt was too terrible a reality to face. And so he didn't.

Hannah had no such qualms.

She had defeated one enemy only to discover another rising from the ashes of the first. Rosamond Sinclair was as bad as her son, albeit in a different way. She was responsible for misery, death, and destruction. She would be responsible for more.

Just because Noah didn't want to face it didn't make it any less true.

Hannah shook her head wearily. "Who are you, Noah Sheridan?"

He stared at her, his gaze pleading, beseeching her. "Hannah, please. I'm your husband. I'm Milo's father. I'm the same man I've always been."

"That's what I was afraid of."

Noah blanched. He looked stricken, as if she'd slapped him. He opened his mouth to argue, but nothing came out.

"Dad?"

They both looked up.

Milo stood in the hallway outside his bedroom. He wore Spiderman pajamas. His dark curls stood up all over his head. He wiped sleep from his eyes. "Are there bad guys out there? I wanna help fight the bad guys."

Noah stepped back into the house and stood between Milo

and the opened door to shield his view. He rubbed his face with the back of his arm. "Everything's fine, buddy. I promise. Why don't I tuck you back into bed?"

Milo looked at Hannah. "Will you do it?"

She didn't have to force a smile. Not for Milo. Never for Milo. "Sure, baby. I'm right here."

Ghost trotted after them as she took her son's small hand and led him back to his room. Milo clambered into bed and squeezed himself against the wall. He gave her a shy glance, the painful longing of a boy for his mother so apparent on his face that she nearly wept.

She climbed into the bed beside him, and he snuggled against her—his head on her upper arm, his warm body tucked into hers. He still fit perfectly.

He looked up at her with his big dark eyes. He hesitated, a little unsure. "Will you sing to me?"

"Always, sweetheart."

He smiled. Then he said it, the words she'd longed to hear. "Thanks, Mom."

Her chest squeezed so tight, for a moment she couldn't breathe. She swallowed the lump in her throat, blinked back the wetness in her eyes, and began to sing Leonard Cohen's "Hallelujah."

As she sang Milo back to sleep, Ghost settled himself in front of the open bedroom door. His head up, expression alert. Watching over them, like he always did.

For a long time, she lay there. Relishing the presence of her child beside her. Smelling the clean shampoo scent of his hair, feeling the little boy shape of him.

She stared up at the ceiling, her mind a jumble of competing thoughts, her heart a tangle of conflicting emotions. She hadn't been sure what it would be like, but she hadn't imagined this.

She hadn't known it would all be so hard.

The entire time she'd fought and bled and struggled to get home, she'd envisioned home as a sanctuary, a refuge to shelter from the storm invading the rest of the country.

But it wasn't. It had been naïve to believe it.

Nothing that truly mattered in life came easily. That was as true before the collapse as after. Nothing was owed to you. Nothing. Not love. Not freedom. Not even family.

Relationships weren't a given. They weren't a right. They were made. They were forged through blood, sweat, and tears. Through time, energy, and commitment. Through good times and bad, through hope and despair.

Love had to be earned. So did freedom. Sometimes it had to be earned again and again. If you weren't careful, it slipped right through your fingers.

Hannah had suffered and lost too much not to live free. She knew what oppression looked like. Chains weren't always visible.

She wouldn't go back to that. She wouldn't raise her children in bondage.

She would fight with everything she had in her—with teeth, nails, and blood. With her own life.

It was worth the risk. Worth the cost. It had to be.

56

LIAM
DAY FORTY

"Get your butt inside where it's warm," Quinn said to Liam as she opened the front door wide. "We've been waiting for you."

Liam paused in the doorway. Beneath his coat, he wore the plate carrier he'd confiscated from Desoto, along with his M4, which he carried on a two-point sling.

The gash in his ear stung, but it had scabbed over and was healing well. His back ached with a dull pulsing pain, but it was endurable. He would endure.

It had been forty days since the EMP attack. Forty days for the country to unravel into complete anarchy. It was the beginning of February. In southwest Michigan, that meant another month of hard winter, maybe even two.

Quinn motioned for him to come inside her grandmother's house. Liam stepped inside, and she shut the door behind him.

Warmth from the crackling fire soothed his chapped cheeks. He took off his hat and gloves and stuffed them in his pocket. A few cats curled around his ankles, meowing plaintively.

Ghost greeted Liam with a brief muzzle press against his

palm, then returned to his patrol of the house, moving from the living room, kitchen, hall, and bedrooms before returning to the living room again.

Liam looked around the circle of tense faces that greeted him. Hannah sat on the sofa, holding Charlotte, with Annette King on one side of her, Molly on the other. Molly's cane rested beside her Mossberg 500 shotgun.

Dave Farris, Samantha Perez, and Mike Duncan and his son Jamal sat in wooden chairs that had been brought in from the kitchen.

Bishop stood sideways near the window, checking the street and yard, the modified AK-47 Liam had given him carried low in his hands. Jose Reynoso leaned against the framed archway between the kitchen and living room so he could keep an eye on the back door. He held a shotgun.

Noah Sheridan was conspicuously absent. Liam couldn't say that he minded.

"What's all this?" Liam asked.

"Quinn's been busy," Bishop said with a wry smile. "She's been recruiting."

"I'm aware," Liam said.

Quinn had tracked him down daily, showing up at Hannah's old house, bouncing on her heels on the front porch like a giddy puppy until he relented and opened the door. Twice she'd found him on his solitary walks and pestered him for two hours.

So much for a bit of peace and quiet to think.

She wanted him to teach her to fight, just like Hannah had. The kid had grit and spirit; he'd give her that. She was sarcastic and mouthy, too. He kind of liked her.

"Enough is enough," Hannah said, steel in her voice. "What's happening is wrong. It's beyond wrong. We have to stop it."

Two nights ago, the militia had raided Winter Haven.

Twenty-seven families were rousted from their beds and driven from their homes. Only the militia and those few citizens who'd proven their loyalty to Rosamond Sinclair had been allowed to stay.

People like Darryl Wiggins and Noah Sheridan.

The community food bank remained open—and well-guarded—at the middle school, but the militia maintained an updated list of who was approved to get supplies, and who was turned away.

At least a quarter of the town had made it on the blacklist for one reason or another. With the Crossway church supplies gone, people were already going hungry.

No further attempts had been made on Liam or Bishop's lives. Liam wasn't naïve. Another assassination attempt was coming. It was only a question of when.

Mattias Sutter would not let this go. Neither would Rosamond Sinclair.

Liam didn't fear them. He'd be ready.

"What are you saying?" Liam asked.

"We gathered you here tonight to ask for your help," Molly said. She locked eyes with Quinn. "It's time to do something."

"You said you couldn't fight the militia by yourself," Quinn said. She spread her arms wide, gesturing at the people seated around her. "You need soldiers. Here they are."

Liam stared at her.

"I'm in," Bishop said without hesitation.

A few people looked at him in surprise.

"I didn't think you were a man of violence, pastor," Mike Duncan said.

"In this fallen world, violence is an unfortunate necessity," Bishop said. "The question is not whether violence is good or bad. But what is violence in service of? Is what you're fighting for worthy?"

He half-turned from the window, his expression grave but determined. "No one else should lose their family. To me, that is worth fighting for."

Quinn dipped her chin at him in acknowledgement and turned to Reynoso. "Officer Reynoso?"

Reynoso scratched at the stubble on his jaw and nodded. "I'll admit it, I didn't see it at first. But I hate what this town is turning into. It's time to end this."

"Same," Perez said fiercely. "You can count on me. Hayes will be in, too. He's a bit lazy and liked his donut runs too much, but he's good people. He'll be on our side."

"I'm not a soldier, but I know my way around a hunting rifle," Dave Farris said.

"I don't, but I know several people at the shelter who do," Annette said. "They're as upset as we are. They might be willing to fight, too. I'll help in any way I can."

"So will we," Mike Duncan said. "Just tell us what you need."

Quinn fisted her hands on her hips and turned her gaze on Liam. "Well?"

Liam understood that Rosamond Sinclair and the militia would not stop. He knew their kind. They were corrupted by greed, drunk on power.

They would not relent until they'd seized as much power as they could. And then they would take even more.

With their bump stocks that modified semi-automatic rifles into near automatic weapons, they would mow down anyone in their path. No one was safe. Not Atticus Bishop. Not feisty Quinn, and especially not Hannah.

If Rosamond Sinclair ever discovered that she and Ghost were the ones who really killed her son, both of them would be set firmly in her sights.

Could Liam really allow that to happen? Could he really

abandon this small town to tyrants and thugs masquerading as saviors?

He rested his hand on the pistol grip at his hip. "You'll likely lose. People you love will die. A lot of people."

"Did I mention that he's also an optimist?" Hannah said.

He shot her a disgruntled look.

Her smile only widened, her eyes shining, almost merry.

"The odds aren't in our favor," Liam said.

"So, you're saying it's not impossible," Quinn said.

"I like her enthusiasm," Hannah said.

"I bet you do," Liam grumbled. "She's as relentless as you are. You're both like a dog with a bone when you've got an idea stuck in your heads."

Quinn beamed. "Thank you."

The mood was sober, the room crackling with tension, but it was far from bleak. There was hope here. Joy and humor. Love.

"Will you stand with us?" Hannah asked, her steady gaze pinned on his.

Liam couldn't look away. Something warm and bright unfurled inside his chest.

He finally understood it, his role in all of this. Why he hadn't been able to bring himself to leave Fall Creek, even after he'd safely delivered Hannah and Charlotte home as he'd promised.

His particular talents were needed in this broken world in ways they hadn't been before. His skills were needed. *He* was needed.

He was the sheep dog. The guardian. The one who stood between the innocent and the wolves who would devour them.

This was who he was. Who he'd always been.

He'd lost himself along the way. Scarred by war. Traumatized by the events of Chicago. Haunted by mistakes and losses.

And yet, somewhere in the wilderness of Manistee National Forest, he'd been found.

Not by himself, but by Hannah. Hannah with her dogged determination and tenacity, her iron will beneath that softness, somehow simultaneously gentle and fierce as a wildcat.

If anyone had an excuse to retreat from humanity, she did.

Hannah's pain should have crushed her. It should have destroyed her. Her faith shattered beyond repair. But it wasn't. She wasn't.

She'd chosen life. She'd chosen faith, trust, and hope. Love.

Here she was, ready to fight for those she cared about, ready to defend her community. She had chosen to become a part of something bigger than herself.

And so would he.

Hannah watched him, the ghost of a smile on her lips. It was like she could read his mind, like she knew what he was thinking before he did. She already knew what he would say.

Her presence steadied him, strengthened his resolve.

"Yes," Liam said. "I will."

Everyone looked at each other, nodding in grim approval. They understood the odds stacked against them. Close to fifty armed men against a rag-tag group of citizens.

They were outmanned and outgunned. They were willing to fight anyway. And Liam would lead them.

Reynoso's radio spat static. So did Samantha Perez's. They both reached for it at the same time.

Reynoso clicked the press-to-talk button first. "Reynoso here. Come in."

Static hissed. A high, frantic voice burst from the speakers. "It's Hayes. We've got a 10-33! All hands on deck! Fall Creek is under attack!"

KYLA STONE

The End

AUTHOR'S NOTE

Thank you so much for sticking with me and supporting this series even as reality seems to be mirroring fiction more and more. I hope that the apocalyptic scenarios I write about remain firmly in the realm of the imagination.

This was my "quarantine book," written entirely during the shut-down here in northern Atlanta. I'm surprised that I managed to string together enough coherent sentences to form a novel. At times, it felt like I bled for every word.

Some of you also know that I'm moving from Atlanta to Michigan this summer (Yep, I apparently love writing about winter so much that I'm moving back...just kidding. We're moving to be closer to my parents). I've been madly revising and editing in between packing and searching for a house.

On top of that, 2020 has been a difficult year for everyone—a dumpster fire is more like it. I am saddened by the violence and division, for those who've gotten sick and those who've lost their jobs.

I pray that we can come together and figure out a better, brighter future moving forward. Despite my tendencies toward

Author's Note

cynicism and the often brutal topics I write about, I do believe in hope. I believe that if we're willing to work for it, the best parts of humanity will prevail.

All that being said, I loved my time with Hannah, Liam, Ghost, Quinn, and the rest of the Fall Creek crew. This book was rewarding in so many ways. I cried with Hannah, felt her terror, and cheered with her when evil Pike was finally vanquished. I hope you were as satisfied with his end as I was!

There is plenty of excitement and edge-of-your-seat action waiting for your favorite characters in book #5! Until next time, be safe and take care!

ACKNOWLEDGMENTS

Thank you so much to my awesome, amazing, and fantastic BETA readers: Fred Oelrich, Melva Metivier, Wmh Cheryl, Jessica Burland, Sally Shupe, Annette King, Joanna Niederer, and Cheree Castellanos. Your thoughtful critiques and enthusiasm are invaluable.

To Michelle Browne for her line editing skills and Nadene Seiters for proofreading. And a special thank you to Jenny Avery for catching those last pesky errors.

Thank you so much to George Hall, a real life Special Forces hero who helps me bring the character of Liam to life. Thank you for taking the time to talk me through fight scenes! Your expertise makes this a better book.

To my husband, who takes care of the house, the kids, and the cooking when I'm under the gun with a writing deadline. To my kids, who show me the true meaning of love every day and continually inspire me.

Thanks to God for His many blessings. He is with us even in the darkest times.

Acknowledgments

And to my loyal readers, whose support and encouragement mean everything to me. Thank you.

ALSO BY KYLA STONE

The *Edge of Collapse* Post-Apocalyptic Series (EMP):

Chaos Rising: The Prequel

Edge of Collapse

Edge of Madness

Edge of Darkness

Edge of Anarchy

Edge of Defiance

Edge of Valor

The *Nuclear Dawn* Post-Apocalyptic Series (Nuclear Terrorism):

Point of Impact

Fear the Fallout

From the Ashes

Into the Fire

Darkest Night

Nuclear Dawn: The Complete Series Box Set

The *Last Sanctuary* Post-Apocalyptic Series (Pandemic):

Rising Storm

Falling Stars

Burning Skies

Breaking World

Raging Light

Last Sanctuary: The Complete Series Box Set

No Safe Haven (A post-apocalyptic stand-alone novel):
No Safe Haven

Historical Fantasy:
Labyrinth of Shadows

Contemporary YA:
Beneath the Skin
Before You Break

Audiobooks:
Nuclear Dawn series:
Point of Impact
Fear the Fallout
From the Ashes
Into the Fire
Darkest Night
Edge of Collapse series:
Chaos Rising
Edge of Collapse
Edge of Madness
Edge of Darkness

ABOUT THE AUTHOR

I spend my days writing apocalyptic and dystopian fiction novels, exploring all the different ways the world might end.

I love writing stories exploring how ordinary people cope with extraordinary circumstances, especially situations where the normal comforts, conveniences, and rules are stripped away.

My favorite stories to read and write deal with characters struggling with inner demons who learn to face and overcome their fears, launching their transformation into the strong, brave warrior they were meant to become.

Some of my favorite books include *The Road*, *The Passage*, *Hunger Games*, and *Ready Player One*. My favorite movies are *The Lord of the Rings* and *Gladiator*.

Give me a good story in any form and I'm happy.

Oh, and add in a cool fall evening in front of a crackling fire, nestled on the couch with a fuzzy blanket, a book in one hand and a hot mocha latte in the other (or dark chocolate!): that's my heaven.

I love to hear from my readers! Find my books and chat with me via any of the channels below:

www.Facebook.com/KylaStoneAuthor
www.Amazon.com/author/KylaStone
Email me at KylaStone@yahoo.com